JILL SHALVIS

Second Chance Summer

headline
ETERNAL

Published by arrangement with Forever,
a division of Grand Central Publishing.

First published in Great Britain in 2015
by HEADLINE ETERNAL
An imprint of HEADLINE PUBLISHING GROUP

1

Cataloguing in Publication Data is available from the British Library

ISBN 978 1 4722 2299 2

Printed and bound in Great Britain by CPI Group (UK) Ltd, Croydon, CR0 4YY

MIX
Paper from
responsible sources
FSC
www.fsc.org   FSC® C104740

Headline's policy is to use papers that are natural, renewable and recyclable
products and made from wood grown in sustainable forests. The logging and manufacturing
sources. The packaging and bindings of our titles are expected to conform to the
environmental regulations of the country of origin.

New York ~~bestseller~~ Jill Shalvis is the author of many novels, including her acclaimed Lucky Harbor and Animal Magnetism series. The RITA winner and three-time National Readers Choice winner makes her home near Lake Tahoe.

Visit her website at www.jillshalvis.com for a complete book list and daily blog, and www.facebook.com/JillShalvis for other news, or follow her on Twitter @JillShalvis.

Jill Shalvis is adored by readers:

'A fun, light-hearted romance that is full of humour. Jill Shalvis is one of my go-to authors' **Sarah (*Feeling Fictional*)**

'This book just made me happy!' **Peabody**

'The equivalent of drinking a yummy hot chocolate curled up in front of a roaring fire' **Danielle @ *What Danielle Did Next***

'Made me laugh, made me cry' **Amazon Customer**

'Beautifully written, full of warmth, humour, friendship and romance. I LOVED IT' **Mrs. S. J. Parkes**

'Simply irresistible' **Trekker22**

'Jill Shalvis can seriously do no wrong in my eyes'
Lesley (*My Keeper Shelf*)

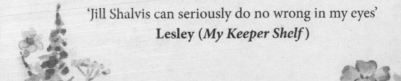

By JILL SHALVIS

Second Chance Summer

Chapter 1

After fighting a brush fire at the base of Cedar Ridge for ten straight hours, Aidan Kincaid had only three things on his mind: sex, pizza, and beer. Given the way the day had gone, he'd gladly take them in any order he could get them.

Not in the cards.

He and the rest of his fire crew had finally managed to get back to the station. They'd been there just long enough to load their plates when the alarm went off again.

"What the hell!"

"Gonna break the damn bell and shove it up some-one's—"

"This is bullshit..."

Whoever said no one could outswear a sailor had never lived in a firehouse. Ignoring the grumbling around him, Aidan pushed his plate away and met his partner Mitch's gaze.

"Gotta be a full moon bringing out the crazy," Mitch said.

"Maybe the crazy just follows you," Aidan suggested.

In turn, Mitch suggested Aidan was number one. With his middle finger.

They'd been playing this game since first grade, when Mitch had stolen Aidan's lunch and Aidan had popped him in the nose for it. As punishment they'd had to pick up and haul trash for the janitor for two weeks.

The two of them had become best friends and had spent the next decade being as wild and crazy as possible.

Eventually they'd grown up and found responsibility, going through the fire academy and now working as Colorado Wildland firefighters for their bread and butter, volunteering on the local search-and-rescue team as needed. And here in Cedar Ridge they were needed a lot. Lost hikers, overzealous hunters, clueless novice rafters—you name it, they'd been called to save it.

Tonight's fire call came in as a possible suicide jumper off the courthouse, which at five stories was the highest building in town.

As they pulled up, they could see a woman had climbed out a window on the fifth floor. She stood on a ledge that couldn't have been more than a foot wide. Wearing nothing but her bra and panties.

"Well, at least Nicky left her Victoria's Secrets on this time," Mitch noted.

Nicky was a bit of a regular.

And Mitch was right. The last time Nicky had gotten upset was after finding the town's councilman she'd been sleeping with going at it on his desk with his assistant. She'd stripped all the way down to her birthday suit before covering herself in Post-it notes. Aidan wondered what had set her off this time.

"I changed my mind," she screamed, jabbing a finger down at them. "I don't want to die! He's not worth it!"

No Post-it notes this time. A bonus. The police had blocked off traffic, but the scene was still chaotic.

"Somebody get up here and save me!" Nicky yelled. "If I fall and die, I'm going to sue every one of you for being so freaking slow! Honest to God, what does a girl have to do to get a rescue around here?"

"So she's changed her mind," the captain said dryly to Aidan and Mitch. Aidan and Mitch exchanged glances. No one could reach her from inside the window. And climbing out on the ledge wasn't an option; it was too narrow—and decomposing to boot. And thanks to the layout of the building and the hillside, their truck couldn't get close enough to the building to be effective either.

They all knew what this meant. One of them was going to have to follow the half-naked crazy chick out onto the ledge. There were a few problems with this.

Aidan and his team had a reputation for being unflappable and tough as nails, but the truth was, plenty unnerved them—including a half-naked crazy chick on a ledge five stories up. They'd just learned to do whatever needed to be done, no matter what.

"Let the fun begin," Mitch muttered.

Plan A was for the captain to head inside and attempt to talk Nicky back inside the window. Since Plan A had a high potential for going south, Plan B was to be run simultaneously—head to the roof and begin setting up rigging for an over-the-roof retrieval.

Through it all, Nicky never stopped screaming at them, alternately begging them to hurry and hurling insults their way.

Then came the cap's radio message: "Yeah, so she's declining to crawl back in the window because there's no press here yet. Last time she was front-page news."

Onward. The team found a good anchor spot on the roof. As Mitch and Aidan were the two most senior members of the unit, one of them always took lead. Mitch looked at Aidan. "Okay, go make like Spider-Man and rescue the damsel in distress."

"Why me?" Aidan asked.

"It's your turn."

"Hey, you're the one who likes her undies," Aidan pointed out. Not that he objected to a rescue, any rescue, but this one had shit show written all over it.

"I weigh more than you do," Mitch said logically.

Only because he was six foot four to Aidan's six two, but whatever. The team got the line set up, and then Aidan got into his five-point harness and hooked himself to the first of the two lines. Mitch hooked up to the second one just in case Aidan got into trouble, and the rest of the unit prepared for go time.

Aidan dropped over the edge. The plan was to rappel him down until he hung ten feet above Nicky. He'd then kick out from the building at the same time that his team lowered him eleven more feet, bringing him to just below her, putting him between her and the fifty-foot drop. He'd attach a harness to Nicky, and the team would give them enough slack so that Aidan could rappel down with her.

And the team indeed lowered Aidan to just above Nicky. Aidan kicked out. But as usual, nothing went to plan. Just as he started to swing back toward the wall, Nicky leapt off the ledge like some rabid raccoon and wrapped herself around him.

Not more than a hundred and ten pounds, she clung to him like a monkey as they hurtled at neck-breaking speed toward the wall. Aidan managed to grip her tight and twist in midair so that he was the one to slam into the brick.

Even as lightweight as she was, it still hurt like hell.

"Jesus Christ," Aidan heard the captain and Mitch say in stereo as they watched helplessly—one from above, one from below, at the window.

They didn't know the half of it. With Nicky's legs wrapped and locked around Aidan's waist, her arms squeezing his head like a grape and her breasts literally suffocating him, he couldn't breathe. Somehow he managed to turn his head sideways to suck in some air, but he still couldn't see. "I've got you," he said. "I'm not going to let go, but you need to loosen your grip."

Nicky was too busy screaming in his ear to hear him, not loosening her grip at all. "Omigod, don't you fuckin' drop me or I'll sue you the most!"

Mitch had dropped over the edge as soon as Nicky leapt onto Aidan's back. He was rappelling down as fast as he could, laughing all the way. Aidan couldn't see shit but he could hear him clearly, the asshole.

"Got his six," Mitch said into the radio as he came even with Aidan, still laughing. "Though I can't tell where Aidan ends and Nicky begins."

You can kill him later, Aidan promised himself. "Listen to me," he said to Nicky. "I've got you. I need you to stop yelling in my ear and look at me."

She gulped in a breath and relaxed her hold only enough to look at him. Her eyes were wide, wet, and raccooned from her mascara.

"I'm not going to let go of you," he assured her, staring

into her eyes, doing his best to give her an anchor. "You hear me, Nicky? No one's falling to their death today."

She nodded and started to cry in earnest at the same time. Aidan preferred her screaming.

"She's not attached to anything," the captain reminded them via radio.

"You don't have to worry about that, Cap," Mitch responded. "She's not letting go of Aidan."

Nope, she wasn't. She'd embedded her nails into him good, and her legs were crossed and locked at the small of his back, but at least he could breathe. "Just get us down," he said.

As the team lowered them, Mitch kept alongside, offering encouragement, cracking his own ass up as they went.

On the ground, Aidan's new companion was peeled off of him and taken away for further evaluation. Aidan took his first deep breath since the rescue had begun. Aching in more muscles than he'd realized he even had, he gathered his gear.

"You okay?" their captain asked. "You took a few hard hits up there."

"I'm fine." He could feel where he'd have bruises tomorrow, and he was pretty sure his back had been scraped raw from the demolition derby collision with the brick wall, but he'd had worse.

Mitch grinned at him. "Man, you just had your bones totally jumped by a nearly naked chick. We almost had to resuscitate you. 'Fireman Asphyxiated by Boobs, news at eleven.'"

Their captain eyed Mitch, and then Aidan. "You remember we have a strict no killing each other policy?"

Aidan reluctantly nodded.

"I'm going to lift that rule for a one-time exception," the captain said, cocking his head at Mitch.

Mitch's smile faded. "Hey."

But the captain had walked away.

"Whatever," Mitch said to Aidan. "If you kill me, you'll never find out what I know."

Aidan slid him a glance. "You never know anything."

"I know lots, starting with a rumor that you're about to get a blast from the past."

"What?"

"Yeah I hear Lily Danville's back," Mitch said.

Aidan froze at the name he hadn't heard in a very long time. Years. Ten of them to be exact.

Mitch raised a brow. "Gray hasn't mentioned it?"

No, Aidan's older brother had not told him a thing, which raised the question.

Why?

"How did you hear?" Aidan asked.

"Lenny. He caught the gossip at the resort. Your family runs the place, how did you not hear this?"

Lenny had gone to high school with them and now worked at the Kincaid resort as a big-equipment driver. Aidan stared at Mitch, unable to process that everyone had known before him.

Lily Danville... Damn. Turning, he started to walk away.

"It's no big deal," Mitch said. "It's not like you're see-ing Shelly anymore, right? You're a free agent, so if you want to try to get Lily back... Hey, wait up."

Aidan didn't wait. And it was true he wasn't seeing Shelly anymore. Technically, they'd never been "seeing" each other. They'd had a satisfying physical relationship whenever they both felt like it, and neither of them had felt like it in over a month now. He hadn't thought about her once since.

But Lily Danville…

He hadn't seen her in forever, and yet he still thought about her way too often.

"Hold up," Mitch called out. "Your half of the gear's still—" He broke off when Aidan kept walking. "Seriously?" And when Aidan didn't so much as look back, Mitch swore and worked to gather the load, making some of the newbies help. He was quiet on the ride back to the station but only because they weren't alone and also because he was playing a game on his phone.

Aidan reached over and swiped his finger across Mitch's screen.

Mitch swore, nearly lost the phone out the window, and then turned to glare at Aidan. "You owe me a Candy Crush life."

"Tell me more about Lily being back."

"Oh, *now* you want to talk? You done pouting then?"

When Aidan just gave him the I-can-kick-your-ass gaze, Mitch grinned. "You know you were."

"It's all over Facebook," one of the guys said from the back. "The news about Lily."

"Aidan forgot his password," Mitch said. "A year ago."

Aidan ignored him, mostly because his brain was on overload. Lily. Back in town…

He'd long ago convinced himself that whatever he'd felt for her all those years ago had been just a stupid teenage boy thing.

Seemed he was going to get a chance to test out that theory, ready or not.

Chapter 2

Fake it 'til you make it, that had always been Lily Danville's motto. And it'd always worked too.

Until the day it didn't.

Which was how she found herself driving through the Colorado Rockies low on gas, money, and dignity.

She really hated when that happened.

But she could throw herself a pity party later. For now it was survival of the fittest—or in her case, not quite as fit as she used to be.

She planned to work on that.

It'd been a damn long time since she'd driven the narrow, curvy highway into Cedar Ridge, ten years to be exact. But she had it memorized, including the dangerous and terrifying S-curve near the top of the pass.

Hundreds of feet of sheer face rock shooting straight up to the limitless blue sky on her left and a stomach-tightening drop-off on her right with nothing but a tiny rail between her and certain death.

Once upon a time, Lily had known every inch of these rugged, isolated peaks, including the most infamous of all of them—Dead Man's Cliff. Hell, she'd once hiked up the back side of the dangerous peak and then free-climbed down the face with no more gear than her own wits, which, granted, in her teenage years wasn't saying much.

Luckily, she'd grown up enough to recognize danger. There would be no free-form rock climbing in her near future. Hiking, most definitely. Risking her life? No, thank you.

As she made it over the last summit before coming into town, Lily rolled down her window and sucked in the mountain breeze. Yep, June in the Rockies still smelled like cedar and pine and air so fresh it hurt.

Or maybe the pain came from being back for the first time in a decade. Her gut twisted at the thought and all the implications that came with it. Telling herself that it was hunger and most definitely not grief, she drove into the town proper. There were ten thousand residents scattered across a county that easily had far more wild animals than people. This didn't include the influx of crazy that went on during ski and board season. During those times, Cedar Ridge's population could triple in size. Most of the tourists spent their time up on the slopes, though, a five-minute drive and two thousand more vertical feet above town.

Lily had no intention of going any farther up the mountain. At all.

Ever.

Instead, she pulled into the first of the three gas stations in town and took a glance at herself in her rearview mirror.

Ack. Her hair had started off decent only because she'd flat-ironed all the natural frizz out, but somewhere between California and Colorado she'd gotten hot and had twisted the unruly mess up on top of her head, holding it there with the stylus stick from her tablet. Strands had escaped and rebelled back to their natural habitat of Frizz City.

Hmm. Not exactly runway-ready after two days on the road. But really, who cared? Probably no one would even remember her.

Buoyed by the thought, she stroked a hand down her clothes to smooth out the travel wrinkles. She wore a sundress and cute blazer out of habit, because that's how they'd done it at the San Diego beauty salon where she'd worked until The Incident. They'd dressed nice to match their upscale clientele, a uniform of sorts.

And now being dressed nice was also her superhero cape. She figured if she looked well put together on the outside, people would assume the inside matched...

For the record, it didn't.

Stretching after the long drive, she looked down at herself. Crap. She rubbed at the four suspicious stains on her blazer that might or might not be fingerprints directly related to an earlier Cheetos mishap. Note to self—give up Cheetos or buy some wet wipes to keep on her. She shed the blazer and eyed the sundress. Damn. There were two more Cheetos finger spots on a thigh. She licked her thumb and tried to rub them out, but this only made it worse. Apparently some things, like Cheetos finger stains and the searing pain of grief, couldn't be fixed.

She was shedding her hard-earned urbanness moment by moment, transforming back to the rumpled, come-what-may, adventurous but oblivious mountain girl. She started to get out of the car, but stopped when her cell phone buzzed an incoming call from Jonathan, her childhood best friend.

"You here yet?" he asked.

Physically, yes. Mentally…well, she was working on that. "Sort of," she said.

"What does that mean?" He paused at her silence. "You know you can do this, right? That you're one of those rare people who can do whatever they need to?" he asked.

True, she'd learned this very skill at an early age, the hard way. But what she needed felt overwhelming and daunting—something that would get her out of the rut that was her life. "I might have come up against my limits this time," she admitted in the understatement of the day. Hell, understatement of the *year*.

"Buck up, Lily Pad," he said. "Things are about to get better. I promise."

"Yeah." She shook her head. "And how exactly is that going to happen again?"

"Because you've got me at your back now," he said, a smile in his voice. "Trust me."

She could trust him, she reminded herself, warming a little as she sighed. Besides, what choice did she have? "Okay, but you'd better be right."

"Always am," he said. "Always am. See you soon."

Lily disconnected and started to get out of the car but realized her feet were bare. She looked around, but apparently along with her city shell she'd also lost one of her wedge sandals. Maybe it was wearing an invisibility cloak. The search led to some swearing and a lot of digging into the luggage in the backseat, and she finally grabbed the next thing she came to.

A pair of Uggs.

She had to laugh as she slid her feet into them. Uggs with a sundress. In San Diego dressing this way would have raised eyebrows, but it was par for the course in Cedar Ridge. Or at least it had been. Torn between hoping things hadn't changed and that they had, she headed into the convenience store, planning on getting in and out without seeing anyone she knew.

There were a handful of other customers in the place, but no one looked familiar. Grateful for small favors, she grabbed an armful of her two favorite food groups—chocolate and salt—then made her way to the front counter to check out.

The convenience store clerk gave her a big eyebrow raise as she dumped her loot on the counter, but either he had sisters or a girlfriend because he didn't say anything as he started to ring her up.

She didn't recognize him, but that didn't surprise her. Ten years was a long time. The thought brought a new wave of anxiety and had her grabbing one more thing that she didn't need—a package of cookies from the counter display.

"Nice," the clerk said without a smidgeon of judgment in his voice as he rang her up. "I especially like the way you've got the entire junk food pyramid represented here. That's not easy to do."

She had a pack of donuts, two pies—one lemon, one cherry—a pint of caramel delight ice cream, a family-size bag of chips, and now cookies as well.

"Bad breakup?" the clerk asked.

"No." Only a little bit of a lie. Because there was bad and then there was *bad* bad. And hers had definitely been *the latter*.

"Smoking too much wacky-tobacky?" he asked.

She could one hundred percent understand why he might think so, but she again shook her head in the negative. No, she was attributing this junk food fest to getting fired from the upscale San Diego salon where she'd worked until three weeks ago.

Apparently she was going to eat her feels about that whole situation.

"Maybe you're having a party?" the clerk asked and flashed a smile. "FYI, my name is Cliff, and I like parties."

"Sorry," she said. "No party." She took a moment to eyeball the rack of candy bars on display.

Cliff laughed. "Listen, don't take this the wrong way or anything, but you have repeat customer all over you, so you should know that we're open twenty-four seven. Which means you really don't have to buy us out of stock right this very minute. Also, at midnight the candy bars go on sale—two for one."

"Do I look like the sort of person who'd go out at midnight for a sale on candy bars?" she asked.

"Oh, yeah."

She sighed and handed over her debit card, aware that a line had formed behind her. Not glancing back, she said a quick little prayer that her card went through the first time and let out a breath of relief when it did.

Getting fired sure had put a crimp in her style.

"Do you want a bag?" Cliff asked. "We charge for them now. Ten cents each."

She had at least a dozen bags in the back of her

car. Not that she'd remember them. "Not necessary." Since she always forgot her bags, she was an expert and scooped the loot into her arms. Everything fit but the bag of chips.

Cliff helpfully added them to the top of the pile. Lily thanked him, pressing her chin down on the chips so as to not lose any of her precious cargo. "Got it," she assured him.

Cliff lifted his hands and she started to leave, side-stepping to avoid bumping into the customer coming up to the register. Lily was halfway to the door when something made her glance back at the line.

Which was how she saw the very last person on earth a woman wanted to see when she felt like roadkill, didn't have on her good moisturizer or her lucky lip gloss...

The guy who'd once upon a time starred in all her fantasies as the man of her dreams: Aidan Kincaid, wearing cargo pants and a dark blue T-shirt with a Search and Rescue emblem on the pec, a radio on his hip, looking dusty and hot and tired and sexy as hell.

Her heart began a slow and way too heavy beat, and she whipped her head around to face forward again.

"Lily? Lily, is that you?" a woman just in front of her asked.

Lily blinked at her.

"Mrs. Myers," the fiftyish woman said helpfully. "Your high school English teacher." She beamed. "Why, I haven't seen you in years. How are you doing, dear?"

Lily's mind raced, leaving her unable to formulate a thought past her instinct to flee. She'd hated English. She'd paid her sister to read the books and write her papers, and in return, Lily had done all of Ashley's math and

science *and* taken on her work hours at the resort their
dad had run. "Uh…"

"Is your mother still happily retired and traveling
around?" Mrs. Myers asked. "I lost track of her after…"
The woman trailed off and her face filled with sympathy.
"After…everything," she finished gently.

There Lily stood in a dress and Uggs and crazy hair,
with Aidan probably watching this entire debacle, and
Mrs. Myers wanted to casually discuss the single most
soul-destroying incident that had ever happened to Lily.

Over a mountain of crap food that she was holding on
to with her chin. And those Cheetos stains weren't going
anywhere…

Thankfully, Mrs. Myers's cell phone rang, and she got
busy searching for it in a purse the size of Texas.

Lily let out a breath and stole a quick peek at Aidan,
nearly collapsing in relief because he didn't appear to
see her.

Miracles did happen…

Before her luck could run out, she said a quick "Nice
to see you" and hightailed it to the door.

Chapter 3

Lily Danville was most definitely back in town. Because he couldn't help himself, Aidan watched as she rushed to the door balancing an armful of junk food. Nice to know some things hadn't changed.

Clearly she was trying to avoid him—a plan he could get behind. He had no desire to take a walk down Memory Road either, especially when that road had ended in a spectacular crash with no survivors.

Just the walking dead.

Still, after all these years she looked the same, hauntingly vulnerable and yet somehow tough at the same time. It was that willowy, curvy body coupled with those drown-in-me green eyes that she so carefully didn't turn his way.

She almost got away, too, and then neither of them would have had to face each other, but someone jostled her at the doorway. Lily staggered backward, right into a five-foot postcard display of the Colorado Rockies.

The entire thing began to wobble.

With a gasped "Oh, no!" Lily reached out for it, sacrificing her bag of chips to do so. The bag hit the floor and then a package of donuts slipped out of her arms as well, landing next to the chips.

And that was it. The domino effect came into play, and sure enough the cherry pie went next.

The very last thing to go was the postcard display itself, falling over with dramatic flair, scattering postcards and Lily's armload from here to Timbuktu, leaving her standing there, a junk food massacre at her feet.

"Damn," Cliff said. "That always happens."

"I'm so sorry!" Lily bent and began to scoop up the postcards.

"No worries," Cliff assured her. "Seriously, I'll get it."

Very carefully *not* looking at the line where Aidan stood, she shot Cliff a grateful smile and vanished so fast that Aidan had himself half convinced he'd imagined the whole thing. Except the postcards sprawled across the floor said otherwise.

So did the odd ache in his chest.

He moved to help Cliff, whom he knew from last summer, when the guy had accidentally set this place on fire.

Cliff grinned as together they righted the display. "She was kinda hot. A mess, sure, but a hot mess, right?"

Aidan made a noncommittal sound and pulled out some cash to pay for the soda he'd come in for.

"Wait," Cliff said, and picked up a package of cookies Lily had left behind.

And a set of keys.

"Hot Chick forgot these," the clerk said. "Could you run them out to her for me?"

Shit. The very last thing he wanted to do was go have

a one-on-one. Especially since clearly she didn't want to talk to him any more than he wanted to talk to her.

"I can't leave the store, man," Cliff said. "You're a firefighter, you rescue people all the time. Go rescue the hot chick, she'll probably be *super* grateful." Cliff waggled his brow. "You're welcome."

Shit. Aidan took Lily's keys and forgotten cookies and strode out of the store. As expected, Lily was still in the lot, sitting in her car, thunking her head against her steering wheel and muttering something he couldn't hear through her closed window.

He shook his head, braced himself, and knocked on the glass.

Lily startled and smacked her head on the sun visor. Rubbing the top of her head, she turned and glared at him.

He lifted his hand, her keys dangling from his fingers.

She stared a moment and then thunked her head on the steering wheel again.

"How long are you going to pretend you don't see me?" he asked.

"Forever?" she asked.

"It's just a set of keys."

When she still hesitated, he revealed the cookies in his other hand, jiggling them enticingly.

As he'd suspected, that did the trick. She opened her car door a little bit, just enough to stick her hand out for the goods.

Aidan dropped both the cookies and the keys into her palm and then made his move, quickly crouching between the opened door and the driver's seat so that she couldn't shut the door on him—though she did give it the ol' college try.

* * *

Damn, Lily thought. He'd always been fast. Whether on a pair of skis on snow or water, or just on his own two legs, the three-time Colorado state champion short-distance runner knew how to move. "You're in my way."

"What are you doing here, Lily? Visiting?"

"No."

"What then?"

No way in hell was she going to admit what had happened to her. Nope. Not saying it out loud. Ever. "Move," she said instead.

Eyes locked on her, he gave a slow shake of his head.

He wasn't moving.

He hadn't shaved that morning, she noticed. Maybe not for a handful of mornings, and the scruff gave his square jaw a toughness that suggested the wild teenager had long ago become a man. She saw now that his T-shirt also had a Colorado Wildland Firefighter patch on the sleeve. The last time she'd seen Aidan, he'd been hoping to get into the fire academy.

Seemed someone had gotten his dream.

"Move or I'll run over your foot," she said, and to prove she meant business, she shoved the key in and cranked the engine.

"You'll run over my foot?" he repeated, eyebrow raised, one side of his mouth quirking in a half grin that was filled with wicked trouble. No wonder half the population of Cedar Ridge had always been in love with him. The other half were either men or dead.

"Grew some claws in San Diego, I see," he said, voice low and amused.

And that amusement got under her skin in a big way.

She told herself she didn't care what he thought, but that was a big lie. She drew a deep breath and went back to her "fake it 'til you make it" attitude. She would simply fake being unaffected by him. Easy enough, right? She released the emergency brake.

"And still impatient as hell." Aidan stood up real slow, on his own damn time schedule.

Just as he did everything.

Once upon a time that had hurt her, deeply, and all because of that damn smile that she'd never been able to resist. But she'd grown up. Gotten smart. Surely she could resist him now as easily as she could resist the cookies he'd hand-delivered to her.

Except she wanted those cookies more than she wanted her next breath. And the worst of it? She had absolutely no illusions about her ability to resist him at all.

Which meant she'd have to avoid him like the plague.

Unfortunately that was a feat she'd never managed. Not the time she'd been a freshman and had come across him kissing an older girl in the alley behind the apartment building where they'd both lived—and not the peck sort of kiss either. Nope, they'd been really going at it, the girl moaning like she'd been eating the very best bag of chips she'd ever tasted.

Nor the time a couple of years later when he and his older brother, Gray—both shirtless and in low-slung jeans—had been working on a muscle car in that same alley all summer long, either fighting or drinking pilfered beers and laughing, their lanky bodies hot and sweaty.

And certainly not the summer after she'd graduated, when she'd finagled a dance with him at the annual festival on the lake, a slow dance—and even after the music stopped, they'd swayed to the beat, unable to break eye contact. She'd been shocked at the heat they'd generated and had wondered if he'd felt the same.

And then he'd kissed her, and it sure seemed like he'd felt plenty, because the kiss... Oh, the kiss. Magical, sensual, erotic... She'd pressed into him, willing to take whatever he could give.

But he'd held back, which at the time she had thought was so sweet. She'd thought he hadn't wanted to pressure her, that they could take things slow.

Until the next day. Lily's sister, Ashley, had come into Lily's room all dreamy, confessing that she had the biggest crush on her assistant ski coach.

Who happened to be one sexy Aidan Kincaid.

Ashley had been sure he liked her back.

That had stung, but it was nothing compared to what followed.

I managed to survive it all, she reminded herself now. Staring into Aidan's melted chocolate eyes, she repeated in her head, The past belongs in the past, the past belongs in the past... Still holding Aidan's gaze, she revved the engine—her car engine, not her internal engine, because that part of her wasn't going to rev for him ever again.

Nope, never. She simply couldn't live with herself if she fell for him again.

With that same small smile still playing on his mouth, Aidan lifted his hands in a stance of mock surrender and took a step back.

Which meant she couldn't very well run him over now. Instead she let her tires chirp as she accelerated out of the parking lot like the hounds of hell were on her heels.

Because in a way, they were.

Chapter 4

Aidan stood watching Lily spin out of the parking lot in a little Honda, as usual leaving chaos in her wake.

And in his gut.

And maybe also in his heart, something he'd admit never. There'd been a time when he would've smiled at just the sight of her, and as she was the daughter of the former manager at a neighboring resort, Aidan had seen her a lot.

She'd been quiet but not shy, smart but a lousy student. Her mountain skills rivaled his. She'd earned them working hard for her dad, *very* hard.

She'd never complained.

He'd loved that about her.

She'd been a bundle of contradictions, and he'd loved that too. He'd also loved how much she'd given to her family, not to mention how tough she was, both mentally and physically.

Her sister, Ashley, had been only a year younger, and

they'd pushed each other hard, competing over every-thing. Ashley had been the outgoing, vocal one, but Lily's charms had been more internal, an inner warmth behind her adventurous spirit that Aidan had been inexplicably drawn to.

He hadn't seen a glimpse of that adventurous spirit or warmth just now.

Nope, the only emotion coming from those light green eyes of hers had been temper and lots of it—aimed at him. He had no idea what she had to be so pissy about. Ten years ago he'd been the one she'd left in her dust, his heart ripped to shreds.

He felt stupid remembering it now, but he felt like they had some kind of connection there on the mountain, in a way he'd never connected with any other girl before.

Or since.

They'd been two adventurous souls, kindred spirits. Or so he'd thought. He'd always been the glue that had kept his family together, and with her he didn't have to work so hard. It had been easy, and he'd felt real contentment. Being with Lily, he could relax and just be. When she'd left, he'd lost all that, and nothing had come easy to him ever since.

Not that any of it mattered now. He'd gotten over her a damn long time ago, a fact he had to remind himself of several times as the worn tires on her car spun a little pulling out of the lot. A city car, not meant for the nar-row, treacherous mountain roads and conditions in the Colorado Rockies.

Maybe she'd forgotten how they did things up here. Maybe she wasn't staying long, though there'd been that cryptic "No" when he'd asked if she was visiting.

It didn't matter. What she did was none of his business.

He pulled out his cell and checked to make sure he hadn't missed any calls. His schedule for the fire season was three days on and one day off, which was today. But S&R had no such schedule. He was often on call for S&R and when notified, he'd go at a moment's notice if he wasn't already on a fire call.

Since he hadn't missed anything, he called his older brother. Gray ran Cedar Ridge Resort and knew everything about everyone in town. He was an eighty-two-year-old lady hiding in a thirty-one-year-old man's body. And he had some 'splaining to do, since he'd apparently known about Lily being back but hadn't mentioned it.

"Mom okay?" Gray asked, in lieu of a greeting.

Their mom, Char, had taken a fall last week and re-injured her bad hip, not that she'd let either of them know how much pain she was in. The woman might look frail on the outside, but on the inside she was The Rock.

"This isn't about Mom," he started. "It's—"

"If it's not about Mom, you've got two seconds," Gray interrupted. "Penny's on a twenty-minute break, I haven't seen her all week, and I have plans for every single one of those twenty minutes."

Aidan could hear Penny's soft laugh in the background and grimaced. Gray had been married to his high school sweetheart going on seven years now. Apparently afraid they were starting to act like old marrieds, they'd decided to spice up their marriage. Just last week Aidan had walked into Gray's office without knocking and found them role-playing *Fifty Shades of "Gray."*

There was some shit you just couldn't unsee. The next day Aidan had installed a dead bolt on Gray's office door and begged him to use it. He could only hope they would.

"Oh, and before I hang up on you," Gray said, "Lenny's an idiot. He got a DUI last night."

Shit. This made strike two for Lenny—strike one had been getting caught having sex inside one of their machines on the night shift. Worse, a DUI meant that his driver's license would be revoked for a minimum of ninety days. Aidan shook his head. Lenny was the best of the best when it came to taking care of their equipment, but that didn't mean shit when it came up against an arrest history. "You want to suspend him until he gets his license back?"

"No, I want him to not be an idiot." Gray sighed. "Yeah, he has to be suspended at the very least. He's lucky you suggested that. I was thinking of firing him on his bad attitude alone."

"I'll deal with it."

"Good. I'm going to go get laid now."

"Wait," Aidan said. "I think there's something else you forgot to tell me."

"Not into guessing games at the moment."

"Here's a hint. Lily Danville."

Silence from Gray.

"Jesus." Aidan rubbed the bridge of his nose. "You really did know. You knew she was coming here and you didn't tell me."

More silence from Gray.

"Answer the damn question," Aidan said.

"You didn't ask me one."

"Why didn't you tell me?"

"Been busy," Gray said. "And that's not the question you really want to ask."

True, but he refused to voice it. Instead he looked up at the sky. No place had skies as big and all-encompassing as Colorado. Things could change in a blink at this altitude, but for the moment the sky was a stark, glorious blue without a single cloud marring it for as far as the eye could see. Which wasn't all that far because the sharp, jagged outline of the Rockies blocked a long-distance view. "How long have you known about this?"

"A few weeks."

This staggered Aidan. "Are you kidding me?"

"Look, not everything's about you, okay? And I have it on good authority that this, her being here, has absolutely nothing to do with you."

"Then why didn't you tell me?" Aidan asked.

"I—" Gray broke off, and Aidan could hear Penny murmur something in the background. Unfortunately for him he could make out the words along with Gray, which included a very explicit, very sexual request.

"Holy shit, Pen," Gray said, his voice low and soft the way it only got with his wife. "Don't take that off yet. Don't move. Not an inch." Then he was back with Aidan. "Gotta go."

"Not until you tell me why she's here."

"*Really* don't have time for this right now, man."

"He really doesn't," Penny piped in. "What he *does* have time for, my dear brother-in-law, is a quickie. Since I know you don't want details, we're going to hang up now. Oh, and don't forget the board meeting in twenty minutes, and the staff meeting after that for the upcoming Tough Mudder event."

"I'm coming," Aidan said.

"Me too," Penny said cheerfully, and disconnected the call.

Aidan shook his head and rubbed his eyes to dispel the images of Gray and Penny knocking it out, but he'd probably need an entire bucket of bleach for that.

And shit. He still had to call Lenny, who answered sounding hung over.

"*What?*" Lenny snapped, not friendly.

"We need to talk," Aidan said.

"No can do, compadre. Got a date with my bed."

"It's important," Aidan said. "It's about work."

"I called in sick today. I'm off the clock."

"Sick or hung over?" Aidan asked.

There was a pause. "We used to agree those two were one and the same."

"That was before we got responsibilities," Aidan said.

"Aw, shit," Lenny grumbled. "Don't talk down to me, man. And I haven't had any caffeine yet. This conversation is way too heavy without caffeine."

Aidan scrubbed a hand down his face. Lenny wasn't taking this seriously, but Aidan felt a huge responsibility. He'd been the one to vouch for Lenny when he'd needed a job. "I'm coming over after my meetings," he said, reluctantly realizing that this was going to require a face-to-face.

There was another beat of silence and then all levity drained from Lenny's voice. "Just say what you want to say."

"Not what I *want* to say," Aidan said. "But what needs to be said. This DUI is strike two—"

"You're counting?" Lenny asked in disbelief. "You? The guy who once got arrested for possession of pot?"

Aidan had been sixteen and stupid. No doubt. But he'd grown up in the decade plus since then.

Way up.

"Lenny, you got a DUI when your job is to drive large pieces of equipment. Our insurance company—"

"Skip the legalese," Lenny said. "I get it. You hired me when no one else would. You're a saint, I'm a world-class fuckup."

"You're not—"

"Let's not sugarcoat anything," Lenny said. "I messed up last night and I know it, okay? It won't happen again."

"Lenny—"

"I promise you, A."

Aidan closed his eyes. Lenny'd had it rough. He'd grown up with a distant great-uncle who'd preferred the assholery technique of parenting. He'd recently been dumped by his girlfriend. Lenny needed this resort job, and he needed Aidan's friendship. Which wasn't so hard to give when Aidan could still remember all the times Lenny had stood at his back. When they'd been accused of cheating on a math test in seventh grade. When he'd gotten in a fender bender with a local cop. When he'd found out he had two younger brothers and a sister, and that his dad was a spineless bag of dicks. "A DUI for you has consequences," he said reluctantly. "Your job requires you to have a license."

"Shit." Lenny blew out a breath. "I was barely over the legal limit—"

"This isn't up to me," Aidan said. "It's a done deal."

There was a long silence. "You firing me?"

"No," Aidan said. "But you have to be suspended until you get your license back, and it can't happen again."

"I know. I'll get this straightened out and be done with it."

Aidan only hoped that was true. They disconnected, and he eyed the time. He'd hoped for something big to stall him so he couldn't hit the board meeting, but since that hadn't happened, he got into his truck to make the drive up Pine Pass Road to the lodge at Cedar Ridge Resort. In winter this could take twenty minutes or more, but today, in early summer with no weather to slow him down, it took five.

Gray handled the day-to-day running of the resort, one of the last family-owned mountain resorts in Colorado. Though "owned" wasn't exactly accurate. Thanks to their dear old dad, they had a very large balloon payment due next year and it was breathing down their necks.

If they went under, they'd lose the only place they'd ever called home, not to mention the fact that they seasonally employed half the town of Cedar Ridge. A mass unemployment would hurt more than just the Kincaids.

Not that they'd get any help from town. Cedar Ridge wasn't that big, but the people in it had long memories, and over the years Aidan had heard it all.

Those Kincaids will never amount to anything.

Those Kincaids, they'd hustle their own mama.

Those Kincaids run with the devil.

Hard to argue the truth. If it'd been just Aidan, he wouldn't give a shit if the resort crashed and burned. To him, the legacy and his father's memory were tainted by the vastness of the man's betrayal. Aidan had absolutely zero loyalty to his dad. But for his siblings and his mom, who'd been hurt way too much, he'd do anything and everything, even though the Kincaids could've been pictured in the dictionary under *dysfunction*. But one thing they did and did well was stick together.

Always.

To get themselves out of the financial mess they could have gone the corporate route and sold out, getting stockholders—but none of them were all that fond of institutions or rules. So, by unanimous decision, they'd gone the hard route.

Status quo for a Kincaid.

Probably today's so-called board meeting would also be status quo—which meant it'd be Gray and Aidan and their half brother Hudson yelling at each other while their half sister, Kenna, watched YouTube on her phone. But just as Aidan pulled into the lodge's parking lot, his cell buzzed.

An S&R call, which had him pumping his fist, because only one thing could get him out of the meeting and he now had it.

A lost mountain climber on Palisade Peak.

Aidan responded to the text with his ETA and put the truck into gear again. Halfway back to town was the local fire station, which they shared with the county's S&R team.

Aidan's home away from home.

Within five minutes he was geared up and heading out with his unit. He'd cleared his mind of everything, the board meeting, his ongoing concern about his mom and her physical health, and especially the sexy blast from his past in a deceptively soft, beautiful package named Lily Danville, and got down to the only constant in his life—work.

Chapter 5

Lily drove up Pine Pass Road, her heart thumping harder and heavier with each beat. For the hundredth time she glanced down at the address on her GPS, saw she was still going the right way, and kept at it, jaw tight.

The thing about GPS, it didn't really reveal hills and valleys. Everything looked deceptively flat on the screen. She'd seen the name of the street and assumed the salon was the one she remembered being downtown.

She'd been wrong.

So wrong, she thought, gut quivering as the elevation climbed and she began to suspect her final destination.

She hadn't been on this mountain in a long time, or any mountain as a matter of fact. Not a single one since that terrible day when Ashley had died.

And then her dad.

Which had been reason number one and reason number two for leaving Colorado.

But her problems went far deeper than regrets or avoiding her old stomping grounds. What she hadn't realized, what Jonathan had failed to mention, was that it appeared the Mane Attraction hair salon wasn't in town at all but part of the Cedar Ridge Resort.

As in *on* the mountain.

But that wasn't even the real problem. Nope, that honor went to Aidan Kincaid himself, reason number three for her leaving this place and never looking back.

And now she was on his family's property.

It's temporary, she reminded herself. *This job, being here, it's only until you get a call back on your resume for another job anywhere other than here.* Still she pulled over and called Jonathan. "You were vague about the salon's exact location," she said, with what she thought was remarkable calm. "It's not the one downtown."

"No. That place went out of business five years ago."

"I'm going to the resort, aren't I?" she said.

"Yep."

She put a hand to her pounding heart. "Oh, my God. Jonathan, I can't. You know I can't." But even as she said it, she knew she had to. She'd sent out approximately thirty resumes over the past few weeks and though she stalked her email hourly, she had nothing else on tap. Nothing, nada, zip.

She also knew why. Yes, she'd managed to claw and fight her way to the very top of the food chain at one of San Diego's premier salons, but she'd also had it all ripped from her with shocking ease.

Thanks to trusting her boss, who had asked her to leak some "confidential" client information to the press about a celebrity, a *big* celebrity—one known for her gorgeous hair. They'd done it before, lots of times. It was common practice. So she never thought twice about it—until it had backfired and *she'd* taken the fall. And thanks to the paparazzi fallout, no matter how great her resume looked, she'd been forced to move two states over, all the way back to Colorado, before she could get another job. A temporary—and pity—offering from the only person she'd kept in touch with here in Cedar Ridge.

Jonathan, who happened to run Mane Attraction.

"Now, you listen to me," he said very gently, very calmly—clearly a man used to dealing with hysterical women. "You know you're good. The very best cosmetologist I know. And I need the very best, Lily Pad. Granted, it's not a manager position like you had, because that's *my* job. But I need you while Cassandra's off to have her baby. It'll be a walk in the park for you compared to the clientele and work you've been doing in San Diego, and by the time Cass is ready to come back, hopefully you'll have heard back on a permanent job somewhere you actually want to be."

"But—"

"But for now you're here," he said. "I'm all you've got, and not to be a complete dickwad, but I'm going to make the most of that. I need you."

She closed her eyes. "I ran into him."

"Who?" Jonathan asked and then gasped dramatically. "*No.*"

"Yes."

"And it was no big deal because you're all done up California-style, right? You're wearing fab clothes and makeup, looking totally irresistible so that he rues the day he let you go, yeah?"

Lily blew out a sigh.

"I'm reading volumes into that sigh, Lily Pad."

"You should be," she said. "First of all, no one let me go—I left. And second, being here..." She swallowed hard. "I don't know, Jonathan," she whispered. "I'm not sure I can do this."

"Well, pull on your big girl panties, because you're already doing it." He softened his voice. "Listen, I get it. I lived next door to you, remember? But it's been a long time, sweetheart. It's okay to move on, to have a life for *you*. It's okay to be happy back here, and maybe even rediscover your love of this place."

There was so much there that she couldn't touch. So much. Mostly because it was all true. So she concentrated on the part she could control. "But what if what happened in San Diego follows me—"

"It won't. You were thrown under the bus by your boss and boyfriend. No one would do that to you here, not even an opportunist like me. I've got your back. You're the sweetest, kindest person I know, Lily."

"You need to get out more," she said, uncomfortable with the praise.

"Shh. I know of what I speak. So...how did he look?"

"Who, Aidan?"

"No, the tooth fairy," Jonathan said. "Yes, Aidan. How did he look?"

"Sexier than sin on a stick," she admitted miserably. "The bastard."

Jonathan laughed in agreement. When it came to all matters sexual, Jonathan was a free agent, playing for whatever team suited him in the moment.

"It was like time reversed itself," she said. "It took

me right back to when...when I left. I want to blame him, but of course I can't. Especially since it was all my fault."

Jonathan stopped sounding amused. "Nothing about what happened was your fault," he said fiercely. "Not Ashley dying on the mountain, not your dad's heart attack, *nothing*."

Lily nodded, which was dumb, since he couldn't see her. But her throat was too tight to talk.

"Lily? Tell me you didn't stay away all this time because you think you're responsible."

She opened her mouth and then shut it.

Jonathan swore with impressive skill. "You're no more responsible than the mountain itself," he said.

"Not true." Everything had been a dare between Lily and Ashley, a challenge. God forbid they play Barbies or have a tea party together, like so many other little girls. Nope, they'd goaded each other through life at full speed, fighting for their parents' attention, grades, skiing, climbing, and once upon a time, Aidan.

"Lily—"

"Listen, I've gotta go," she said, unable to discuss it. "I'm heading into a tunnel, bad connection."

"There are no tunnels in Cedar Ridge."

Committed to her lie, Lily used the back of her throat to fake static. "Hello? Sorry, Jonathan, I'm losing you."

"Uh-huh," he said dryly. "You need more phlegm in that static, babe."

With a grimace, Lily disconnected. She pulled back onto the road. A few minutes later she passed by the resort, which looked busy.

They were in the middle of high summer season, which

drew in everyone from bikers to kayakers to climbers to office dwellers on vacay.

Just past the resort, her GPS binged, letting her know that she'd come to the address that Jonathan had given her for housing. He'd told her that the efficiency apartment came with the job, and when she pulled up in front of a large barracks-like building, she got why.

It was employee housing for the resort.

Lily's unit was on the second floor, and she'd gotten a one-room apartment. She'd assumed that meant one bedroom, but nope. It meant one room. As in the kitchen, dining room, living room, and bedroom were all one big open space.

Big being a bit of a stretch.

Out the back window, she had a view of the lake. From the front window, her view was the parking lot of the resort and the base building.

And the mountain.

She could see most of Cedar Ridge from here, including Dead Man's Cliff far off to the right. Technically it wasn't part of the Cedar Ridge Resort property. In fact, Dead Man's Cliff was closed off to climbers and skiers alike, having been deemed too dangerous since the early 1960s. The only thing allowed there was on-trail hiking.

This hadn't stopped the daredevils from going up and attempting to free-climb the face. But true to its name, it'd killed more than one adventure-seeking idiot.

Ten years ago that idiot had been her sister.

Lily's chest tightened. Well, what did she expect? She'd known she would stir up all sorts of emotions by coming back here. Still, it was harder than she'd imagined.

Turning away from the window, she changed her shoes

and her intentions. Suddenly she needed to show the mountain she wasn't afraid. She was going to go for a hike. Not a climb. Just a simple, easy hike. And if she got to the spot where Ashley had left the trail and tried to climb across the face of Dead Man's Cliff and fallen to her death, then she'd stare that place down and...hell. She had no idea.

But since she had nothing pressing other than obsessing about how she'd ever thought coming back here might be a good idea, she geared up and headed out.

It took her a good half hour to force her feet to move past the trailhead. Twice she turned back but stopped herself.

She could do this.

It was another two hours before she got to the well-known fork in the trail at the base between Cedar Ridge and Dead Man's Cliff, and she was breathing heavily from exertion by the time she did.

Decision point.

Left, and she'd get to an extremely popular hiking trail that would take Lily to about nine thousand feet and give her an incredible, awe-inspiring view.

Right, and she'd get to Dead Man's Cliff. The trailhead had a sign posted that read:

EXPERIENCED HIKERS ONLY
DANGEROUS CONDITIONS
NO FACE CLIMBING
STAY OFF ROCKS AND OUTCROPPINGS

For most, this served as enough of a warning. But for the daredevils, it was an active dare.

And a death wish, of course, for those who chose not to listen...

Like Lily, when she'd been younger and far more stupid. Once upon a time she'd wandered all over this mountain looking for a way to challenge herself and she'd found it here. Hiking up to the top of Dead Man's Cliff and free-climbing on the face was the one thing she'd been able to do that Ashley hadn't, and remembering how she'd bragged about it backed up the air in her lungs.

Because of course Ashley couldn't possibly let the unspoken dare go. Nope. She'd had to attempt to beat Lily, as she did at everything.

And she'd died because of it.

Lily's heart started a heavy, fast beat as she stared at the sign another moment and then...

Took a step back.

Maybe back then she'd had no fear, but that had changed. Big-time. Feeling responsible for your sister's death did that to a person.

And your dad, too, a little voice inside her added. *Don't forget.*

As if she could. He'd collapsed at Ashley's funeral from a heart attack and had died en route to the hospital.

With them both gone, Lily's mom had decided leaving town was the best way to heal. She retired and sold the house. So Lily had taken off, too, meeting up with her mom once a year, or as often as their paths crossed—not easy, since her mom loved to travel. Lily was only back in Cedar Ridge now because she needed the job. But standing at the trailhead she suddenly knew she'd also come back for something else—to somehow find forgiveness.

Maybe then she could finally really move on.

She was still standing there when her phone rang. Not recognizing the number, she hit IGNORE. A minute later came a text from that same number:

If you're looking for something bad for you, try me instead.

Lily stilled. She didn't have to be told who it was, she could hear Aidan's voice as she read his words. But how…? Where…?

She whirled around, searching above her for the security camera she hadn't realized was out here. Though it made sense. In the past ten years, Cedar Ridge's popularity had boomed. It was much more remote than the most well-known Colorado ski parks, but for the people who wanted extremely challenging, rugged, and out-of-the-way adventure, it was here at Cedar Ridge for the picking.

She couldn't find the camera, but knowing she was being watched, she hit REPLY:

How did you get my number?

She got a reply in seconds. *Jonathan.*

She growled, then hit DELETE and left. A few minutes later she received another text:

Good choice.

Funny, coming from Aidan. Oddly enough, back when she'd known him, he hadn't been a natural risk taker. He'd been sharp and ready, willing and up for anything, and maybe a tad bit feral—but though he'd often found trouble with his brothers, he'd been smart about his walk on the wild side.

In truth, he had been her complete opposite.

Still was. Now he'd become the risk taker—firefighting, S&R—and she the cautious one.

And he was sitting in front of the security feeds somewhere, watching her, aware of what she was doing and knowing she'd failed.

Her thumb hovered over DELETE, but somehow her wires got crossed and she typed a response instead: *Just out trying to acclimate to altitude again.*

His reply was immediate: *You were born acclimated.*

Yeah, maybe he was right. But she was no longer that girl he'd known, kissed, and found lacking.

And yet, here she was taking on her biggest adventure of all. Coming home to where she no longer had a home, where she was constantly reminded of why she'd left in the first place, forcing herself to face her demons and grief.

And then there was once again seeing the first man to have ever stolen her heart.

Stolen.

Stomped on.

Run over.

Which meant that maybe she still had a little bit of risk taking inside her after all.

Chapter 6

That hat evening Aidan strode to his truck after a hell of a long day, his eyes gritty with exhaustion, his stomach rumbling from eating nothing but a few PowerBars all day long.

The lost hiker call had turned out to be a false alarm, and Aidan had ended up making the board meeting after all, which was how he'd seen Lily on the monitors, hiking toward Dead Man's Cliff.

He'd been surprised, though he shouldn't have been.

If he'd lost one of his siblings on the mountain and had left Cedar Ridge shortly thereafter, it'd probably be one of the first places he'd want to go see upon his return as well.

But he wouldn't want to do it alone.

He'd started to go up after her when he'd gotten another S&R call—a three-year-old had wandered out his back door into the woods and vanished.

It'd taken several heart-stopping hours to find the kid

three hundred yards from his house, asleep at the base of a huge cedar tree only a few feet away from a steep drop-off.

Now Aidan was finally heading home. An evening thunderstorm was moving in, and, as always in the Rockies, it moved fast. In the five minutes that passed while he stopped for a desperately needed soda, the sky had darkened considerably. Thunder rolled in with the rain, loud booms that made the earth shudder. Already the roads had become slick and dangerous, but that didn't give him pause. Cedar Ridge was rustic, remote, and isolated, and only the hardy and the durable lived here.

He wondered whether Lily was still hardy and durable. Not that it mattered. He'd been there, bought the T-shirt, and gotten left behind, not for the first time either. The first time it had been his father who'd left. But Aidan had a steep learning curve and worked hard never to repeat a mistake.

Allowing himself to care about Lily again would be just that—a big mistake.

Lightning flashed, followed by another rumble of thunder that had the road beneath his tires trembling. The other vehicles on the road kept as steady as he did. Yep, durable stock in these parts. And Aidan and his family were just about as durable as they came. People said they were untamable and born troublemakers.

They'd be right on all counts.

He rolled up his window, because the evening air held a sharp chill now, a reminder that spring had barely left and could make a reappearance in an instant. The season had been particularly heavy and wet this year, leaving the mountains lush and green and thick with new growth.

Once things dried up, it was going to be a hell of a fire season.

Not that there was any other job he'd prefer. Maybe it was the adrenaline junkie in him, maybe it was just his need for fast-paced action and nonstop adventure, but he thrilled to the insanity that was wildland firefighting.

He drove through the resort's lower parking lot past the employee housing and offices, which made him think of Lenny. He'd tried calling him again to check on him, make sure he was okay.

Lenny had ignored the call.

Aidan continued on past the base building that held the mountain café, their equipment rental and sales shop, a general store, and the beauty salon. He turned onto the private service road that circled the resort. His truck bumped along on the dirt road, up past the lodge that housed ski and avalanche patrol, first aid, and the ski school to the very last building.

Originally the three-story log cabin had been the ski lodge. Built in 1920, it held plenty of personality and old rustic charm—emphasis on old. In other words, it was a true POS. There'd been a reason his family had abandoned it for a new ski lodge, but because it was a historic building they hadn't been allowed to tear it down.

So Aidan and his siblings had made it their home—or as close to a home as any of them had ever had.

Not that it was ever as cozy as the word *home* implied. They were the Kincaids, after all, and there wasn't much coziness about Aidan or his pack of wild siblings. Although they were a lot less feral than they used to be.

Cedar Ridge Resort had gone into a tailspin after their dad had started traveling a lot back when Aidan was two years old. Then around the time Aidan became a surly teenager, the truth had come out. Richard Kincaid hadn't been traveling for business, he'd married another woman and started a second family.

And then a third.

To say that discovery of this had been hard on their mom was an understatement. When the dust had cleared, Richard was gone. He'd walked away from all of them.

Char had done her best to keep the resort going, but her injuries had never completely healed quite right, which made managing on the mountain tough. Plus, she'd had her hands full trying to get the wild, rebellious boys under her roof through school without killing any of them or letting them kill each other. The twins had shown up when they were twelve, and Kenna, from a third family of Richard's, came a few years later, just before her twelfth birthday, for the ski circuit. The kids, all of them, had been her priority, and she'd done the best she could.

Gray had taken over for her as soon as he could, gathering in all the wayward half siblings.

They'd all stuck together—except for Jacob, who'd taken off at age eighteen and joined the army. He hadn't been seen or heard from since, a fact that drove Hudson nuts.

In the meantime, Gray, along with his Midas touch and business degree, had worked his ass off. Not to mention pushed, prodded, and bullied the rest of them into doing the same. It'd taken a lot of blood and sweat and maybe a few tears—not that any of them would admit to such a weakness—but they were operating in the black.

Barely.

It was a start. And Gray was still cracking the whip hard, coming down on everyone around him. Always had, probably always would. He was the toughest son of a bitch Aidan knew, and he had only one weakness.

A five-foot-two domino named Penny.

Okay, so they *all* had a weakness for Penny, as she'd long ago worked her nosy self into each of their hearts.

The entire lot of them were like a pack of kittens, they couldn't stand to be together but they couldn't stand to be apart either. In the end, secretly starving for togetherness while fighting daily, they'd divided the building up for all of them into four living quarters. Aidan and Hudson were on the bottom floor. Kenna had taken half the second floor, the other half being full of all the crap they'd accumulated over the years. The third story was for the marrieds, Gray and Penny.

Char lived in a small condo in the town proper and rarely ventured up here to the resort because it brought back bad memories for her. Aidan had the same bad memories, but he was good at locking his shit down tight.

He parked his truck and jogged up the front steps. He keyed his way in and walked through the foyer, shedding his sweatshirt and shoes as he went.

They used what was formerly the lodge's lobby as a living room/secondary office/great room, and the large room was most definitely lived in. The huge, overstuffed and battered leather couches in a wide V in front of a wood-burning stove held a variety of different remotes and several throw blankets, not one of them folded. There was also a flat-screen TV, a sound system, and two dead potted plants gifted to Aidan by an ex who'd been attempting to domesticate him.

And then there was the coffee table, currently littered with trade magazines and more than a few empty glasses that no one would claim because if you got caught leaving anything out, you had to clean the entire place.

Penny's rules. And every one of them was afraid of Penny, so those glasses would not be claimed by anyone with a brain.

The first thing Aidan heard was yelling. This came as no surprise. The Kincaids didn't have much in the way of volume control. Yelling was what happened when they were on top of each other night and day. Hopefully at some point they wouldn't both work together and live in the same building, but for now, for better or worse, no one had made the effort to move away. Maybe because they'd grown up without much family and were making up for lost time. Or maybe it was sheer laziness.

Home. Sweet. Home.

By the time he shed his gear and stood in the middle of the living room, where he could also see into the kitchen, the yelling had stopped. He found Gray face-first in his fridge and Kenna sprawled on the couch. Aidan tossed his keys into some fancy bowl Penny had put on the coffee table. "What the hell's wrong with your own places on your own floors?" he asked.

"I don't have a couch yet," Kenna said.

Like Hud and Jacob, Kenna hadn't grown up in Cedar Ridge. Her mom had brought her to Colorado for the skiing, and it hadn't been long before she'd joined the professional snowboarding circuit and become a world phenom by age fifteen. After that, she hadn't set down roots anywhere until she'd imploded her life last year. Publicly. *Very* publicly.

She still wasn't on the people train. The only socializing she tolerated was her half brothers, and even then only barely.

"You can stay," Aidan told her and looked at Gray. "But not you."

Gray scowled. "Why not me?"

"You're eating my food."

Kenna snorted. "That's because he texted Penny asking her what was for dinner and she texted back that his dinner was in the cookbook, any page, and that the ingredients were all at the store."

"So I came here," Gray said, mouth full as he foraged, holding up salami and cheddar cheese. "You and Hud stock the good stuff."

"It's called the deli aisle," Aidan said. "Also at the store."

"Penny won't let me have salami or dairy," he said. "Says it makes me gassy. You should see the stuff in our fridge, it's all green and 'healthy' shit that"—he used air quotes—"cleans our colon."

Aidan grimaced. "That's—"

"*Disgusting*," Kenna filled in. "And let me perform a public service announcement here and tell you that you seriously overshare." She stood up.

Gray pointed at her. "Stay."

"Um, yeah, hi. My name is Kenna and I'm the boss of me. Not you."

"Goddammit," Gray said. "You're not going back to your cave and holing up for another night."

"Again," she said icily, heading toward the door. "I call my own plays."

"Hold up," Aidan said, and snagged her hand before

she could escape, pulling her around to face him. "What's going on?"

Kenna gave him a pointed look that said, *Ask Gray.*

Behind her, Gray circled his finger around his ear—the universal sign for crazy.

Jesus. "I'm not playing kindergarten teacher today," Aidan told them both. "Someone's going to have to use their words."

Gray stuffed three pieces of salami into his mouth all at once, and then let out a groan. "Oh, my God—this is the real deal, fully loaded with all the fat and everything. Damn, I almost forgot what I've been missing…" More groans and moans.

Aidan shook his head. "You sound like you're starring in a Red Tube video."

"That's because this salami's almost as good as sex," Gray said, and the moment the words escaped he whipped around, clearly making sure Penny hadn't shown up and overheard him comparing their sex life to salami.

Kenna shook her head. "You're so whipped." She tugged free from Aidan. "Okay, I'm out."

"What's the rush?" Aidan asked. Gray wasn't the only one worried about her.

She sighed. "I'm not in the mood for another fight."

Aidan slid a look in Gray's direction. His brother's jaw was doing that tightening thing it did when he was pissed and trying to control himself. "Seriously," he said to them both. "What's going on?"

"I'm tired," Kenna said. "I just want to go to bed, but Gray here thinks I'm acting like an old lady and should hit the town."

After her self-destruction last year she'd turned herself

into a hermit. They'd been trying to work on that with her, but the truth was, they just wanted to fix her and she didn't appear to be in all that big of a hurry to be fixed. "I could give you a ride," he said casually. "Want to go get a drink?"

"Hell no," she said. "The last time we had a drink, you tried to give me the sex talk."

"No, I tried to tell you not all men think with their—"

"Stop!" she said on a rare laugh, covering her ears. "The first time was bad enough."

"How about if I take you up to Mt. Hennessy?" he suggested.

There'd been a time when she'd loved to go four-wheeling up to Mt. Hennessy with him. The faster they'd gone, the louder she'd laughed in sheer delight. At the top, they'd sit on the edge, their feet hanging over the crevice a thousand feet below and they'd just...be. In a rare moment of openness, she'd once told him that had been her favorite thing to do next to strapping on her board and taking any double X diamond run on Cedar Ridge.

But now she just shrugged her indifference.

"Come on," he coaxed. "I'll even yell into the crevice and maybe nearly get arrested by Hud again. Just for you."

Kenna smiled a little at the memory of Aidan taking her up there last year. They'd taken turns yelling themselves hoarse into the canyons, laughing at the echoes. They'd been so loud that someone had called the cops on them, saying someone was screaming bloody murder. Hudson had responded to the call and been pissed to find two of his siblings screwing around.

"Good times," he said, nudging her shoulder with his.

Her smile vanished, and she sighed. "Maybe another time." She met his gaze. "You look pretty done in, A."

Aidan felt Gray take a second, longer look at him as well. "I'm fine," he said.

"You're not," Kenna said, laughing a little. "You're as screwed up as I am and we all know it." She patted his cheek like *he* was the baby sister. "You do know you don't always have to take care of me, right? You can work on taking care of yourself."

With Gray still looking at him like a bug on a slide, Aidan tugged lightly on Kenna's ponytail and bent a little to look right into her eyes so that she really heard him. "I know I don't have to take care of you. I *want* to."

She sighed again, and he prepared for her to roll her eyes, but then she surprised him and walked into his arms. She even let him hold her tight for a beat before pulling free.

She wasn't back on the touch train yet either.

And then she was gone.

"Shit," Gray said, staring at the door. "She's not getting any better."

"Yeah, but she's not getting worse," Aidan said. He took heart in that.

The front door opened again, but it wasn't Kenna coming back. It was Hudson. He was in uniform, holding half a bagel and a to-go cup of coffee.

Gray gave him a brows-up glance.

Hudson ground his teeth.

"Yes or no?" Gray demanded. "You play, you pay."

"Shit," Hudson said, and looking pained, he kicked off his shoes, shoved the bagel into his mouth, and still holding his coffee, he untucked his shirt. He was leanly muscled, emphasis on the lean. Without the shirt tucked in, his pants sagged down on his hips, revealing a strip of pink satin beneath.

Women's panties.

Gray grinned.

Hudson shook his head. He'd had to wear the women's panties or lose a bet. The Kincaid brothers had a long-running joke that had started out with a tie Gray had gotten as a gag gift. It'd had penises on it. Gray loved to have it delivered to either Hud or Aidan, and the rule was that the recipient had to be seen wearing it before he could deliver it to one of the others.

Penny—not a supporter of the penis tie—had nipped that shit in the bud when she'd shoved the thing into the office paper shredder.

After that they'd switched to underwear. Aidan couldn't remember why, exactly, other than that it was funny. Now, once a month or so, whoever had last been punk'd would purchase and have delivered a particularly embarrassing pair of undies, and they had to have proof that they were worn the day post delivery no matter what.

Gray, who'd sent this particular pair, shook his head. "Dude, pull your pants back up, what if Penny walks in?" So far they'd managed to keep her out of the loop on the undies thing. No sense in bothering her...

At Gray's question, Hudson just shrugged—which loosely translated meant, *Penny isn't here, so why should I worry?* At the movement, his pants sagged beneath his ass. Completely unself-conscious, Hudson frog-marched through the place with his pants still at his ankles, vanishing into his room.

Aidan's stomach rumbled loudly, and Gray tossed Aidan the package of salami. "Feed that beast. And how did that last call turn out? The kid?"

Aidan shoved some of the meat into his mouth. "Got him home to his hysterical mom in one piece. Can't say the same for the husband, though. He was supposed to be watching their son while Mom was out shopping. He'd gotten into the game, and the kid walked out the door right beneath his nose."

Gray winced. "That's going to hurt." He took the salami back from Aidan and grabbed some bread and a knife. He added mustard, mayo, cheese, lettuce, and some tomato, then handed the sandwich to Aidan.

Aidan wasn't the only caretaker in the family. He looked down at the sandwich. "Aren't you going to cut off the crusts for me, Mom?"

"Bite me, bitch."

"I should," Aidan said. "Explain the Lily thing."

"I did."

"How about in a way that actually makes sense," Aidan said.

"The salon needed an experienced stylist and cosmetologist," Gray told him. "I told you Jonathan was looking for someone."

"Yeah, but you didn't tell me he was going to hire Lily."

"Because you didn't call me back."

Aidan shook his head. "When?"

"A couple of weeks ago," his brother said, with a vague wave of his hand as he dove back into Aidan's fridge. "You were on a call fighting that Eagle Peak fire or something."

"You mean when I was gone for nine straight days working twenty-four seven fighting that seventy-five-thousand-acre fire, trying to save a hundred homes and uncountable livestock?"

"Maybe." Gray pulled out some leftover Chinese. He sniffed it, shuddered and grimaced, then shoved it back into the fridge. Next he found a plate of brownies and his eyes lit. "*Score.*"

"What about our rule?" Aidan asked. "The no working with exes rule." He yanked the plate from Gray's hand. "And those are mine. A woman brought them by the firehouse. For me."

"The statute of limitations regarding working with exes is long over as it applies to Lily," Gray said, and managed to steal a brownie off the plate, licking it to claim it.

"Are you serious right now?" Aidan asked. "How old are you?"

Gray grinned. "And plus, Lily's not a real ex. She's more a *fantasy* ex."

That it was mostly true just pissed Aidan off. Yeah, okay, so he'd fallen hard and fast for Lily. Unfortunately the recovery from her leaving without so much as a Dear Aidan letter hadn't been nearly so fast.

"Did you ever find out what she thought she was doing up near Dead Man's Cliff?" Gray asked around a mouthful of brownie.

"We both know what she was doing. She wanted to see the last place Ashley had been."

"Well she didn't. She didn't get more than halfway up there."

"She will," Aidan said with certainty. Lily was tough

to the very bone, and she didn't give up. At least the old Lily wouldn't have given up. "What I don't get is why Cedar Ridge now, after all this time?"

"Now, see, if you followed Buzzfeed you'd know why," Gray said smugly, licking residual chocolate from his fingers.

"What's Buzzfeed?"

Gray shook his head. "One of these days you need to do something on your iPad other than watch porn. Lily was working at some fancy spa in San Diego where the rich and famous go, not just for hair but stuff like Botox and chemical peels too."

"What the hell is a chemical peel?"

Gray shrugged. "Beats me, but they do it, all far away from the Hollywood eye. Lily had worked her way up from cosmetologist to assistant manager. Then it got out that some celebrity client used hair extensions or some such shit like that, which was a problem because she's in all these shampoo commercials. Word is that Lily leaked it."

"She lost her job over hair extensions?"

"That celebrity's kinda known for her soft tresses. The news that her hair isn't real has the potential to backfire for both her and the salon, which lost a lot of credibility."

Aidan went brows up. "Tresses?"

"Shut up," Gray said. "I'm married. I know shit like the word *tresses*. And yeah, Lily got canned. Not only that, she was blacklisted over it. Seems that Hollywood's got a long reach. Anyway, she needs this job. She's got a bunch of resumes and feelers out, but so far no one's willing to touch her. And Jonathan said it's only a temp thing, until Cassandra has her baby and finishes her maternity leave."

"That's such bullshit, Lily'd never do something like that."

Gray shrugged.

Aidan stuffed in the last bite of his sandwich, thinking about Lily and how she must feel. "Anything else I should know about?"

"Yep. Shelly's in your bed."

Aidan nearly choked. "And you're just now telling me this?"

Gray shrugged, snatched another brownie, and headed for the door. "She's sleeping."

Shelly was a local bartender and had been on their S&R team for a while until she'd broken her ankle last year. She and Aidan were long-running friends with benefits minus the friends part. They were also on-again off-again, currently mostly off.

He had no idea why she'd be here now, but he could guess. Kicking Gray out, he headed down the hall. Maybe sex with Shelly and eight straight hours of sleep was just what he needed.

He opened his door and stopped in the doorway.

Wearing nothing but his sheets, Shelly sat up in the center of his bed with a come-hither smile. "I forgot why I was mad at you," she murmured.

"Because I work too much," he said.

"Oh, yeah." She affected a pout. "Seems silly now, though, doesn't it? I read about that search and rescue of the little girl you saved from the river last week. You jumped off the bridge like it was nothing. It was…amazing," she said a little breathlessly. "I think I need to be searched and rescued too."

Telling himself he was game, he kicked off his shoes

and pulled off his shirt, and then hesitated, suddenly feeling the need to stall. "Let me take a shower first."

She got up on her knees and crawled toward him, hooking a finger in the waistband of his pants and reeling him in. "Search and rescue me first," she whispered breathlessly, "then shower."

Thinking that should be sexy as hell, he bent to kiss her, but...couldn't. "*Shit*," he said.

Shelly stared at him and then got off the bed. She bent for her clothes, pulling them on in jerky movements. "You know," she said, no longer breathless, "if you weren't in the mood, you should've answered my text."

He pulled out his phone for the first time in hours and indeed found her unread text. "Shit," he said again.

"You're a jackass, you know that?"

Aidan scrubbed a hand down his face. Lily hadn't even been back in town twenty-four hours, and she was already screwing with his head. As much as he wanted to get laid, all he could see were her moss-green eyes when he closed his own. "I'm sorry, Shelly."

She looked shocked. "*Good-bye* sorry, you mean?"

He couldn't believe he was going to do this, turn away a sure thing with no strings attached. "Yeah. This isn't working for me."

Shelly paused. "Let me get this straight—all the casual, easy sex isn't working out for you?"

"No," he said. "It's not."

She was looking and sounding pissy now. "Your job is your life, Aidan, and I get that. You've said you don't have time for a real relationship, and I get that too. I don't want one either. But I do want honesty. I deserve that much."

She was right about his job being his life. But he also *did* want a real relationship…someday. And though they were compatible in a lot of ways, Shelly wasn't the one he wanted a relationship with.

Just as he wasn't the one for her either.

"You do deserve honesty," he said. "And okay, yeah, this is about more than my work, but I don't know what exactly it is. That's the truth," he said when she gave him a skeptical look.

She stared at him, the temper still clear in her eyes. "You're funny and hot and magic in bed, but I don't play second fiddle, Aidan. Not even for you." She slipped into her sandals and headed toward the door. "You're going to miss me, you know."

But when she was gone and he looked at his empty bed, he felt nothing but a little ping of relief that he could have the entire thing to himself.

Chapter 7

The next day, Lily woke up early because her toes were missing. When she cleared the cobwebs from her brain, she realized she was still in possession of ten toes—they were just frozen. Overnight, the temps had dropped, and she could in fact see her own breath inside her apartment.

Damn. It'd been a long time since she'd experienced the fifty-degree drop between night and day that Colorado called normal. Huddling under the covers, she wished for a magic blanket warmer. Or a really warm man.

The image that came to her wasn't her usual fantasy of Channing Tatum and Chris Hemsworth.

It was even more embarrassing.

Aidan. Naked. Heated. Willing and able to share that heat…

Gah.

She grabbed her phone and distracted herself with her daily morning chore—checking her email for a response to one of her resumes. Any response at all would do. But, like yesterday and all the days before that, she had zip.

Sucking in a breath, she braced herself for the rush of cold before sliding out of bed. The early light drew her to the window, where the mountains backdropping the resort seemed to mock her.

She yanked the shade down.

Yesterday she'd unloaded her suitcases from her car but hadn't unpacked. So she dug through them until she found a sweatshirt and pulled that on over her PJs. She added wool socks and then stood in the middle of her apartment hugging herself. There was no central heater in the place, just a woodstove.

With no wood.

The welcome letter on the counter read:

Utilities come with the rent. The stacked wood by the dumpsters is free. So is the Internet.

We hope you'll take advantage of some of the recreation the resort offers this summer season; biking, climbing, rafting, kayaking, a ropes course... the sky's the limit.

Enjoy your stay.

That would be easier to do if she were back in San Diego, where it didn't get cold at night. Or ever. Where she could insulate herself from her past with a nice, solid thousand miles between herself and Cedar Ridge with all its memories.

Including Aidan Kincaid.

Shivering again, she stomped into her Uggs. Then she opened her front door to peer out and see how far away the woodpile was. At least a hundred feet away off to the left, she discovered, next to two large dumpsters. She looked down at herself; oversized sweatshirt, hood up, PJ shorts in pink plaid with KISS IT on her butt, wool knee socks, and her Uggs. Own it, she decided, and ran down the stairs to the woodpile.

The first piece weighed far more than she remembered it would. She grabbed two more pieces and then the worst possible thing happened.

Something slithered out from behind one of the logs in her hands. At the way she screamed, one might assume that a bear had come trolling along looking to eat her up. But no, not a bear.

Worse.

It was a snake, and it touched her arm.

Tossing the wood away from herself, Lily gave another scream and did the snake dance, the one that looked like maybe she was having a seizure. This lasted a full minute before she got ahold of herself.

Torn between the snake willies and possible humiliation if anyone saw her, she decided humiliation was worse and forced herself to calmly smooth down her clothes. Nope, nothing to see here... Casually she turned to send a glare to the snake.

It was gone.

Well, crap. Because now she had a bigger problem. How could she pick up the wood now knowing that the mofo was hiding in there, watching her from obsidian eyes, waiting for his big moment to give her another heart attack.

She kicked one of the logs. Nothing. Okay then, she thought, and gingerly picked it up. And then another, carefully stacking them in her arms as if they were fully locked and loaded bombs. "He's long gone," she whispered to herself as she headed to the stairs. "He went on vacay. Somewhere warm."

A lie, as it turned out, because the thing dropped from the wood in her arms and slithered across her boots.

Game over.

She screamed even louder than before, tossed the wood, and started to run away, her feet scrambling like a cat on linoleum.

"Lily."

She jerked to a halt in shock. *No.* But sure enough when she turned around, there Aidan stood in the parking lot, framed by the morning light and looking gorgeous, the bastard. He wore dark sunglasses and a long-sleeved Henley with a Cedar Ridge Resort emblem on one pec. And his faded jeans, low slung on his hips, had a rip in one knee that she'd bet was genuine and not manufactured that way. Leaning back on his truck, arms casually crossed, he seemed amused by her snake dance, but not particularly happy to see her.

Well, the feeling was entirely mutual, she thought grimly.

"Need a snake inspection?" he asked.

Yes. If she was being honest, she wanted a serious snake inspection and also, at least in her dreams, she wanted it to involve his hands on her. All over her— Gah. "*No.*"

At her emphatic tone, he went brows up.

"What are you doing here?" she asked, not having to fake the irritation in her voice. She *was* irritated, starting to sweat, and—dammit—also a little turned on. Stupid sexy guy jeans.

"I was on my way to my office," he said.

She slid a look at the resort's office building and met his gaze again. "You work here too?"

"I help Gray run the place."

This was curious. "You used to say you'd join your father's business when you were cold and dead. Or when *he* was cold and dead," she said, "whichever came last."

He lifted a broad shoulder. "Things change."

That simmered between them for a moment, past and present commingling uncomfortably.

"You find what you were looking for up there on the mountain yesterday?" he asked casually.

What was it about him that made her want to both kiss him and yell at him at the same time? *Because once upon a time you wanted him and he...wanted your sister.* Oh, yeah, it was all coming back to her now, and her spine snapped straighter. "I told you," she said. "I was just trying to get my sea legs."

He wasn't polite enough to just nod and let her have the lie. Instead he called her out on it. "Or you were thinking of Ashley," he said with a gentle directness that nearly broke her.

She paused a moment to swallow hard. "I guess I just wanted to say good-bye," she finally said.

His expression tightened a little at this. "You were going to free-climb the face?"

"No. I'm not in any sort of climbing shape," she said. "Nor used to the altitude either. I was just going to hike to the top. But as it turns out, I'm not in shape for that either."

He studied her a long moment. "I'm surprised."

She wasn't sure how to take that. "I've been stress eating and not exercising like I should—"

"No," he said. "I meant I'm surprised you're back. When you left, you vowed to never return."

Oh. That. "Things change," she parried softly. Back then she'd lived for the outdoors, suffering through school and work, counting the minutes until she could escape. In the winter she'd been required to be on the ski team for the resort her father managed—not as fun as it might seem. In fact, it'd been brutally competitive and incredibly demanding, to the point that she'd had no life.

But in the off-season, she'd been free.

So she'd hiked and had discovered her first real joy—being alone on the mountain. She'd quickly gotten bored with the trails and had begun challenging herself with rock climbing instead, using no ropes just her fingers, toes, and wits, until there'd been no place on or near Cedar Ridge that she hadn't explored, including the aptly named Dead Man's Cliff.

Looking back on it now, it was a miracle that she'd lived to tell the tale. But she hadn't been the only one enjoying her solitude.

She'd often come across Aidan out there. In fact, if anyone had known that terrain better than she did, it was him. After that night at the summer festival, she'd thought that maybe they'd explore the mountain together.

And then each other.

But then Ashley had claimed him first, and he was the one thing Lily had hoped to never compete with her sister for. Especially after she'd died.

Aidan was watching her from those dark glasses, thoughts hidden, though she had the feeling her own thoughts were as clear to him as crystal. "Tell me about the resort," she said, before he could ask her any questions.

He shrugged. "Not much to tell. Gray took over the management. It took a few years, but he runs a good ship and we turned it around."

"We?" she asked.

He smiled grimly. "Turns out we Kincaids are good at pulling ourselves out of the gutter. We're like cats, nine lives and all that."

"And good at landing on your feet," she said.

He bowed his head in silent agreement.

"You're a busy guy," she said. "Firefighting, and the resort."

"And Search and Rescue."

It all made perfect sense for him. He'd always been at his best on the mountain, and that he'd made a real life for himself on it in every way gave her both a sense of pleasure for him and an ache for herself, one she couldn't put her finger on. "And the other Musketeers?" she asked, referring to his half siblings, Hudson and Jacob, and their reputation for trouble.

Aidan smirked at the "Musketeers" and said, "Hudson works ski patrol in the winter and works with me at S&R as well. And he's a cop in the off-season—"

She laughed, she couldn't help it. Hudson, the scourge of Cedar Ridge, becoming a cop of all things.

And Aidan actually flashed a grin as well. "Yeah, I know. Go figure, Hud on the right side of the law. He takes a lot of shit for that. I think he likes it."

"And Jacob?" she asked. "Don't tell me he's a cop too."

His smile faded. "No. At least I doubt it." He paused, then shoved his fingers through his hair. "He hasn't been home in a while. A long while."

There was pain in his gaze now, and regret. "I'm sorry to hear that," she said, and dropping the subject that was none of her business, directed her attention back to the wood.

"Need some help?" he asked.

Need? *No.* Want? *Yes.* But she'd never been good at admitting that. "I'm fine." Tearing her gaze off of him she glared down at a piece of wood. She kicked it again, not once but *twice*.

No snake.

She gingerly picked it back up.

"You forget how to survive out here?" he asked.

She glanced at him over her shoulder. "What are you talking about?"

He gave her a slow once-over, gaze lingering on her bare legs, which had certain body parts leaping to life that had no business doing so.

"Loading wood in…" He looked her over again, and his lips quirked. "PJ's and no gloves. Not the Lily I remember."

"Well, if one thing's true, it's that I'm definitely not that same girl you knew." She kicked the second piece twice too.

No snakes.

She picked it up, carefully, because Aidan was right. She should be wearing gloves. Spiders lurked in the wood stacks as well as snakes, and the last thing she needed was a bite. She carried the two pieces of wood up the stairs, nearly tripping when she heard his muffled snort of laughter behind her.

"*Kiss it?*" he asked.

Remembering her shorts, she felt her face flame. Ignoring that, and him, she moved to her front door, dropped the wood in a little stack, turned for more, and—

Ran straight into Aidan, who also had a full armload of wood. "Door," he directed.

She had no idea how it was that she was both annoyed and yet turned on by his bossy, take-charge tone, but she obediently shifted aside and opened the door. Aidan carried it all into her place and neatly stacked it next to the woodstove. "More?" he asked.

"No." She watched as he rose to his full height and felt her good parts quiver again. Dammit. "Thanks."

"Anytime."

The air between them thickened. "So," she said. "You were surprised to see me."

"Yeah. I was surprised to see you."

"No one told you I was coming?" she asked.

He met her gaze. "No, though it would've been nice to hear it from you."

"We hadn't communicated since..." She trailed off. Since Ashley's death.

No, that wasn't quite true. He'd tried to get ahold of her after the service. She'd picked up one of his calls, and neither of them had known what to say.

The awkwardness of that conversation had stuck with her enough to cut the ties entirely.

"You got in to Boulder," he said, referring to the University of Colorado's pursuit of her. "Onto their ski team. A huge big deal."

"Yes," she said, trying not to grimace at the memory of being accepted into the one and only school Ashley had desperately wanted to ski for. It was guilt that had kept her from going, plain and simple. "So?"

"So you didn't go. Instead you became a cosmetologist."

She paused and arched a brow, going for a misdirect. "You think I'm beneath being a...cosmetologist?"

"I'm just curious about the transition," he said easily.

"I decided Boulder wasn't for me."

"Why?"

She wasn't used to the questions. It'd been a long time since anyone had gotten close enough to want to know about her personal life at all. Yeah, there'd been her ex, Michael, but it'd been more about work with him, and they'd never really gotten into each other's pasts at all. And now she wasn't sure how to answer Aidan's question. "I was never a great student, we both know that."

"Did you think Ashley would be upset at you for going?" he asked.

She had no idea how he did it, how he always put his finger right on her thoughts. Her private thoughts. "Maybe at first."

"Lily," he said with devastating gentleness.

"She was the one who wanted to go to college, Aidan. She was meant for it, not me."

"Bullshit." He was leaning back against the doorjamb, feet crossed, hands in his pockets, a casual pose, but there was nothing casual about his expression.

He didn't like where she was going with this.

"I'm not stating an opinion here," she said. "I'm stating fact."

"So Ashley was smart," he said. "So what? So are you. Boulder wouldn't have accepted you otherwise. Tell me you've since realized that, Lily."

She shrugged. "It took awhile, but after cosmetology school, I started working full-time at the spa, as low on the totem pole as I could possibly get, of course. That frustrated me," she allowed. "I did all the grunt work and then finally was given more to do but didn't get any of the credit for it. So I went back to school at night and took some business classes. By the end I was practically running the spa myself." Not that she'd gotten credit for that either...

"I hope like hell it hurt them when you left," he said.

So did she...

"Did you like it there?" he asked. "San Diego?"

She'd thought so. Until she'd come back here. She hadn't realized in all those years that she'd never really felt like she was home. "I missed the snow."

He chuckled. "Can't tell by the car you're driving."

"Yes, well, you always were a car snob." She paused. "And I don't plan to still be around by the time I need four-wheel drive."

"You just got here," he said. "In a hurry to leave already?"

"I'm only here until a permanent job comes through. I'm looking at this as a little break."

"From the bad press you mean."

She sighed. She shouldn't be surprised he'd heard.

His smile faded. "You get a bum rap, Lily?"

She met his gaze, extremely tired of dancing around this subject. "Are you asking me if I ratted out one of my clients for money?"

He shook his head. "I know you wouldn't rat out anyone."

The words, unwavering, sucked the air from her lungs. "You don't know me anymore," she reminded him.

"I know enough." This was said with steely certainty.

The blind faith in her actually made her throat burn. Her eyes, too, and for a moment she couldn't speak, afraid she'd burst into pathetic tears. "But it *was* me," she said softly. "My boss asked me to leak it in order to get the salon's name in the press. But it backfired and so…" She shrugged.

"And so you took the fall for it."

She nodded.

"So your boss was a real stand-up sort of person, then."

She'd thought so, at first. Michael had run the salon, been her friend, her sometime lover, and sometimes her boyfriend. And not only hadn't he stood at her back, he'd fired her and then blacklisted her as well. "It's actually done a lot," she said. "Where a celebrity calls ahead and wants their arrival or departure noted in the press. It keeps them in the public eye and relevant."

Aidan never took his eyes off of her. "So then why didn't your boss come clean? She could've saved you a lot of problems by doing so."

"He. Michael," she corrected. "And I don't know, other than Michael turned out to be someone other than I thought."

He studied her a moment. "This guy was more than your boss."

This startled her.

"Turns out I can still read you," he said quietly.

"Lucky me."

"So you going to tell me what's wrong?"

"Other than I hate snakes and you saw me in my PJs? Nothing." She lifted her chin and defied him to contradict her.

She should have known better. Like Ashley, he'd never met a challenge he didn't face head-on.

He moved toward her, right into her personal space.

She took a step back and came up against the wall.

This didn't stop him. He kept his forward momentum until they were toe to toe. And then while she was still standing there a little dumbfounded and also something else, something that felt uncomfortably close to sheer, unadulterated lust, he put his hands on the wall on either side of her head.

This both escalated her heart rate and stopped her lungs from operating. "Um—"

"You had your chance to tell me what's wrong with you," he said. "You passed. Now I'm going to tell you what's wrong with me."

Oh, God. Talking would be a bad idea. As for a good idea, she had only one, and before she could consider the consequences, she gripped his shirt, hauled him down, and kissed him.

He stilled for a single beat and then got on board quick, pulling her in, sinking a hand into her hair to tilt her head to the angle he wanted, and taking over the kiss.

The next thing she was aware of was the sound of her own aroused moan, and she jerked free.

The corner of his mouth quirked. "Did you just kiss me to shut me up?" he asked.

She blew out a sigh. "It made a lot more sense in my head."

He grinned, one of those really great grins that made something low in her belly quiver. Needing some space, she pushed him, even though her instincts were telling her to pull him in tighter instead of pushing him away.

"Back to what's wrong with me," he said, still looking amused. "It's you."

She opened her mouth to say something, but he set a finger against her lips. "My turn," he said, and lowered his head and kissed her.

And oh. Oh, damn… There were some men who just knew how to kiss, the kind of kiss that could send a woman reeling. The kind of kiss that could take away problems and awareness and…and *everything*. The kind of kiss that could shatter her into a trillion little pieces. The kind of kiss that somehow both calmed her body and soul even as it wound her up for more.

Aidan was that kind of kisser. Shocking, really, to also realize that in between their first kiss all those years ago and now, that there'd been nothing like it for her.

Aidan pulled back a fraction of an inch, opened his eyes, and stared into hers.

She stared back because wow. *Good.* So damn good, and for one glorious moment there she'd let her lips cling to his, let the memories of him and all that he'd meant to her wash over her.

And those memories had all been…epic.

Until the end.

Finding her sanity, she pushed him again. For a beat he didn't move, just looked into her eyes.

And then, on his own terms, he stepped back.

She pointed at him. "That was…"

He arched a brow.

"Never mind what it was," she said. "We aren't going there."

His smile was grim and utterly without mockery.

"Agreed." But then he hauled her up to her toes and kissed her again.

And again.

And only when she was a panting, whimpering mass of jelly did he finally let her go.

"What was that?" she managed.

"Hell if I know." He shoved his fingers through his hair, looking uncharacteristically baffled.

She stared at him, a little startled to realize he was no more eager for this than she. Had she done what she hadn't imagined she could, hurt him when she'd left? "Then we won't make the mistake of repeating it," she said, shocked to find the words hard to say. Once there'd been nothing she'd wanted more than him, and she'd really believed it could happen.

But then Ashley had died and Lily hadn't been able to find her footing in an upside-down world. She'd walked away from Cedar Ridge and Aidan, and it had hurt nearly as much as losing Ashley had. She didn't want to go through anything like that, not ever again. So she opened the front door in a silent invitation for him to leave.

He didn't. He just met her gaze, his own hooded, giving nothing away of what he was thinking. "I know you're so stubborn that you'll freeze to death before asking for help," he said. "But I'm going to ask anyway—do you need anything else?"

"No," she said abruptly, and then sighed. "No," she repeated, softer now. "Thanks."

He held her gaze, shook his head, and then he was gone.

She closed the door behind him and settled a few hard-earned pieces of wood into the stove.

And that's when she realized. She did need something—

matches. But Aidan had been right, she'd freeze to death before opening the door and catching him on the way to his truck to ask if he had any. Nope, she'd have to relive kissing Aidan to keep her warm until she got to the store. The thought heated her just as well as any fire.

Chapter 8

Aidan's cell went off in the middle of a really great dream where he had the kiss with Lily playing on repeat. And damn, she'd tasted as sweet as he'd remembered. It'd nearly killed him to pull away.

He loved the way she'd held still after, staring at him in shock and wonder, how her tongue had come out to lick her lower lip as if trying to make the taste of him last.

He'd had to force himself to let go of her. But in his dream he didn't have to let go. And she didn't push him away either. Nope, instead she pushed him down onto her bed and—

His phone buzzed again. Damn. Reaching out in the dark, he squinted at the screen. Incoming text calling him for an S&R—a missing camper.

He dressed and ran into Hudson at the front door, hair crazy wild, his eyes hooded from sleep.

"Hey, Princess," Aidan said. "You look like shit."

Hudson flipped him off as they jogged out to Aidan's

truck and hit the road, driving straight into a wall of fog in the still-dark morning.

"Zero visibility," Hudson said, looking at his weather app.

"No shit," Aidan said, looking out the windshield.

Hudson handed him a granola bar.

"What's this crap?" Aidan asked.

"Just eat it before I cram it down your grumpy-ass throat."

Aidan ate the granola bar. Not because of Hud's threat but because he was starving. And when he was done he tossed the wrapper at Hud's head.

Hud caught it without taking his eyes off his phone. Impressive. The guy had been a skinny and sickly eleven-year-old kid when his mother brought him and Jacob to Cedar Ridge. Char, suffering in her own right, had taken them in, since it was clear their mother wasn't mentally stable enough to handle them. From that day forward Hud had followed Gray and Aidan around with hero worship in his eyes. Unused to any sort of outdoor lifestyle, he'd often ended up hurt and stuck indoors. Char, who'd loved them all equally, had a soft spot for Hud. She'd babied him, earning him the nickname Princess.

Hudson had grown a couple of feet and a whole bunch of muscle since then, but, to his eternal frustration, the nickname had stuck.

"You really do look like shit," Aidan said.

"I was online all night," Hudson admitted.

Aidan knew Hud had been searching in earnest for his twin brother, Jacob. Not that they'd found hide nor hair of him.

More recently, and for more complicated reasons,

Hudson had also been searching for their dad, much to Aidan's frustration. He didn't want that asshole within a thousand miles of here. "Please tell me you were up all night watching that cartoon porn again and *not* searching for Dad."

In the way he'd been doing since he was a kid, Hudson set his jaw. And the big brother in Aidan sighed, knowing he'd come up against the brick wall that was Hudson's stubbornness. "We've been over this, man. We don't need him."

"We do," Hudson said. "And it's not porn, it's called anime. It's an art form."

Aidan shook his head. "Whatever. Just concentrate on finding Jacob. Forget Dad."

"I can do both."

"But you don't need to," Aidan insisted. "We don't need Dad here right now."

Or ever.

Hudson slid him a glance. "On a scale of one to goat-fuck, how stubborn are you going to be about this?" Hud asked.

Aidan just gave him a hard look.

"So goatfuck then," his brother muttered. "Perfect."

They pulled up to the incident command center and joined the fray.

"Gonna be like hunting a needle in a haystack," Hudson said, squinting at the fog.

No doubt. During the summer months they had more rescues than any other time of the year. With its sheer rock face for climbing, challenging trails for hiking, and some decent rapids, Colorado was a magnet for what they called weekend walkers—people who were office-dwellers during the week and adventure-seekers on the weekend. They were the main reason things stayed so busy for S&R and the fire department.

Depending on the runoff from the surrounding creeks and estuaries, the river rapids could go from an easy class two up to a class four in a blink, making it all too easy to run into trouble. And in spite of the carefully posted warnings, the signs were all too often ignored. It was as if people lost all common sense the moment they smelled fresh air and got onto a dirt trail.

Today's trouble came courtesy of a group of six girl-friends who'd gone on an overnight hiking expedition to Eagle's Cove. They'd decided to prank the sole single girl in their midst into thinking she was being tracked and stalked by Bigfoot because he could smell her virginity. Terrified, she'd run off, heading into the woods.

And had not been seen since.

This had been at midnight, but the girls hadn't called it in until four a.m. because they thought she'd been playing a return trick on them by disappearing.

Plus, they hadn't wanted to get in trouble.

But then a bear had crossed their paths, and they'd all run screaming into the night, racing all the way back to base, convinced their friend had become Bigfoot bait.

Aidan wasn't too worried about the bear sighting. They'd most likely seen a black bear, known to be meek and mild-tempered—unless you got between a mama and her cub. That always changed the game. Hoping for the best, Aidan and Hudson geared up with the others on their team. Mitch had caught an extra shift at the fire station so he hadn't made it, but the rest of them headed out into the predawn light.

There'd been plenty of June snowstorms over the years, and it was definitely cold enough for one today, but there was no precip in the forecast.

Small favors.

Two hours into the search, the sun had come up and they'd found the girl's bandanna hanging off a branch. She'd gotten as far as the base of North Peak.

Problem was, this sat at a crossroad and they had no way of knowing which way she'd gone. Alone in the dark, frightened, she could've chosen any of three options.

The team split into pairs, each taking a different direction, with Aidan and Hudson continuing north. A quarter of a mile later they found a torn piece of sweatshirt material snagged on another branch.

"Shit," Hudson muttered, and they both looked up farther north—to Dead Man's Cliff.

Had the girl left the trail and tried to climb the rocks down? The trail did vanish into nothing in a few spots, it was entirely feasible to get turned around and completely lost in less time than it took to blink.

"This is no place for a novice," Hudson said.

Hell, it wasn't a place for an expert. Dead Man's Cliff had claimed far too many lives, and yet people *still* ignored the warning signs posted everywhere and purposely left the trail and risked their lives.

Aidan had seen far too many deaths in this area, but the one that always stuck with him, and in fact still gave him nightmares, was Ashley Danville's. He had to shove that thought aside or he wouldn't be able to do his job. They radioed in their new information and kept going.

An hour later they found another breadcrumb—the missing girl's shoe.

"Not a good sign," Hudson said, the master of understatements.

"She was moving fast," Aidan said. "Probably scared out of her mind."

Hudson pointed to yet another STAY OUT OF THIS AREA sign. "Why do we bother with these?" He shook his head. "Maybe she hasn't seen any of the *Scream* movies, the ones where the girl who runs off on her own dies a horrible death."

They kept going. An hour later, Aidan stopped again. Shoving his sunglasses up on top of his head, he crouched down next to a low-lying manzanita bush and stared at the shoe that matched the one they'd already found, this one dotted with some blood. "Shit."

Hudson echoed the sentiment and radioed it in.

A few minutes later they heard the thumping beat of the search chopper flying overhead.

Their radios crackled in stereo as the report came in from the helo. The missing girl had just been spotted one hundred yards north of Aidan and Hudson's position, off the side of the trail, where she'd apparently fallen and was clinging to some undergrowth.

Aidan and Hudson raced to the spot and peered over the side.

Yep, there she was, twenty feet down, conscious and hyperventilating by the looks of things. "Shannon," Aidan called down while Hudson prepared the rope, harness, and attachment point. "How you doing?"

She burst into loud sobs while simultaneously cussing out her coed sisters with enviable creativity.

"It's okay, we've got you now," Aidan told her. "Just hang tight, we'll be right there." He looked at Hudson. "Hit it."

"Not me," Hudson said, nudging the harness at Aidan. "You know I don't do criers. This one has your name all over it."

Aidan snatched the harness. "What makes you think I do criers?"

"Have you met the women you date? Teri, Breanne, Molly, Shelly—" Hudson ticked off Adrian's exes on his fingers.

"I never *dated* Shelly," Aidan said, slapping Hudson's helping hands away.

"Banged then," Hudson said.

Aidan straightened the harness and narrowed his eyes at Hudson. "And how is it you get to escape all the crazy?"

"It's a talent I picked up by watching you and doing the opposite," Hudson said.

The rest of the team arrived. As Hudson belayed him down, Aidan kept his eyes on the girl. "Keep your head down," he told her. "Don't look up or you'll get rock dust in your eyes."

So of course she promptly looked up and got rock dust in her eyes. She screamed and slid down another few feet. "Omigod, I'm losing my grip! I—"

Aidan snatched her just as she let go. "Got ya."

Still screaming, she managed to climb his body, gripping him with both arms and legs like a monkey.

Déjà vu…

"Shannon," he said firmly while keeping his voice purposely low so that she'd have to strain to hear, theoretically shutting up in the process. "I've got you. You're safe."

She stopped screaming. With a noisy sniff, she met his

gaze, her face puffy and mascara ravaged, as the team pulled them up. "Are you married?" she asked.

"No."

"Do you want to be?"

By the time they got Shannon down to the base of the mountain, a rather large crowd had gathered. Any rescue on Dead Man's Cliff was always big news in Cedar Ridge. Other than that time the *Housewives of Beverly Hills* had come through town complete with their television camera crews, Cedar Ridge's biggest claim to fame was the cliff and the lives it claimed.

The group of Shannon's sorority sisters looked worried, and for good reason. They were probably about to get their asses handed to them in a sling.

You play, you pay, Aidan thought, knowing it all too well. He and his brothers had been pulling shit on each other forever.

"Remember when Gray locked us in the Cat?" Hudson asked, obviously thinking along the same vein. "We found the keys and drove it into town in the middle of the night in the snowstorm from hell. Good times."

"Good times?" Aidan asked. "We nearly went to juvie for grand theft. We would have if my mom hadn't made Gray stand up before the judge and tell how he'd locked us in."

Hudson grinned wide. "We *all* got our asses handed to us on that one. It was fun."

"We were grounded for months," Aidan reminded him.

"Yeah. Together." Hudson shrugged. "I had the time of my *life*. You let me drive, remember?"

Yeah, Aidan remembered. Mostly because Hud had nearly killed them on Pine Pass Road when they'd narrowly avoided more than one tree. But he knew that compared to Hudson and Jacob's rough childhood, nearly going to jail as a cocky fourteen-year-old with his big brothers at his back might indeed have been the time of his life.

They made their way through the crowd, but Aidan stopped short at the sight of the woman standing off to the side of the others, chewing on her thumbnail, a haunted expression on her face.

Lily.

His chest squeezed. Nothing about this woman should reach him, nothing, and yet he couldn't seem to help himself. It was the kiss—stupidity at its finest. He'd gotten a taste of her, and it was messing with his head. "*Don't do it, Kincaid*," he muttered.

"Do what?" Hud asked, and followed Aidan's gaze. "Ah. That's what."

"Give me a minute." Ignoring the instincts that had kept him alive on more than one occasion, and despite being exhausted, starving, and on his last ounce of energy, Aidan walked over to Lily. "Hey," he said. "What are you doing here?"

She looked away, but not before he caught the flash of worry she'd been masking. The rescue had brought back horrific memories for her, of that he had no doubt.

"Just wanted to make sure everyone was okay," she finally said.

She sounded calm, but he could feel the tension simmering beneath the surface. He felt for her and the nightmares this mountain must bring. "We got her," he said, voice softer now, feeling things when he didn't want to. Way too many things. "She's going to be okay."

She nodded. "Good."

Walk away. You've done your duty, now get the hell away from her. "How about you?" he asked instead. "You going to be okay?"

"Always am."

More like she'd always had to be. Their gazes held for a single heated, tension-filled beat, and that's when he knew something else as well—he was all kinds of screwed. Upside down, sideways...every which way, because just as she had in the past, Lily drew him in with those eyes, her voice, the outer toughness she showed the world, the inner vulnerability she did her best to hide.

And damn if he didn't want to kiss her and then drag her back to his place caveman-style and show them both what they'd been missing out on. He tried to remind himself that their time, if they'd ever had one, had long since passed. Which was proven when, without another word, she broke eye contact and walked away.

Chapter 9

Lily managed to get to the Mane Attraction at nine a.m. on the dot, half an hour earlier than her official start time. She liked to be prepared. Unlike, say, how it felt to run into Aidan again. Nope, she was as unprepared for that as one could get...

The salon was located in the bottom floor of the big lodge at the resort, next to an equipment rental and sales shop. The place itself was small and cluttered but warm and welcoming nevertheless. There was one client room for waxing, and everything else was done out in the main room of the salon.

In other words, no real privacy.

"Not what you're used to, I'm sure," Jonathan said as he walked her around.

True enough. The place was nothing like Lily was used to. In San Diego they'd had 10,000 fabulous square feet, every inch designed to soothe and calm and rejuvenate the spirit.

They'd been a five-star salon and proud as hell of it.

Jonathan gestured to the three hair stations. "Pick your spot."

Pick her spot? "Don't you have more staff coming in?" she asked.

"Today it's just you and me, Lily Pad."

She stared at him.

He sighed. "Cassandra's not supposed to be on her feet for more than a half hour at a time, so she's not working anymore until after she pops. And then there's my part-timers, Terika and Rosa, but they're not in today either."

"What days are they in?"

"Well," he said with a grimace. "That varies. Terika's mad at me right now."

"Why?"

"Something to do with a late night, too much Jack Daniel's, and a really awkward morning after." He sighed. "It's complicated."

I bet. "And Rosa?"

"She scares me."

Lily laughed, but Jonathan didn't. "You serious?" she asked.

"As a midget at a nudist colony," he said.

Lily shook her head and spent a few minutes selecting a station and getting her stuff all set up. They shared a wash station, and everyone had to answer phones, since they didn't have a receptionist. Definitely not five star, but then again this wasn't SoCal. Needs here were different. Things were simpler.

For the last ten years, she'd thrown herself headlong into the San Diego culture and lifestyle. But the Rocky

Mountain way of life came back to her in less than fifteen minutes. The lack of fake niceties, the laid-back atmosphere...all of it.

It took her about five more minutes to realize that the Mane Attraction needed some major modernizing: new supplies, brighter lighting, new equipment, and a better system all around.

Which became obvious two hours into her shift, when she blew a fuse after attempting to straighten a client's hair while another client sat under a dryer. She found Jonathan in the back office grabbing a snack. Chips and dip, and her mouth watered.

"Damn," he said. "It's a sad moment when you lose a chip in the dip and you send in a recon chip but that breaks too."

"Stop it, you're making me hungry," she said, and grabbed a chip "What kind of dip?"

"Ranch."

"Low fat?"

"Hell no," he said. "Life's too short for fake butter, dip, or people. Call the landlord about the blown fuse. The number's programmed into the phone."

Knowing full well who the landlord was, Lily balked. "I don't think—"

"It won't be him," Jonathan said. "It'll be Gray."

So she made the call, and indeed got Gray, who was calm and efficient. She had no idea if that was because he could hear the panic in her voice that he might try to strike up a conversation or because he just didn't care. In either case, he didn't try to make the call personal. He simply promised to send someone within the hour.

The front door opened, and Jonathan's next client

walked in. Char Kincaid—Aidan's mom. She gave Lily a big hello hug and seemed genuinely happy to see her.

"You look great," Lily said.

Jonathan smiled at Char. "For a feeble old woman, she sure does."

"Jonathan," Lily gasped in horror.

Char laughed and spoke in the soft Southern accent she'd never lost, not even after living in Colorado for forty years. "No, he's just making fun of my boys because that's what they think."

Lily stared at her. Char was in her late fifties and trim with lovely chestnut-colored hair and warm chocolate-brown eyes that matched Aidan's. She walked with a cane, but otherwise seemed fine. "They think you're feeble?"

Char laughed. "Well, to be fair to them, you're seeing me on a good day. I've had some hip trouble again. Took a fall and needed surgery. But I'm on the mend. Unless you ask Aidan and Gray. I tripped last week and they nearly sent for an ambulance. They worry like a couple of grannies. Baby," she said to Jonathan, "would you mind if Lily fixed me up today?"

"Not even a little," Jonathan said.

Lily smiled as she went to work on Char's hair even as a part of her ached. The Kincaids stuck together through thick and thin. For the last ten years she'd been independent. On her own. No one counted on her, and she didn't count on anyone either.

It was best that way.

Or so she'd told herself. But she couldn't deny just a little bit of envy at what the Kincaids had in one another. "They worry because they love you and want you to be happy and safe," she said.

Char nodded. "I know, and of course I feel the same way. It's just that it's all amping up again—the resort, the past, and I can't stop it or help them. I worry, too, about them."

Lily met Char's gaze in the mirror. "What's amping up again?"

"Oh, never mind my ramblings." Char waved her words off like she regretted uttering them in the first place. "It's just me being silly. You're doing a great job on my hair, honey"

Lily took in Char's expression, carefully blank now. Clearly she'd said more than she'd wanted. Lily wanted to push, wanted to…what? Help? She could barely help herself.

And then there was Aidan.

She didn't need to know what was going on in his life. She was here to earn some money until a real job came through.

That was it.

She was not here to reminisce or daydream about Aidan. Besides, if she was going to think about him at all, it was to hope that he'd taken one look at her and was even now pining away for what he could've had all those years ago.

Later, when Char left, Lily took a walk-in customer. She was finishing up the cut when the door opened again, to another woman.

"The special please," she said, waving a coupon from the week's paper. "The young rejuvenating facial. I want to look thirty."

"Mom," Jonathan said. "It's a facial, not a magic wand."

She rolled up the paper and swatted him with it. "Fine. I'll take forty." She gave Lily a hug. "And you! How lovely to see you again!" She turned to Jonathan. "So… you can make me look forty, right?"

"How about gorgeous?" Jonathan asked his mom. "Does gorgeous work for you?"

"Aw." She grinned at him. "Always can count on you. Love you, baby."

"Yeah, yeah," he said. "That won't get you out of leaving a tip." He nodded at Lily. "You want my specialist to do this. She's the best woman for the job. Plus, I hate giving facials."

Lily loved skin care. Actually, she loved all the different aspects of what she did: cutting and coloring hair, skin care, all of it. There was just something about making people feel good that made her feel good. She loved the easy, fast people connections, too, especially since in her everyday personal life she didn't tend to make such easy, fast connections at all.

She never had.

She gave Jonathan's mom a facial that did indeed make her look gorgeous. Then she did an eyebrow wax for a woman who'd worked for Lily's dad years ago.

"Such a shame how he went," the woman said, her eyes closed while Lily worked. "That heart attack. So sudden. And in his prime too."

Lily stilled. "Yes," she managed. "A shame."

"He was a good man," the woman said, not noting Lily's discomfort since her eyes were still closed. "And your sister too," she went on. "Such a tragedy. You okay with being back, honey?"

Lily was still having trouble finding her words. But her

client had opened her eyes now and was looking at her expectantly, so she put on her best "I'm good" expression and nodded. She even added a smile, which she thought was a good touch.

"Are you?" Jonathan asked quietly after the woman had left. "Good with being back?"

"Don't start," she said.

"So you're not. Damn, I knew it." He slid an arm around her and pulled her in for a hug. "What can I do, Lily Pad? Anything for you, you know that, right?"

"Yeah." She hugged him back, drawing on some deeply needed strength. "I'm working on being okay, I promise. I think I just need some more time to adjust."

A truck drove up. The man driving it parked right out front in the no-parking zone like he owned the place and ambled into the shop.

Aidan. The only man she didn't want to see, wearing sexy jeans faded in all the stress spots that she abso lutely wasn't noticing and a T-shirt that said KEEP CALM AND SKI ON.

"Mm-mmm," Jonathan murmured for her ears only. "I tell you what. Channing Tatum and his gorgeous wife both own my heart, but Aidan's a close third. The girls are going to be bummed. We love it when Gray sends Aidan to fix stuff."

"Not this girl," Lily said. She blamed the kiss. "And this place is falling apart," she said, trying to redirect. "You should be as irritated with him as I am."

"No can do." Jonathan was not only an equal opportunist when it came to sex, but he was also eternally optimistic. "I'm a lot of things, but irritated isn't one of them."

"But he—"

"Shh."

Oh, for God's sake.

"Hey," Aidan said in greeting to Jonathan before his gaze then slid to Lily.

She stood her ground instead of running in the other direction as her feet wanted.

"Lily," he said with a nod and absolutely no indication that he'd played tonsil hockey with her just yesterday. "One of you called?"

Lily glanced over at Jonathan, who was very busy looking at Aidan like he was the sun and the moon and maybe also a lemon meringue pie. She gave him a nudge that was really a shove and then spoke for both of them since apparently she was the only one of them immune to Aidan's dubious charms. "We need some renovations," she said.

Aidan raised a brow. "We."

"Jonathan," she corrected and then shook her head. You know what? She worked here too now, and so far she liked it, dammit. It'd been weeks since she'd liked where she was. More than weeks. Way too much more. "And okay, me too," she said, claiming the place in spite of herself.

Jonathan grinned and blew her a smooch.

"There's a problem with the electrical," she told Aidan. "We can't run two blow-dryers at the same time. A pretty big problem for a salon."

"Absolutely," he said easily. "What else?"

"Nothing," Jonathan said, pulling three sodas out of the mini fridge they kept stocked for clients. "We're good."

Lily glared at him. "The private patient room needs some plumbing help. The sink drips."

"Drips," Aidan said, taking one of the sodas and popping it open.

"Yes. It's annoying."

He smiled. "Annoying."

"To the client, yes," she said. "It's annoying. They're here to relax and be pampered. A dripping faucet isn't relaxing."

"Understood," he said. "Anything else?"

Huh. She didn't remember him being this agreeable. "And the lighting. It's not bright enough in the client room, and too bright and harsh out here."

Jonathan choked on his soda.

But Aidan just looked at the overhead lighting and nodded. "You also need a new paint job."

"Yes," she said, surprised. Huh. Maybe this was going to go a lot easier than she'd imagined. "Thank you," she said genuinely.

Jonathan was smiling at Aidan like he'd just brought Christmas. "She's something else, right?" he asked Aidan.

Aidan looked at Lily. "Definitely something else."

She gave him a long look that made him grin.

Jonathan too. "I'm thinking of putting her in charge just so I don't have to be."

Aidan nodded. "I'm sure you'll be in good hands."

Well dammit, it was hard to hold on to a good mad with a compliment like that, but she gave it the ol' college try.

"Get me a list of the work you need done," Aidan said. "I'll talk it over with Gray and see what we can do."

"Maybe we could just deal with Gray directly," Lily said.

He gave a slow shake of his head. "Why?"

She tried not to notice how his T-shirt had stretched it-self nearly beyond its limits to cover his broad shoulders. Or how the shirt was only partially tucked in at his abs. Or that he smelled fantastic. "It'd make things easier," she said.

"For who?"

She stared at him. Was the air suddenly too thick to breathe or was that just her? "Me," she admitted.

He cocked his head. "Maybe I'm not interested in making things easier for you," he said so casually that it took a moment for the words to process. By the time it sank in, he'd changed out the blown fuse and was gone.

Jonathan was still grinning.

"Why are you smiling like that?" she asked, irritated.

"Because this is going to be fun."

Lily was pretty sure this, whatever *this* was, was going to be the exact opposite of fun.

Thanks to some idiot throwing a lit cigarette out his win-dow on Highway 74, Aidan and the entire fire department spent the next three days fighting a blaze fifteen miles away on Mt. Rose.

Finally a violent rainstorm rode in like a tumbleweed and saved the day, helping them beat the fire into submis-sion.

When he finally got home, he felt disgusting. He stripped on the way to the bathroom and then stood be-neath the showerhead for a full thirty minutes—the best thirty minutes he'd had in days.

He'd no sooner turned off the water and wrapped him-self in a towel when his phone buzzed an incoming Face-time call from Gray. He hit ACCEPT and when Gray's face appeared, Aidan went on the immediate offensive. "No," he said, before his brother could speak.

"I didn't even ask you anything." Gray looked at his bare torso and grimaced. "And Christ, put on some clothes."

"I just got out of the shower. And you didn't ask me anything—yet," Aidan corrected. "I'm just warding you off at the pass."

"I don't only call you to get you to do something," Gray said.

"Yes you do."

Gray opened his mouth and then shut it. "Shit," he finally muttered. "Fine. I need you to do something."

"If it doesn't involve a beer and then an entire night of sleep, forget about it," Aidan said.

"It's Mom."

The only two words that could have Aidan rustling through his dresser for clean clothes instead of hanging up on his brother. "What is it?" he asked. "She didn't fall again—"

"No," Gray said quickly. "Healthwise she's fine."

Neither of them liked to talk about Char's physical limitations. On the night that their father had left, they'd had a big fight. She'd hit him with a frying pan, but then he came after her, and she'd fallen and broken her wrist and hip. They'd both been arrested for battery and assault, and his father had taken off afterward, never to be seen again.

His mom had healed, at least physically, although her hip had never been the same. After she reinjured it last week, the doctor said she was supposed to limit her physical activity for the next month.

"She's...on a date," Gray said.

Aidan blinked. "What?"

"Yeah, she's wearing that blue dress she saves for weddings and everything. I tried to talk her out of it and she…"

"She *what*?"

"Laughed at me," Gray said, looking butt-hurt. "Gave me some line about how our generation has lost all sense of romance. She said she was like a fine wine and deserved to be uncorked and aired out."

Aidan stared at him.

"I know, dude, my ears are still burning too. So you're up. And don't even try reasoning with her. She's completely unreasonable and illogical. She says she's going dancing."

"Dancing?" Aidan repeated. "She's supposed to be taking it easy. She can't go dancing."

"Thank you," Gray said. "Penny thinks I'm being overprotective."

The phone was suddenly wrestled away from Gray and then Penny's face appeared. She took a good look at Aidan and smiled.

Aidan cursed, tossed the phone aside, and ditched the towel for a pair of jeans.

"Gimme that," Gray said to his wife. Then he reappeared, though he was still glaring at Penny, who was laughing.

"Does he have clothes on yet?" she asked.

"Yes," Aidan said, buttoning his jeans and grabbing a T-shirt. *Jesus.*

"Too bad," Penny said, and got serious. "Now listen to me—both of you have to leave your poor mom alone. She's going out to The Slippery Slope tonight with Marcus Dolby. She's a grown woman who's perfectly capable of taking care of herself."

"Wait a minute," Aidan said. "Marcus?" He couldn't think of anyone less likely to go dancing than the resort's equipment manager.

"Yep," Penny said. "He asked her out. She thinks he's cute. She said that since she hasn't gotten any action in a few decades, she wants to get back into the game before her womanly parts wither up and die from misuse."

Both Aidan and Gray winced.

"Your turn," Gray whispered covertly to Aidan.

"*Fine*," he said. "I'll handle it."

"*Good*," Gray said, and disconnected.

Shit. Aidan jammed his feet into shoes, grabbed his keys, and headed out into the rain to drive to The Slippery Slope.

He checked the bar first and damn. Yep, there was his mom at the far end, hair done, siren-red lipstick on, and laughing at something Marcus had just said to her.

Aidan snarled and headed over, stopping short when Jonathan stood from a barstool and offered a hand. "Hey, man, heard that last fire was a bitch. Join us? Drinks on me."

Aidan turned to Jonathan's companion and froze.

So did the companion.

Lily was sitting there in a little black dress, looking like a million bucks, even if her eyes were telling him to just keep walking.

And of course his mom took that exact moment to lift her head, and with the uncanny instinct that could only come from a mother, leveled her eyes right on her son.

Chapter 10

Aidan spared the brief thought that he'd rather be back on Mt. Rose trapped by the fire than sandwiched between his mother and Lily. One was the only woman on earth whose wrath scared him, and the other was the sexiest pain in the ass—er, blast from his past. While he stood at the bar in rare indecision, he felt someone at his back.

Gray.

"Sneaked out of the house," his brother whispered. "Penny's engrossed in a *Supernatural* marathon and a tub of popcorn. It'll be hours before she surfaces."

Aidan broke eye contact with his mom only to have his eyes lock in on Lily like she was a homing beacon. "I said I'd handle it," he whispered back.

"Yeah," Gray said. "And it looks like you're doing a bang-up job of it just standing here too. You going to make a move or keep pretending you're invisible?"

One of the bartenders came up to them, smiling sweetly at Gray and completely ignoring Aidan.

Shelly.

Ah, so the night *could* get worse.

"What can I get for you?" she asked Gray.

He ordered a beer and then looked at Aidan. "The same for you?"

"Yeah, thanks."

"Oh, I'm not serving him," Shelly said to Gray.

Gray grinned at her.

Shelly winked at him and sauntered off.

"A real fan of yours, I see," Lily noted dryly.

Gray laughed, fully enjoying the show, the ass. "Don't worry, man, she'll bring you a beer. She likes her tips too much not to."

Aidan could only hope that was true.

"But she'll probably spit in it first."

Aidan sighed. "Yeah. Thanks."

At the other end of the bar, Char stood up. She pointed two fingers at her own eyes and then at her boys before heading down the back hall toward the restrooms.

Her date, Marcus Dolby, was looking both relaxed and amused as he sipped his beer.

"Go," Gray said. "Make our move."

Aidan slid his brother an incredulous look. "Are you crazy? She just let us know she's onto us."

"Just do it," Gray said in his annoying big brother voice.

"Do what?" Jonathan wanted to know.

"It's about her date," Gray said. "He's gotta go."

"You're going to try to scare him off?" Jonathan asked. "I know Marcus. He's not scared of much."

"Not scare exactly," Gray said, and paused. "Maybe intimidate. Just a little bit."

"That's...horrible," Lily said.

"She's not in a dating place," Aidan said. "She's... healing."

"She's fine," Lily said, and when Aidan and Gray just stared at her she said, "She is! I did her hair for tonight and she's great, actually."

Shelly snorted as she walked by on the other side of the bar. "You gotta keep in mind that these two geniuses think their dear mama's too old and feeble to do the nasty. A bad hip is a setback not a deterrent."

Aidan shuddered.

Gray looked...well, gray. He gave Aidan a little push. "Get on with it. I gotta get back before Penny runs out of popcorn."

Aidan walked the length of the bar and sat down on the empty barstool next to Marcus.

Marcus nodded at him.

Aidan nodded back.

"What happened?" Marcus asked. "You lose at rock-paper-scissors?"

Aidan's gaze slid to Gray. "Uh—"

Gray jerked his chin as if to say, *Go on, do it.*

Lily rolled her eyes.

Marcus grinned and leaned back. "Well, let's hear it already."

"Hear what?"

"All the reasons why you think I shouldn't date your mom. Does it have anything to do with the fact that I work for you?"

"No."

"What then?" Marcus asked.

"She's not up for it, for one thing," Aidan said. "You shouldn't have asked her out. You—"

"First of all, she asked *me*." Marcus smiled when Aidan just stared at him slack-jawed. "That's right. And I jumped on the chance. She's funny, she's warm and wonderful, and if you want the truth, she's sexy as hell."

Aidan scrubbed a hand over his face.

Marcus laughed softly as he leaned in closer. "Things don't shrivel up just because you turn the big five-oh, you know. In fact, some things just get better with time. Your mama is one of them."

Aidan closed his eyes. "I will pay you to stop talking."

Marcus laughed again. "And I'll pay you to still be sitting right here when she comes back from the restroom, because we both know she's going to be pissed as hell at you." He just grinned when Aidan made a sound of frustration. "Tell you what," Marcus told Aidan. "You walk away right now and I won't mention this to her."

"Mention what?"

They both stilled at Char's voice and then turned in unison to face her.

She stood, hands on her hips, glaring at Aidan. "Son," she said evenly in that mom voice that mothers the world over have perfected.

"Hi, Mom."

"Let me guess," she said. "You're here to say, 'Have a good evening, love you, Mom,' right?"

"Yes," Marcus said, before Aidan uttered a word. "That's exactly what he told me he was here to tell you." Then he set his big hand in the middle of Aidan's back and shoved him off the stool.

Aidan stood, towering over his mom but still feeling like he was two feet tall.

"Aw," his mom said, softening, enveloping Aidan in a

warm hug. "That's sweet of you, baby." Then she put her mouth to his ear. "Now I know that you and your brother are so full of poo your eyes are brown, so you listen up good. If you screw this night up for me, I'm going to put an ad in the paper saying you're ready to get married and have kids and that *all* singles should apply. Especially the criers, the stage-five clingers, and poetry lovers."

Aidan shook his head. "Been awhile since I've seen the ruthless side of you."

"I know. So in case you've forgotten, I'll remind you that you should be afraid, very afraid." She cupped his cheek lightly and then tapped it—not so lightly. "Now go away, baby. The adults want to get back to their date."

"Fine. Have it your way. But be careful, Mom, okay?" He leaned down to brush her cheek with a kiss and knew he didn't imagine the way she clung to his arm just a moment longer than necessary.

Aidan made his way back to Gray. Lily and Jonathan were still there, as was Shelly, all of them watching him like he was better than a sitcom.

"Well?" Gray asked. "Did she understand—" He broke off, staring over Aidan's shoulder across the bar. "What the— Aidan, why is Marcus putting his arm around Mom? And now he's leaning in and— Shit, he's going to kiss her! He *is* kissing her! What the hell did you say?"

Aidan just shook his head and looked at Shelly. "I really need a drink."

She smiled evilly and produced two beers. Aidan reached to take one.

She slapped his hand away from it. "Not that one. That one's Gray's." She handed it to his brother. Then she held out the second.

Aidan stared at it. "Do I even want to know what you've done to this one?" he asked.

She smiled. "Nope."

Shit. He set the beer down.

Lily stood and kissed Jonathan on the cheek. "Well, this has been enlightening, but I'm out."

Aidan started to follow her, but Gray stood up and got in his way.

"What are you doing?" Aidan asked.

"Stopping you from making your second mistake for the evening."

"Hey, talking to Mom was *your* bright idea," Aidan said.

"Yeah but you're the one who screwed it up."

Aidan blew out a breath. "Whatever, man. Get out of my way."

"Fine." Gray lifted his hands in surrender. "Apparently you haven't gotten in enough trouble tonight. You need more. Go for it."

Aidan shoulder-checked him on his way toward the front door and then was stopped again. He turned, ready to rumble, but it wasn't his brother, it was Jonathan. "Listen, about Lily," he started.

Shit. Aidan liked Jonathan, he really did. But if the guy was about to try to lay some kind of claim on Lily and then ask Aidan to back off, they were going to have a problem.

He got that such a thing made no sense at all. He didn't have any plans to go after Lily for himself, so it shouldn't matter one little bit if Jonathan did.

But it did matter.

A whole hell of a lot. "What about her?"

Jonathan paused, searched Aidan's gaze, and smiled. "Never mind. You already answered my question."

"Wasn't aware you asked one."

Jonathan looked away and then back to Aidan. "I'm about to overstep my friendship boundaries with her to tell you something because I think you need to know it. Don't disappoint me, okay?"

Aidan narrowed his eyes. "Is she in some sort of trouble?"

Jonathan relaxed his shoulders and smiled. "Yeah, you're not going to disappoint me. You do know why she's back, right?"

"She lost her job."

"And to face her past," Jonathan said. "Which we both know sucked. She blames herself for what happened to Ashley."

"She shouldn't," Aidan said.

"No shit." Jonathan slid his hands into his pockets. "But have you ever successfully talked a woman out of believing something she wanted to believe?"

Aidan huffed out a barely there laugh. "No."

"Yeah. So good luck with this one."

"Wait—What?" But Jonathan was already walking back to the bar, whistling to himself like he had no care in the world.

Aidan was pretty sure he'd just been tasked with relieving Lily of her guilt, which was a bad idea.

The worst of bad ideas.

He stepped outside into a summer night mist and found Lily in the parking lot on her bare knees fighting with the lug nuts on her back left tire, which was flat. When she couldn't get them loose, she smacked the tire with the wrench.

"Yeah, that's not exactly how to fix it," he said.

Her back to him, she went still and tipped her head back to stare up at the misting sky. "Seriously?" she asked it. "What have I ever done to you?"

"Who are you talking to?" he asked.

"Karma. Fate. God." Getting to her feet, she swiped the rain from her face with a forearm and turned to face him. "Whoever's listening."

Walk away, he told himself. *Just walk away.*

But he couldn't. One, because he was an idiot. Two, because she had muddy knees and that, combined with the killer dress, did him in. He loved a woman who could get down and dirty.

And three, because there was something in her voice he hadn't heard earlier. A sadness that gripped him by the throat. He hated this for her. She was carrying way too big of a burden, one she didn't deserve.

Christ, Kincaid, don't do it.

But he did. He stepped closer. "Lily—"

"No. Stay back," she said, pointing a finger at him.

He went still. "Why?"

"Because when you come close I do stupid things."

"Like?"

"Like let you kiss me."

"Let me?" He laughed ruefully. "Lily, you just about crawled up my body to get at these lips."

She narrowed her eyes. "Like I said. Stupid." Turning away, she hugged herself tight.

And he felt like a first-class asshole. "What's wrong?" he asked her quietly.

"Other than my tire's flat and not one person has responded to any of my resumes and I've gained five pounds in a few days?" she asked on a mirthless laugh. "Nothing at all is wrong."

"I'm going to fix your tire," he said. "And you'll find the right job soon, you will. And you look…"

She glanced up when he trailed off.

"Amazing," he said.

She blushed and then remained quiet so long he was sure she had no intention of speaking to him again. Then, so softly he had to move closer to hear her, she said, "Today's her birthday."

Aw, hell. He didn't need to ask whose. Ashley's, of course.

Chapter 11

Lily didn't fall apart often. She'd made it through the public humiliation of being fired and having to come back to her hometown a big failure without losing her collective shit.

Well, mostly.

But after seeing everyone at The Slippery Slope tonight, so close and comfortable with each other, she realized that their lives had gone on without her, almost like she didn't even exist.

That's when she'd realized she was...lost. Lost and unsure where she belonged. Especially right now standing next to the hottest guy she knew in a light mist staring down a flat tire and another endless, sleepless night in front of her.

"I'm sorry it's so hard for you to be here," Aidan said quietly.

She closed her eyes. "It's not that." Although it'd be a lot easier if she had any job—or life—prospects. Or an umbrella. She swallowed past the football-size lump in her throat. "It's that I miss her. I miss her so much."

"Aw, Lily," he breathed and when he held out his arms she was just wrecked enough to walk into them. He opened his jacket for her to get closer and she snuggled inside, finding him dry and warm and smelling like heaven.

A sigh escaped her as those strong arms closed around her. And she pressed her face into his chest, letting him hold her up for a moment. For just a moment... "I feel so alone," she whispered, hating that the words escaped, though they were the utter truth and she was tired of holding on to them.

Because she did feel alone. Alone and sad and restless, like maybe she was missing the boat that was her life.

"But you're not alone," Aidan said, stroking a big hand down her back. "There are people here in Cedar Ridge who care about you."

She didn't say anything to this. Mostly because she was remembering how she'd felt like such an outsider at The Slippery Slope. Maybe he was talking about himself caring about her. That would be nice. Yes, she was crazy. She blamed the fact that he smelled delicious and had to tell her hopeful body that she was not going to kiss him again. She couldn't. Not and live with herself. "You want to hear something stupid?"

"Always," Aidan said, voice low, a little rough and a whole lot sexy.

"I pictured Cedar Ridge as standing still the whole time I was gone." She shook her head and leaned back to see his face. "I expected it to be the same, but it's not. Everything's different, everyone's changed."

As if adding an exclamation point to this sentence, Mother Nature chose that moment to turn the mist into rain. Lily let out another mirthless laugh.

Aidan tugged off his jacket and wrapped her up in it. "Come on, I'll drive you home."

"Is Shelly your ex-girlfriend?" Not the question she'd meant to ask, not even close, but she hugged his jacket close and bit her tongue, not willing to take it back.

If Aidan was surprised by the question, he didn't show it. "We saw each other on and off, mostly off, but she was never a girlfriend," he said.

"So there's no...relationship?"

"I haven't had time to be in a relationship," he said. "Now let's go. I'll come back to fix your tire and get the car to you."

That all sounded good, but there was more sympathy in his gaze than she was comfortable with. "Why?" she asked.

He looked confused at the question, like it didn't compute. And for a guy whose job was, literally, to help people, to save them from whatever situation they'd found themselves in, it probably didn't compute. He was programmed to help people, to save their asses, no matter how pathetic the situation.

"Why would I help you?" he repeated slowly, obviously still baffled by her. "Because I can. Because I want to."

But she didn't want to need saving. Not by him, not by anyone. She did her own saving, thank you very much. And if she could've budged those lug nuts, she'd have changed her own stupid tire. "But I don't need saving."

"I hear you," he said, calm and quiet, like maybe he was talking her off a ledge, and in some ways she supposed he was. "But it's raining," he reminded her. "And you're wearing a pretty dress, which you'd get dirty changing your own tire."

She looked down at herself. She'd almost forgotten she was dressed up. Her knees were a mess. And the dress was clinging to her thighs a little bit. Aidan's clothes were doing the same now. He looked good wet. Too good.

"Come on," he said, grabbing her hand, pulling her across the lot before she could think of stopping him.

When he pulled open the passenger door of his truck, she met his gaze. "Okay," she said. "But I want to note that this isn't a rescue. This is a favor that you'll let me return."

"Sure," he said. "Just get out of the rain and in the damn truck."

"No, I mean it, Aidan. You have to let me pay you back somehow."

He dropped his head and muttered something beneath his breath about the entire female race being more stubborn than a pack of Kincaids. "Fine," he said, meeting her gaze again. "You owe me a favor. Get in."

"And you'll let me repay you."

One brow shot up.

"Say it," she said. She was probably proving his point about her being stubborn, but she didn't care. "Say you will, or no go."

He gave her a long, hard alpha-man look she imagined usually worked for him, but she held her ground. It was the one thing she knew about him more than anything else—he was strong, inside and out. Strong willed, strong minded, and she needed to be the same to stand up to him.

Finally he let out a low laugh and shook his head. "You're something else, you know that?"

"I do know," she assured him. "And…?"

His gaze dropped to her mouth and his voice dropped too. "And I'll let you repay the damn favor." Apparently done indulging her, he practically hoisted her into the truck, then leaned in to do her seat belt for her, like that might keep her from running. When she was locked in, he came around to the driver's seat and slid in behind the wheel. He shook his head and sent a myriad of raindrops flying before turning over the engine and cranking the heater. "You warm enough?" he asked.

That he cared enough to ask, coupled with his gruff voice, had her getting there. "Yes," she said. "Thanks to you."

"You have enough wood loaded in your place?"

"I do," she said. Also thanks to him. "I haven't used too much, I've been at work."

"And apparently doing my mom's hair while you're at it," he said, and spared her a glance.

"She looked pretty tonight, don't you think?"

He grimaced. "Yeah."

"And happy." Lily shook her head. "I can't believe you and Gray tried to sabotage her date."

"She's not ready to go out. She's…"

"Feeble?" she asked dryly.

He sighed.

Lily found a laugh. "Aidan, she's fantastic. Really."

"She's not ready for a man in her life."

"Why not?" she asked.

"Why not?"

"Yeah, why not? She kicked your father to the curb a long time ago."

"She's...frail."

"Because of her hip? She says it's feeling better every day. Besides, that shouldn't keep her from dating."

"She doesn't pick the right men."

She stared at him a moment. "That's her choice. You realize that, right?" she asked gently. "Doesn't everyone deserve their own version of a happily-ever-after?"

"Yes," he said meaningfully, and slid her a look.

"Oh, no," she said. "We're not talking about me."

"We should be."

"But we're not."

They drove in silence. Aidan handled his truck like he handled everything in his life—with easy, effortless confidence. It wasn't fair at all. He pulled into the lot of her building, and Lily hopped out of the truck practically before he'd stopped. When she turned back to close the door he was there already standing before her, big and rock steady.

"In a hurry?" he asked, brow raised.

"Yes." In a hurry to not kiss him again.

He smiled. He knew, the bastard, as proven by his next words.

"You don't trust yourself around me," he said, sounding way too pleased with himself.

"I trust myself just fine," she said. "It's *you* I don't trust."

He laughed, looking smug and...damn. Hot. Extremely hot.

"I'm serious," she said. "You have this way of mowing over my roadblocks."

"Are you referring to the present or the past?"

"Both." She pointed at him. "But we're not talking about it."

"Why not?"

Because my sister was in love with you and I can't...I can't go there. "Do you think about her?" she asked before she could access her good sense and keep her mouth shut.

"Yes," he said again, not having to ask who. "I think about her every time I have a call up on Dead Man's Cliff." He met her gaze. "And you, Lily. To be honest, mostly I think of you."

She sucked in a breath at that. She'd thought of him plenty too. But somehow she'd never pictured him thinking of her in return. Shaking her head because it was too much, she took a step back.

He reached out for her, but she lifted her hands to hold him off and shook her head again. "Don't," she whispered. "I...can't."

And then she walked away. Or maybe ran was more like it, taking the stairs blindly. At the top, her fingers shook so badly she dropped her keys twice before Aidan gently nudged her out of the way and opened her door with *his* keys before bending to scoop hers off the floor.

"You have keys to my place?" she asked in surprise.

"I have keys to everything."

Except her heart, she told herself. Nope, he was firmly locked right out of that particular organ. And he'd stay out.

Aidan watched Lily's heart go to war with her head for a beat before gently nudging her inside.

She slipped out of his jacket and handed it back to him.

"Thanks for that. And the ride. Lock the door on your way out?"

"I can't leave you alone. Not on her birthday."

"Yes you can. You just walk out the door."

He gave her a slow shake of his head.

"And you call me stubborn," she muttered beneath her breath, but he was fluent in Annoyed Female Speak, living with Kenna.

"Do you want to talk about her?" he asked.

"No. Not even a little bit."

Wrapping his fingers around her upper arm, he pulled her back around to face him when she turned away. He tried to read her expression and went still with a gut-wrenching pit in the bottom of his stomach. "Does this have anything to do with me?"

A sound came from deep in her throat. Pain? Regret? Hard to say as she pulled free and took a step back, staring at him, clearly shocked. "No, of course not. I don't know why you'd ask me such a thing."

"Maybe because immediately afterward you took off," he said. "And when I called you, you clearly didn't want to talk to me. That was the last I heard from you for a decade until the junk food massacre in the convenience store."

She closed her eyes. "It's not you. It's me. Ashley's accident. It was all my fault, Aidan."

This was somehow worse, the proof that Jonathan was right, that she did indeed blame herself. Feeling hollow at the notion that she'd been feeling this way for *ten* years, Aidan shook his head. "Why would you possibly blame yourself?"

"Because she was just trying to be like me!" She covered her face. "I'd climbed the face and hiked down and she couldn't let it go until she'd done the same." She broke off and swallowed hard before covering her mouth with a hand and closing her eyes. "If I hadn't bragged about it—"

"Lily, that was your relationship with her, competitive to the core. What happened to her up there was an accident. A horrible, tragic accident. But it wasn't your doing."

Her eyes flew open, filled with surprise, and that just about killed him. Hadn't anyone else ever told her these things? She was still staring at him when he took her hands in his and lifted them up to his mouth, where he brushed his lips over her knuckles. "Not your fault," he repeated softly as it all clicked into place and made sense for him.

She'd left because of grief.

She'd stayed away because of guilt.

Not because of him. The knowledge at once changed things for him and also devastated him—for her. "Ashley was book smart but not street smart. We both know that. She didn't have your logic skills, your ability to know your own limits. She was headstrong and self-centered and she did whatever she wanted—not thinking about the cost to anyone, especially you. You can't carry around the responsibility for what happened to her, you just can't. And more than that, she wouldn't want you to."

She pulled free and moved to the woodstove. "It's June and I'm about to light a fire," she said, her back to him. "Definitely not in San Diego anymore, Toto."

Nudging her aside, he crouched before the woodstove and began to build her a fire.

"I can do that," she said.

"I know." He was expertly and efficiently crisscrossing the kindling, then adding the wood on top, doing what would have taken her a good half hour in less than a minute.

"You're good at that," she said, but it wasn't his fire skills she was admiring. It was the easy way he was balanced on the balls of his feet, his pants stretched taut across what was surely the best ass in all of Cedar Ridge.

He rose and met her gaze, and she could feel herself blush because what if he could read her mind?

"I'm good at a lot of things" he murmured.

Dammit.

"Now tell me how you can be one of the smartest people I know and yet really believe you were responsible for your sister's death," he said, switching gears with far more ease than she could. "What am I missing?"

She stared at him for a long beat. "The day before, I'd come home with a scholarship to the University of Colorado at Boulder and an invite to be on their ski team."

"Prestigious ski team," he corrected.

"Yeah, well, it was the last straw for Ashley after the attention I'd received in the recruiting process. And Boulder was the only place she'd ever wanted to go ski, so it was her dream opportunity and I got it a whole year before she could even apply."

Aidan didn't point out that Ashley should've been proud of her sister, so damn proud.

Lily shook her head. "I know what you're thinking, and she would've been happy for me. Later. It would've come to her, really it would have, but in the moment all she saw was that I had something she wanted. I shouldn't have told her like I did, I shouldn't have—" She let out a low sound of regret. "We were already in a fight because she'd been bugging me to take her up to Dead Man's Cliff and I'd refused. It was way too dangerous for her. She was only an intermediate climber at best, but she was determined to beat me at something."

"Listen to me," Aidan said. "All siblings are like that, okay? Hell, Gray and I nearly killed each other a hundred times over when we were growing up. Never mind the bad example we set for Jacob and Hudson."

"This was different," she insisted. "I *knew* the Boulder admission letter would hurt her. She got straight A's through every single semester of high school in preparation and I..." She shook her head. "Didn't. I didn't get A's at all. I wasn't into school. I wanted to be outside."

"On the mountain," he said quietly. "I know. You were out there exploring every single day that you could, which was just about every day in the summer."

She looked surprised. "How...how did you know that? I saw you a few times but...every day?"

He hesitated to tell her. She was like a bird with a broken wing, nursing her past hurts, afraid to forgive herself and be happy. He wanted to soothe, to help ease the pain, but wasn't sure how to do that without losing his heart and soul to her. Again.

"Aidan?"

"Gray and I took turns going up after you," he said. "Making sure you were okay."

She gaped at him. "Why?"

"Because no one should be out there by themselves, Lily."

"I was fine," she said. "I knew what I was doing. I'd been out there hiking those mountains all my life."

"It was your escape," he said. "It was always mine too. We all got that, and no one wanted to impede on the only time you ever had to yourself."

"But you watched me. Which means that I was never really by myself at all."

He ran a finger along her temple, tucking a strand of wet hair behind her ear. He loved the silkiness of her hair and how when she was outside, it always caught the sun, a thousand different colors that he couldn't possibly name. "No, you were never alone," he said, purposely switching up the words.

She studied him, her eyes softening. "I didn't ask for you to watch over me."

"I know. I wanted to," he said, and stroked a finger over her temple again. "I loved watching you up on the mountain, whether on the trail or taking years off my life when you went rock climbing. I saw the love of the place all over your face. We had that in common, Lily. I thought it was just a friendship only. And then that night at the dance when I kissed you and you kissed me back like I was the greatest thing that had ever happened to you…" He smiled a little at the memory. "Best day ever." Lifting his other hand, he slid his fingers into her hair, letting his thumb lightly glide over her.

And damn, he needed to taste her again. Slowly, knowing she'd be stopping him any second, he backed her to the wall and then lowered his head.

She didn't stop him.

Instead she gripped his biceps and tugged him the rest of the way to her, closing the distance to kiss him.

And kiss him…

Slow.

Sweet.

Achingly so.

He told himself he would stand there and let her have her way with him for as long as she wanted, but he underestimated the speed with which she could decimate his self-control. Still he hung on until he knew he was close to scooping her up and tossing her on her bed, from which there would be no going back.

And he wanted that.

God, how he wanted that.

But he wouldn't take it there. He couldn't. Because soon enough she was going to leave. And he didn't want to feel that pain ever again. Heart heavy with regret, he caught her wandering hands in his and slowed the kiss, gentling it. A good-night kiss now, one that was still sexy as hell but not going anywhere.

Lily stilled as if her wits had just come back to her. She blinked and stepped back. "Crap. That shouldn't have happened. Again." She shook her head. "Especially on her birthday." She paused. "You should go."

He wasn't sure he understood the significance of kissing her on Ashley's birthday, but she was right about one thing—he needed to go. He stepped outside and turned back...just as she shut the door.

Smart girl.

Welcoming the cold wet air slapping him in the face, Aidan jogged down the stairs and to his truck.

As he started the engine, he looked up and saw Lily at the window, watching him. But then she must have hit the light because the room went dark.

And he drove off, telling himself it was for the best.

Chapter 12

On the days where there were no morning calls, Aidan and his fire crew had a routine. First they trained, *hard*. This was usually a four-mile run in full gear. After that they cleaned the station and their gear.

Their captain was new this year and still working on earning the guys' respect. He was five foot six in shoes and a hundred and fifty pounds soaking wet, and was not so affectionately referred to as Captain Tyrant.

For a few days the fire calls had been few and far between, thanks in part to some heavy rainfall leaving everything so wet nothing could catch fire.

Which meant Captain Tyrant was on the loose. This morning he'd made them run *five* miles in full gear and then decided that they'd go straight into washing the rigs before hitting the showers.

Not a popular call. Hot and sticky from the workout, everyone immediately began to bitch.

But the captain's jaw was set, which meant there'd be no changing his mind.

So they went to work cleaning. Well, everyone except for Mitch, who'd gone to the shower without hearing the captain's decree.

When the captain heard the shower running he muttered something about "that cocky son of a bitch" and stormed off to the showers, yelling through the glass doors for Mitch to "get your ass out here and help clean the station right this very minute unless you want to run another five miles in full gear and then clean the place by yourself!"

Mitch, who was six foot four and, at two hundred and twenty pounds, quite an imposing figure, strode out wearing nothing but his fire boots.

Well, and a few soapsuds.

He ambled over to the big bay windows, grabbed a squeegee, and went to work scrubbing the glass, his twig and berries swinging in the wind.

The entire crew doubled over, dying of laughter. Everyone, that is, except for the captain, who was looking apoplectic. "What the hell are you doing?" he bellowed.

"Cleaning like you ordered. Sir," Mitch added politely, scrubbing with a whole new level of vigor.

The bay windows stretched from ceiling to floor and faced a restaurant across the street. The restaurant was busy with the breakfast crowd, lots of people going in and out.

And there stood Mitch in all his glory, washing the windows.

He was gathering quite the audience.

"Are you trying to get me fired?" the captain yelled.

Probably this wasn't actually Mitch's endgame, but

going by the considering look that crossed his face, it was clear he wasn't opposed.

By this time the rest of the crew was practically on the floor rolling while Mitch just carried on, his personal attack hose right there if he needed it.

"Get your ass back in that shower!" the captain roared.

"I'm confused," Mitch said, turning to face the captain, body parts going along with the force of gravity. "Get in the shower! Wash the windows! Which is it, Cap?"

The captain turned so red that Aidan started to fear that he might actually stroke out.

"Go! Just go!" the captain bellowed at Mitch, shooing him with wild hands.

So Mitch, with the rest of the crew still laughing their asses off, turned and calmly walked back into the shower.

He was back out five minutes later, fully dressed, hitting the chores as hard as the rest of them.

The captain didn't say another word.

At the end of their shift the next morning when Aidan and Mitch walked out to their vehicles, there were no less than three notes taped to Mitch's truck.

With phone numbers.

Aidan stopped by Lenny's place on the way home to check in with him, which wasn't hard since he lived in the resort's employee housing building.

Lenny didn't answer, so Aidan called him.

"Better be good," Lenny answered, sounding groggy and pissed.

"I'm at your door. Let me in."

"I'm…indisposed."

Aidan dropped his head and stared at his boots. "You said you were going to stop drinking."

"Indisposed with a *woman*," Lenny said. "But good to know where we're at with the trust. I told you I would quit drinking and I have."

Aidan shut his eyes. "I'm sorry—"

"Save it," Lenny said, and disconnected.

Aidan went home to crash but once again found Gray with his big, fat head in Aidan's fridge and Kenna on his couch using his laptop.

"Could've sworn you have a wife to take care of you," Aidan told Gray, tossing his keys to the counter. "And you," he said to Kenna. "What's wrong with *your* laptop?"

"Died. But don't worry, I'm not looking at your browser history. I don't want to see your selection of porn." She leaned back and met his gaze. "I'm looking for work."

"You have work," he said. "You work here at the resort helping Gray." Aidan looked at Gray.

"Yep," Gray said, nodding.

"So you don't need to look for work," Aidan said to his sister.

She just rolled her eyes.

Gray's glance to Aidan said he was baffled but not delegating much brainpower to the situation. "Given all we have on our plate," he said, "I've filed this under the Ain't Broke column."

"Okay, yes, I get a paycheck," Kenna said. "But no one lets me do jackshit. I wanted to drive the big Cat and Gray nixed that. I wanted to teach mountain biking. He nixed that too."

"You wanted to teach the biking team how to navigate Killer Alley, a triple diamond run," Gray said.

"I'm not some fragile little flower, you know," she said.

Maybe yelled. "I used to snowboard at neck-breaking speeds off cliffs for a living."

Aidan slid a look to Gray. "I'm sure we could find you something more…challenging to do."

"That's just it!" she burst out, standing, tossing up her hands. "I don't want you to 'find' me something. I want a real job, not one my brothers give me with a pat on my head."

Gray had been steadily shoving food into his mouth this whole time, but when Aidan gave him a level look, he sighed and swallowed his mouthful. "We can give you a real job. A job without head pats."

Aidan nodded.

"Too late," Kenna said crisply. "I'm applying at all of our competition. You'll have to steal me back if you want me." She shut the laptop and walked out.

Aidan looked at Gray. "You're going to find something good for her, right? Before she really gets another job?"

"Hmphl," Gray said around a bite of Aidan's leftover pizza.

"That was my breakfast."

"Pizza for breakfast'll make you fat," Gray said, mouth full. "And you're single. You can't go fat until you're married." Gray stuffed in another huge bite. "I'm just saving you from yourself, man."

"Well done." Aidan shoved Gray away from the fridge and bent to peer into the depths himself. He was so hungry he could eat a horse. "Hey, you ate Hud's pizza too. He's going to kill you."

Uncharacteristically, Gray shrugged instead of launching into his usual "I can kick both your asses at the same time with my hands tied behind my back" speech.

Aidan narrowed his eyes. "What's up with you?"

Gray shrugged again and opened Aidan's last soda.

"Listen, I'm gonna need you to spit it out because I've gotta date with my bed—and you better not have been a dumbass and let anyone into it again."

Gray just shook his head.

That he didn't hit back on the dumbass comment had Aidan straightening from the fridge to look at him. "Okay," he said. "I'm going to ask you again and you're going to answer me with the CliffsNotes version, you got me? *What's wrong?*"

"She's undercover trying to bring down a gang of boat smugglers."

"Who, the Black Widow?"

"Penny." Gray threw the now empty can of soda across the room, where it landed with perfect precision—not in the window sill above the sink, knocking over the dead flowers someone had brought Hudson on his birthday a month ago.

Aidan let out a slow breath and kept his pichole shut. He was no idiot.

"Did you hear me?" Gray asked.

"Yeah, I heard you. So did the people in China. Look, you knew she wanted to work in insurance fraud investigations before you married her. You can't be mad at her for that."

"I'm not mad at her for being who she is. I'm mad at myself for not being okay with it. You remember last year when she went after those bank fraud idiots and they shot her?"

"Yeah, and they're rotting in prison for it."

"And Penny's still got the bullet wound scar in her

shoulder." Gray's phone vibrated a text. He read it, shook his head, and stood. "She's on her way home with McDonald's. It's a truce breakfast."

"I love McDonald's breakfasts," Aidan said. "*I* should've married her."

"Mine." Gray headed to the door. "Go find your own woman. How hard can it be? I even let one into your bed for you."

"Yeah, well, she was the wrong one."

Gray stopped short and turned to stare at him.

Shit.

"Wrong woman?" his brother repeated. "So who's the right woman?"

"There isn't one. Get out."

But Gray had become an unmovable mountain, staring at him, doing the Kincaid mind meld thing. "Kylie?" he asked. "From dispatch?"

"No," Aidan said.

"Yeah, good thing. She's hot, but she laughs weird. Lori in rentals?"

"No," Aidan said, annoyed but also trying to keep his shit together because giving his brothers, any single one of them, more information than strictly necessary was like giving intel to the enemy. "Drop it."

"Yeah, right," Gray said. "Lily?"

Aidan did his best not to react, but he couldn't still his mind. He still remembered every second of dancing with her beneath a half moon that long-ago summer festival. He remembered kissing her…falling for her.

Then how she'd left the mountain without looking back, forgetting about him with shocking, heartbreaking ease.

Now she was back. And she'd kissed him like maybe she hadn't forgotten him after all…

Which was really fucking with him. "I said drop it."

Gray grinned. "Yeah. It's Lily."

Aidan stalked past Gray, yanked open the front door, and shoved his brother out.

Gray was still grinning wide as Aidan slammed the door on his nose and then bolted it for good measure. But he could still hear his brother chuckling to himself. "Dumbass," he said.

"Yeah. He is," Hudson said from behind him.

Aidan whipped around. "Jesus. How long have you been standing there?"

"Not long."

Aidan relaxed again and headed back to the kitchen.

Hudson waited until Aidan had taken a long pull on a bottle of water to say, "So. Lily, huh?"

Chapter 13

The salon turned out to be an interesting place. Cassandra stopped by daily, eight months pregnant and bored out of her mind. Today she plopped herself into the massage chair they had for waiting clients. When she turned it on, her body shimmied and shook in an alarming fashion.

"Turn that thing down," Jonathan said. "You're going to go into labor."

"That's the idea," she said, turning the chair up.

Jonathan pointed at her. "If you birth that thing in here, I'm going to..." He paused like he couldn't think of anything heinous enough.

And while he was thinking, Cassandra doubled over with a cry.

"Oh, God," Jonathan said, face going white. "What the hell did I tell you?"

Cassandra lifted her face and grinned. "Gotcha."

Jonathan just stared at her. "You're not in labor?"

"Nope."

Jonathan let out a long, slow, shaky breath, a hand to his heart.

Cassandra laughed and kept on with her massage chair antics. She also got her kicks out of announcing every little event, such as "The baby just stuck her foot into my bladder" or "I think I lost my plug" or "Don't get too close, I'm gassy today and there's some hang time."

Lily couldn't imagine the feeling of having someone step on her bladder and she had no idea what a plug was, but she made sure to stay out of Cassandra's personal space bubble so as not to experience any of the hang time.

"Am I wearing pants?" Cassandra asked the room. "I hope I remembered pants today. I don't want anyone to see my cankles."

"Aren't you supposed to be home building a nest or something?" Jonathan asked her, still irritated.

"I'm nesting here," Cassandra said on a yawn. "And it's hard work."

Jonathan sighed and brought her some hot tea.

Lily didn't expect to have clients right away, but she'd underestimated the far reach of the Internet. Jonathan referred people to her, but mostly they seemed to come out of the woodwork wanting her to spill celebrity gossip. Her nine o'clock was a thirty-something mom of two originally from San Diego who now ran a bookkeeping service in Cedar Ridge.

"So you're back home after the big to-do, huh?" she asked Lily. "I thought the celebrities liked when you leaked stuff about them."

Lily kept her sigh to herself. "Turns out it depends on who it is."

Sympathetic eyes met hers in the mirror. "Let me

guess. Your boss told you to notify the paparazzi and then when it backfired, you took the heat."

Lily's throat caught at the simple validation that this shit happened, all the time, and really she hadn't done anything wrong. She was so stunned she couldn't speak.

"Lord, I so don't miss SoCal," the woman said. "Not even a little bit. The land of blonde extensions, orange tans, bleached teeth, fake boobs…you're probably ecstatic to be out of there."

Lily laughed softly. She hadn't thought of it like that, not once. "Yes, actually," she said, surprised. "I am."

Her ten o'clock appointment was Lenny. She remembered him vaguely from high school, but she didn't really know him. Still, this was Cedar Ridge, so even though they weren't well acquainted, they could carry on a conversation like they were old friends.

Small-town living at its finest.

"Look at you," he said with a smile. "You got all hot. Like I want to have you for dinner hot."

She laughed. "Stop."

"Come on," he said, smiling. "I got hot, too, right?" His eyes were warm and frankly appraising, and she laughed again. Lenny had always been drop-dead handsome and he knew it.

"What have you been doing with yourself over the past ten years?" she asked, changing the subject.

He shrugged. "I run the equipment at the resort."

"Sounds like fun."

"It is. You ever go out with a big-equipment operator?"

In San Diego, Lily had been a master of dodging such questions. She never dated the clientele, period. It made for bad business. "I'm on a dating hiatus," she said.

"Hmm," he said, all relaxed and easygoing. "Maybe I could change your mind."

"I don't think so, sorry."

He smiled. "No reason to say no so fast. Just think about it."

She didn't need to think about it, but she didn't want to argue with him. "Sure," she said. "So, do you like working at the resort?"

Something crossed his face but was gone too fast to identify. "Usually," he said. "I'll stick around, at least until the place goes under."

She met his gaze in the mirror. "What?"

"Yeah," he said and shrugged. "Hopefully not. It is the Kincaids, after all, so anything could happen. But don't worry, they're good at landing on their feet. Real good."

When she'd finished his hair he tipped generously, joked that she was making him work harder for a first date than he was used to, and left.

At her noon appointment she was asked if she'd ever seen any of the *Real Housewives of Orange County* stars and if their hair was real.

At her one o'clock, Lily decided to head off the questions from the get-go and steered all conversation toward her client. For her trouble she learned from an ex of Aidan's that he had been voted most likely to never settle down, which was the one thing he'd apparently gotten from his "no-good" father.

At her two o'clock she met Evan, their hair products rep, and learned he had a huge crush on Jonathan, who refused to date him.

When Evan left, Lily told Jonathan he was nuts. "He's

great-looking, employed, and likes you," she said. "What's the problem?"

"He's great-looking, employed, and likes me."

Lily blinked. "Huh?"

"Listen," Jonathan said. "I only go for the head cases. It's my thing."

"Yeah? And how's that working out for you?"

He grinned. "Forget it, Lily Pad. You can't reform me. Head cases bang head cases. It's what we do." He tugged a strand of her hair. "We also hang out together in clusters. Welcome to the cluster."

She sighed. "So we're all crazy? The whole salon?"

"Yes," he said. "And while we're in between clients, I just remembered—I need you to do something for me."

"What?"

"Take over all the product ordering."

Lily blinked. "When you hired me, you said you didn't want me to do anything but handle the clients."

"Well, I was wrong."

She narrowed her eyes. "You also said you're never wrong."

He blew out a sigh. "Just do this, okay? Take over the ordering for me? I totally trust you to handle it."

"That's nice," she said. "But you're not usually nice. What's going on here?"

"You know how you said I should give Evan a shot?"

"Yes," she said.

"Well, the truth is that I already did. And let's just say it wasn't a smooth morning after."

She gave him a bland look. "Didn't we already have this conversation about Terika?"

Jonathan tried to look repentant and failed.

Lily sighed. "How not smooth?"

"We had a great night but he's just so…" He searched for a word. "Sweet."

"That bastard," Lily said.

Jonathan gave a little smile. "He's too good for me, and I'm not going to change my mind. I'm not one to settle down, you know that. I'd just hurt him."

"So you're going to cut off your friendship with him," she said with a shake of her head. "Cuz that's not going to hurt at all, Jonathan."

"That's why we don't tell him. All he needs to know is that my new assistant manager is doing the ordering now."

She went brows up.

"Oh, yeah," he said. "Congrats. You got a promotion."

"Does this promotion come with a raise?"

"It's not that kind of promotion," Jonathan said.

"Uh-huh." She eyeballed the supply wall, where everything they bought was on display for their customers. She'd been wanting to redo that wall for two weeks. "Okay if I make a few changes to our display then?"

"Fine by me," Jonathan said. "And if Evan doesn't like it, we'll tell him I did it."

"Yeah, that's just what Michael told me, and look what happened," she said. "I was out on my ass so fast my head's still spinning."

Jonathan turned her to face him. "Don't lump me in with that asshole. I'd never throw you to the sharks, not without a rescue plan. Besides, much as I'd like to sleep with you, I won't. I can't lose you again."

"You want to sleep with me?" she asked, surprised. "Since when?"

"Since always." He laughed. "Have you looked in the

mirror? Of course I want to sleep with you. Everyone wants to sleep with you."

Lily looked into his eyes. He was selfish and self-centered and a bit of a drama queen, but he was also fiercely loyal and fiercely honest to those he loved. "Fine, I'll take over the ordering. But I'm buying us better coffee."

"See, I knew you were the right person for the job," he said.

Lily's three o'clock arrived. Char Kincaid again.

"I've got another date," she said proudly. "But I can't do my hair as good as you. I need your help." She limped a little, leaning on her cane as she sat in Lily's chair. "Oh, Lord have mercy, it feels great to sit."

"Your injury acting up?" Lily asked, worried.

"Nah. I had to swim for half an hour this morning to atone for the donuts I ate. I've been walking, too, on the easy trails. Need to try to get back in shape before ski season, but I keep working against myself."

"You still get on the trails? And ski?" Lily asked in surprise as she began to work on Char's hair.

"Well, sometimes, but only cross-country skiing these days. And of course I have to sneak it in now. Your mama helps me when she's in town."

Lily blinked and stopped what she was doing. "My mom comes to Cedar Ridge?"

"Couple times a year at least," Char said, and frowned. "You didn't know?"

"No." She'd had no idea, her mom had never said a word. "We get together and get on the mountain," Char said. "Not Cedar Ridge, though. My sons would plotz if they thought I was still cross-country skiing. We go to Eagle Mountain."

Lily could only stare at her. One thing at a time. "But Ashley...," she said, trailing off.

"What about her?"

"She died on the mountain."

"Yes," Char said softly, and squeezed Lily's hand. "And it was awful and tragic and we all hate that it happened. And trust me, no one's forgotten about it. But, honey, that was ten years ago. Life goes on."

"But...how?"

Char's voice was very gentle now. "By knowing in your gut that Ashley would want you to be happy. She'd want you to live your life, Lily, not just mourn hers."

Lily swallowed hard. This was true. Ashley would most definitely want Lily to live her life. She'd want her to kick ass at it too. Probably she was sitting up on a cloud somewhere with a stopwatch, timing Lily on her hikes, yelling at her to do it better, go faster.

"When your mom and I walk, we always talk about her," Char said, smiling as Lily went back to working on her hair. "About how she's looking down at us, probably annoyed that we stop to smell the wildflowers instead of trying to see which of us is faster."

Throat tight, Lily laughed in spite of herself. "You both still get on the trails. And ski," she marveled.

"Well of course we do." Char narrowed her chocolate-brown eyes, so much like her son's that Lily found herself a little transfixed. "Why wouldn't we?"

Lily bit her lower lip.

Char sighed. "Let me guess. My sons are still making it sound like I'm on my deathbed."

"Well, not...*all* the way on your deathbed."

"I swear, those boys... And don't think that I don't

know it's mostly Aidan." She sighed. "He's the one who saw me so fragile, so hurt…" She visibly shooed off the thought. "You know what? I think I've got an idea."

Lily got a bad feeling as she met Char's gaze in the mirror's reflection. "Why do I feel like I should be afraid?"

"Don't be silly. But I'm going to need you to do something for me." This was uttered in Char's full-on Southern accent, making her voice sound like melted butter.

Uh-oh.

"I want you to call my son in here," Char said. "And mess with him the way he's been messing with me."

Yep, she'd been right to be afraid. "Which son?"

Char smiled. "Don't make me lump you in with those idiots, honey. You know which son. The one you're still crushing on."

Lily felt herself go still. "I'm not—I mean—"

"Just call him. For me." She smiled at herself in the mirror. "And oh my, look at me. You sure outdid yourself, my hair looks fabulous. You're not calling yet."

Oh boy. "Aidan's not going to want to come to the salon," Lily said, stalling.

"Well, of course not. He's not big on anything girlie. He only gets his hair cut when his captain threatens to take the shears to him himself. And he doesn't like to be called away from work either. It makes me worry that he's never going to find a girl and settle down and give me grandbabies. Call him, honey. Tell him he's won a free treatment or something."

"But I…" Lily looked around for an excuse to further stall but couldn't find one. "I'm pretty sure he won't want to hear from me."

"I think you're wrong," Char said with a knowing smile. "I've got a feeling that for you he'll do anything, even if it affronts his precious alpha manhood."

Lily thought about the things he'd already done for her: rescuing her keys from the convenience store, loading wood, saving her from a flat tire. And then there were all those times he'd watched out for her on the mountain years ago.

Small things, but they all added up to one big thing—he'd been there for her when she needed him, whether she'd known she needed him or not.

"Oh, and once you get him in here held captive in your chair," Char said, "be sure to tell him I've decided to go into an old folks home and that he and the others can stop worrying about me. Tell him it's in…Greece," she said. "Yeah, that'll mess with him. I love Greek men *and* their food. Be vague on when, though, cuz when is never. You know what I'm saying?"

Lily paused to take it all in. "You want me to tell your son that you're moving to Greece," she said in disbelief.

"Yep."

"Char, I really don't feel comfortable lying to him—"

"Now see, that's the beauty of it—it's not really lying because it *could* happen." Char lifted a shoulder. "Someday. Maybe. You see?"

No, Lily did not see.

Char pushed Lily's phone across her worktable. "Now make it good, okay? You know how to make it good, right? So that he can't refuse coming over and seeing you?"

Lily hadn't the foggiest but she nodded.

Char waited expectantly.

"Oh, you mean right now?" Lily asked, looking to the

empty waiting area. Where was a hair emergency when she needed one?

"Yes, now," Char said. "Better than yesterday, don't you think?"

And now she knew where Aidan had gotten all of his sarcasm. She picked up her phone and stared at it for a minute, like maybe it could somehow get her out of this.

It didn't.

Seriously, not even a dead battery?

"Do you have any brownies?" Char asked. "Because brownies would get him here really fast."

She'd had cookies, but she'd eaten them all. "No."

"Too bad," Char said. "It's just that he's working so hard, and on top of that he's also trying to help save the resort."

"Save the resort?"

"Yes. He Who Shall Not Be Named left them debts."

Lily remembered what Lenny had said. "How come I feel like I'm the only person in town who doesn't know what's going on with the resort?"

"Well, you've been gone a long time, honey," Char reminded her. "But this goes back a ways too. My ex—the son of a bitch—racked up a lot of gambling debts and then took a loan out on the business. None of us knew of course, not for a long time. And by then it was too late. Now the balloon payment's coming due and it's in my name and the boys are killing themselves trying to figure the entire mess out. Gray's been tearing his hair out about it for a couple of years now. They've been working hard on some options, but nothing's come through yet."

"I'm so sorry," Lily said. She knew how much the resort and property meant to the Kincaids. She couldn't imagine how betrayed they must all feel. And Aidan. Her heart hurt for him. "Will they lose the place?" she asked softly, half afraid of the answer.

"They might. The boys are certainly going to have to cut staff this next quarter to try to lower costs." Char's eyes sparkled with unshed tears that she sniffed away. "Okay, listen to me run my mouth. They'd hate it if they knew I was talking about this. They'd also hate to see me cry over it. So they won't," she said with determination, lifting her chin. "But if the worst happens, I'll tell you what, I'm going to hunt that man down myself and finish what I started all those years ago and I'll use more than my frying pan this time."

Lily didn't know Hudson or Jacob as well as she knew Aidan and Gray, but she did know that not a single one of them would let that happen. She drew a deep breath and called Aidan.

"Kincaid," he answered after the third ring, not sounding particularly happy to hear from her.

She held her breath and nearly hung up.

"Lily," he said, still impatiently but with something else as well.

And that something else coiled through the connection, jump-starting her heartbeat and scraping across her belly. And farther south as well. She closed her eyes. "Remember that favor I owe ya?"

He paused. "Yeah."

"I'd like to repay it. Now."

Crickets.

"So if you could come over," she said.

"I just got down off the mountain from a rescue, I'm filthy dirty."

Oh, the images that conjured up in her mind... She shook them off. "It's okay. It won't matter for what I have in mind."

A shorter silence this time, filled with a new kind of tension.

And her nipples went hard. "Aidan? You still there?"

"Your place in ten."

Her place? What the— *Omigod.* "No, I'm at the Mane Attraction! I have a treatment I want to give you!"

More crickets.

"Aidan?"

"In ten," he repeated.

"Okay, good—" But she was talking to dead air. She looked at Char. "He needs to work on his phone etiquette."

"God himself couldn't teach those boys of mine phone etiquette. So is he coming?"

"In ten."

Char smiled wide. "Yep. He likes you." Her gaze went speculative. "So what's your stance on children?"

Lily's mouth fell open.

"Kidding!" Char said, and laughed, the sound a little evil actually.

"He doesn't like me like that," Lily said.

"Honey, let me tell you something about my boy. It takes an act of Congress for me to get him to do anything he doesn't want to do. You follow me?"

Lily was afraid she did but she shook her head no.

"It's the middle of the day and he's busier than a priest in a whorehouse. So if he's coming now, he dropped a million things to do so. For you."

Oh, God. "Why are we doing this again?" Lily asked desperately.

"Because the mess-ees are going to become the mess-ors."

Lily stared at Char. Yep. Evil. "Promise me something."

"Anything," Char said.

"If you ever get mad at me, you'll just kill me dead. You won't pin me to a board and slowly pull off my legs."

Char laughed again, sounding delighted now. "I'd better get out of here."

"Wait— What? I thought you wanted to see your son."

"No, I want *you* to see my son."

"But—"

"Just work your magic, get him to talk to you." Char hugged her. "He needs that, honey. More than you know. He doesn't have anyone in his life to let go to. Oh, and give him a haircut—or whatever treatment floats your boat. God knows he could use a little TLC. But don't forget to feed him the old folks home story." She grinned. "I'll leave my credit card at the front desk. Make sure to wear that pretty little sign on your forehead."

"What sign?"

"The one that says, *Spill your guts to me.*"

Lily was boggled. "I don't have a—"

"Yes, you do. That's what makes you such a good cosmetologist. You listen. You care. It's what he needs, trust me. He doesn't spill his guts to anyone. Ever."

"Maybe he doesn't have any real feelings to spill," Lily said.

Char laughed again. "Aw, now we both know that's not even close to true." She hugged Lily again, winked, and left.

"But what am I supposed to do with him?" she asked Char's empty chair.

The chair didn't answer.

Chapter 14

Aidan was exhausted. The night before he hadn't gotten to bed until midnight, and no sooner had his head hit the pillow than an S&R call had come in.

Two hikers, a newlywed couple from Denver, hadn't checked back into their honeymoon suite for the night at a local hotel. Earlier in the day, the concierge had sent them on a hike and then had worried that maybe they were lost.

When the couple hadn't returned by the next morning, their family and friends became concerned as well.

Dispatch had finally gotten a panicked call from the couple themselves, who'd managed to climb high enough to get cell service. They were hopelessly lost, freezing, freaking out, and hungry.

They were told to start a fire to keep warm while S&R worked their way to them.

The couple had called dispatch back twice. They'd had trouble starting a fire. Dispatch walked them through it, instructing them to find something for kindling before carefully stacking the wood correctly to catch fire.

By the time Aidan and Mitch had located them, the couple indeed had found something for kindling. In spite of being surrounded by hundreds of thousands of acres of forestland filled to the brim with pine needles and fallen twigs, they'd been burning their cash.

Aidan had seen people burn their clothes, their supplies... He'd genuinely thought he'd seen it all. But this was a new one, even for him.

And now Lily wanted to see him at the salon, something about returning the favor, which he didn't care about.

What he did care about was the tone in her voice. Uncertainty. Nerves.

What the hell was up? Sliding his phone into his pocket, he stood up.

Gray and Hudson stared at him.

"Got a thing," he said.

"You're in the middle of a thing," Hudson said. "A management meeting thing."

Aidan kept heading to the door.

"Hey," Gray said. "There's still a few items on the to-do list. What about Lenny?"

Aidan turned back. "He's pissed."

"So am I," Gray said grimly.

"He says he's quit drinking. I'm trying to keep an eye on him. So is Mitch."

"Listen," Gray said, "it might be easier if I take over Lenny watch."

"I brought him on board, I'll take responsibility."

There was a long silence during which Gray and Hudson gave each other a long look.

"What?" Aidan snapped.

"Lenny's a friend of yours," Gray said. "That's what. And he's an alcoholic. Not your fault, by the way. So you don't have to take responsibility for him."

"I said I'd do it," Aidan said.

Gray looked at him for a beat. "Fine. Moving on to Dad." A muscle in his jaw ticked. "Hudson still wants to track him down."

This gave Aidan a gut ache. Track him down? Christ. Just the thought brought a tidal wave of memories. It'd been hot as hell that night he'd found his dad cheating. He could remember the sweat pouring down his face after having the shit beat out of him. Nearly passing out walking home to his mom. But what he remembered most was the look on his mom's face when he told her his dad was cheating on her. Which had been nothing compared to her expression when she discovered Richard had laid his hands on Aidan. He'd never intended for her to know that. Had wished she hadn't figured it out. Because as he'd known it would, it just about killed her.

And then Richard had shown up and that was when Char clocked him with her frying pan...

Gray had been away at camp. He had no idea that a thirteen-year-old Aidan had been the catalyst for the fight. No one but Char knew. Shortly after that, she'd found out about the other kids Richard had deserted, which further cemented her hatred of the man who'd never lived up to his own responsibilities.

One year later the twins had shown up in Cedar Ridge, and Char, being a better person than anyone Aidan had ever known, had taken them in as hers. And then Kenna had come along a few years later.

Aidan had been doubly resolved to keep what had happened between him and Richard a secret after that. Hud and Jacob were so messed up from taking care of their mom instead of the other way around, the last thing Aidan wanted to do was destroy any fantasy memory they had of their dad as well. And then there was Gray. If he ever found out, Aidan probably wouldn't be able to keep Gray from hunting Richard down and killing him.

Nope, the secret was still his alone to keep. "I told you to forget it," he said to Hud. "We don't need him. We never have."

"Yes, we do," Hudson said. "He got us in this mess, and he can figure a way to get us out. His fault, his problem."

"His fault," Aidan agreed. "But *our* problem. Trust me, bringing in the man who's abandoned everything and everyone in his life will be a joke. We've never been able to count on him, how much help do you really expect him to be? No, we do this as always—on our own."

While he and Hudson were going back and forth, they lost Gray, who was staring down at his phone, shaking his head.

"Seriously?" Hudson asked him.

"I'm still listening," Gray said, but thumbed something on his phone.

Two seconds later his phone buzzed again. He looked pained as he read the response.

"Care to share with the class?" Aidan asked banally.

Gray turned his phone to reveal the text conversation:

Penny: PROBLEM. Spider in the clean laundry basket and now it's gone. I have to burn down the house.
Gray: No.

Penny: You're not grasping the severity of this situation. The spider is huge and it's going to eat the cat.
Gray: Then the spider will rightfully take our cat's place
and become our beloved spider cat.
Penny: This is on you. And remember that thing I said
you could do to me tonight? It's off the table.

Hudson grabbed Gray's phone and executed a three-
pointer into the trash.

"What the hell?" Gray said.

"We're talking about finding Dad," Hud said. "I want
to and Aidan doesn't. You're the tiebreaker."

Aidan gave Gray a long look that said, *Side with me or
I'll kick your ass.*

Gray ignored him to look at Hudson. "Shelve it."

"But—"

"Shelve it," Gray repeated. "For now."

At this, Aidan relaxed marginally. Because Hud had
different memories of their dad than he did. Hud had seen
a different side of the man. He'd been too little to remember anything bad, he only knew him as Absent Dad. And
apparently there'd been one early birthday memory that
Hud had held on to, when Richard had brought Hud and
Jacob bikes.

There was no way in hell that Aidan was going to ruin
that memory with the reality that was their father.

Plus, the guy wasn't just a deadbeat dad and an asshole, but also unpredictable, not to mention uncontrol-
lable. If they got him here and he found Kenna, complete
with all the buckets of money she'd earned in sponsor-
ships and endorsements during her snowboarding years,
he'd find a way to bleed her dry too—even though Gray

had managed to convince Kenna to lock her money up in long-term investments. It'd been a hard sell, because Kenna had wanted to give them the money to put toward saving the resort. Gray had refused to use her hard-won money to save their asses, and Aidan agreed.

If they were going down, she wasn't going down with them. "Subject closed," he said now to Hud.

Hudson opened his mouth to argue the point to death, because that's what annoying-as-shit little brothers did, so Aidan cut him off and shook his head. "No," he said again.

"And what," Hudson said, pissed. "You're the end of the line?"

"On this, yeah."

"That's bullshit, A."

"It's the way it is," Aidan said.

"Bullshit," Hudson said again, and stormed out.

"Don't say it," Aidan said into the deafening silence.

"That went well," Gray said anyway.

"You're an ass," Aidan said.

"No doubt," Gray said. "And he's not going to stop. You going to tell me what the real problem is?"

Hell no. But Gray was right. Hud wasn't going to stop pushing, because Kincaids never stopped. Looking for trouble. Finding it. Fucking things up. All of the above, they were masters at all of it.

Five minutes later Aidan opened the front door of the salon just as his cell buzzed. Another Facetime call.

"What the hell are you doing at the salon?" Gray asked.

Aidan vowed to delete the Find Your Friends app off

his phone if for no other reason than to have a private life. "Don't worry, Mom. I'm off the clock."

"You getting a perm? Your cuticles done? A man-scape?"

Aidan flipped him off, ended the call, and entered the salon.

Jonathan came from the left at the exact moment Lily came from the right.

Aidan took in Lily's warm smile and without warning his brain went to war with his dick.

Why is she smiling like that? his brain asked, a little stunned and also immediately skeptical. *She never smiles at us like that.*

Who gives a fuck? his dick said. *She's gorgeous.*

"I'm on this one," Lily told Jonathan.

Jonathan grinned.

"Not like that!" she said quickly, her cheeks flaming. "Go away!"

Jonathan laughed and vanished into the back, leaving them alone.

"So," Aidan said, mentally cracking his knuckles. "You said something about returning my favor." He looked around the salon warily. The place wasn't overly girlie or anything, but Aidan saw lots of things he had absolutely no use for.

Lily smiled. "You look nervous."

He met her gaze and found a light of mischief there that he hadn't expected. "And you look like you're up to something."

She laughed. *Laughed.*

And damn, he enjoyed that too. He'd missed seeing her happy, but now his brain and dick went on high alert for two different reasons. Danger, abort mission, his brain warned. No, she totally wants us, his dick said. "Listen, this returning the favor thing isn't necessary—"

"I promise it won't hurt a bit." But she looked very amused, which put him on guard.

"Uh-huh," he said, looking around, fully expecting one of his brothers to jump out at him. "So what are we talking about here?"

"I just wanted to give you a"—

He went brows up. He had no idea where she was going with the rest of that statement, but once again his brain and dick took it straight to the gutter. Blow job, both said in his head.

—"*haircut*," Lily said at the same moment, and then narrowed her eyes at him. "What did you think I was going to say?"

"No idea." He flashed a rueful smile. "But it was definitely going to be X-rated."

"I should reiterate, that kiss was a mistake. So let's stick with a haircut."

"Which one?"

"Which one what?" she asked.

"Which kiss was a mistake?" he wanted to know, knowing damn well she was full of it. "The one after the snake incident or the one against the wall?"

"Both." Turning away from him she strode to the wash station. She was wearing another sundress, this one with thin straps crisscrossing over her slender, tanned back. She had a tiny infinity sign tattooed on the back of her right shoulder with the initials AD scripted inside.

Her sister's initials.

Lily's high-heeled sandals were strapped around her

ankles and sexy as hell, and the thin, flimsy material of her dress flirted around her thighs as she moved. The entire outer package said fun sophistication.

A complete contradiction to her demeanor.

Once she'd been an open book. What you saw was what you got with her, nothing was a mystery. He'd loved that.

She'd changed.

But so had he.

"I don't get it," he said.

"What?"

"You."

"You don't have to get me," she said, gesturing him to the chair. "Just lie back and accept that this is happening."

In the same way he was supposed to accept that she was back in town for however long she planned to be here, no expectations, no ties?

Maybe she could pull that off, but he sure as hell couldn't. Though he had to give her credit, she knew exactly how to make him sweat.

He sprawled out in the chair. When he was settled in, she said, "After this I've got you booked for a full-body mud wrap."

He sat straight up, not even the hand she set on his chest deterring him. "Hell no," he said, even though he had no idea what a full-body mud wrap was.

"You really need it, Aidan," she said a little too earnestly.

He met her gaze in the mirror. Her eyes were filled with mischief. Yeah, she was most definitely messing with him. "Letting myself go, am I?" he asked.

"Terribly."

They both knew this was a big, fat lie. He ran four or five miles in full gear every single morning: rain, snow, or shine. He was in the best shape of his life. "No full-body anything unless it's your body on mine," he said, and if they hadn't been in a damn salon he might've grinned at the look on her face—a little shock, a lot of arousal.

"How about a facial?" she finally asked. "Or does that insult your manhood too?"

"At the risk of repeating myself," he said. "*Hell no.*"

"Your pores really do need some work," she said. "You're too dry, which is going to age you. And your T-zone is crying for help."

He paused. "Was any of that in English?"

"How about you just sit back, relax, and trust me?"

"With all these instruments of torture at your disposal?" he asked, looking around.

She rolled her eyes and gave him a nudge so that he lay back again.

He let her push him around, but his eyes never left hers as she went to work, running warm water on his hair. It felt amazing, he was forced to admit. But he was distracted by what he could see behind the teasing light in her eyes. "What's really going on here?"

"Nothing," she said, her voice a little too tight.

"Try again," he said. "The truth this time."

She blew out a sigh. "Your mom thought maybe you could use some pampering."

Aw, shit. "Lily, tell me you have not been listening to my crazy mother."

"She's not crazy! And she has your best interests at heart."

"Oh, Christ. You've been drinking her Kool-Aid." He

laughed dryly. "Trust me, the only interest she has right now is in pranking me. So what exactly did she put you up to? Nair in my shampoo?"

She stared at him like he was speaking in tongues. "Your mom is the sweetest thing! She would never—"

"Babe, my mother would sell my soul to the devil himself if it meant she won this round. Now tell me what she wanted you to do to me."

Lily sighed. "She wanted me to tell you she's decided to go into an old folks home. In Greece."

"Uh-huh." He'd sell his own left nut if that were true. No, make that Gray's. He'd sell Gray's left nut. "And?"

"And..." She sighed. "She thinks you're too stressed and need some relief."

"Having my hair cut isn't how I relieve stress," he said.

This rendered her speechless, and she dropped the handheld faucet into the sink. She recovered quickly, though, he'd give her that. And at the touch of her fingers gliding through his hair, he groaned. Damn. She had amazing hands... "Wait." He sat straight up and glared at her. "This isn't some salon voodoo thing where I unknowingly spill my guts, is it?"

She paused a beat too long. "Of course not," she said.

"Shit," he said, staring into her eyes. "It is."

She pushed him down. "You can't seriously be afraid that I'm going to somehow make you talk."

Ha. If she only knew her own power. One touch—hell, one *look*—and he'd give her whatever she wanted.

Chapter 15

Lily took in Aidan's look of discomfort. Normally he ex-uded easy, effortless confidence, so this made her laugh. "You really think I'm going to wave my magic shampoo and somehow force you to spill your guts to me," she said with a laugh.

"You telling me people don't spill their guts in here?" He looked around at the walls as if maybe they were magic too.

"I'm pretty new here," she reminded him.

"You know what I mean."

"Yes."

He tilted his head up and met her gaze. "Yes you know what I mean?"

"Yes, people spill their guts to me. So if you're scared, you know where the door is. And don't worry, I get it," she said soothingly. "Lots of boys are scared of getting their hair cut. Usually they're five and under though…"

That sexy muscle in his jaw bunched, which she did her best to ignore. She also ignored the fact that he had at least a day's growth of stubble there, maybe two.

And that his jeans fit him perfectly, emphasizing his long legs and...the rest of him.

And she quickly realized she had a problem, a big one. His hair was soft and silky and her fingers couldn't get enough of it. To distract herself she poured the girliest-smelling shampoo she could find into the palm of her hand and began to suds him up.

He hadn't taken his eyes off her.

"Close 'em," she said.

He held her gaze for a long beat before closing his eyes—defiant and alpha to the end. But at least now she couldn't get lost in those chocolate-brown depths. Nope. Instead she found herself staring at his mouth, remembering how it had felt on hers. His jaw, rough with that scruff, was square and strong, and as she automatically gave him a scalp massage the way she did everyone, that jaw relaxed a bit and he let out a long breath.

"You're dangerous," he murmured.

Right back atcha, she could've said. When she was done, she stood back and gestured for him to move ahead of her back to her salon chair.

He walked to it as if walking to his own execution.

She laughed. "Stop it. I'll admit I wouldn't mind having you at my mercy spilling your guts, but we both know that's not going to happen." She stopped smiling. "You're too careful for that."

He looked at her reflection in the mirror for a long moment, but didn't respond as he folded his long body into the chair.

"So," she said, hands on his shoulders. "Buzz cut? Or maybe a new color? Both?"

He actually paled.

"Aw, don't worry. I hardly ever nick an ear or screw up a color."

He stared at her. "This is the worst repaid favor in the history of forever."

She laughed again.

"A *trim*," he allowed, trying to not be moved by her laughter. "That's it. You hear me?"

Oh, she heard him. And she supposed it was wrong that she was enjoying this so much, but she didn't care. She shook out her cape and wrapped it around him.

"Lily."

"Sure," she said. "A trim. Whatever you want."

He sat there, long legs stretched out in front of him, his body loose and relaxed, though his eyes tracked her every movement as she stood over him. "You don't trust me," she murmured.

He didn't respond to this and she had to admit, that one stung a little bit. But she gave him a trim and then led him to the private client room. "For our facial."

"Lily—"

"Painless, I pinky swear."

He eyed the bed. "Be gentle with me."

"Lie down, Aidan."

He stretched out on his back on the bed, feet casually crossed, his hands up behind his head. "My safe word's *more*."

She tried to ignore him, but that was all but impossible. She moved to the sink and mixed up their organic facial product—a recipe she was proud to have brought to this salon—and slathered it on his face. She nearly jumped when he spoke.

"So how are you doing?"

She stared down at him and his eyes opened, locking on hers. Not cynical or amused. Just genuinely curious.

"Truth?" she asked.

"Always."

She slowly shook her head.

Making a sound of regret, he reached out and took her hand. "Can I help?"

She didn't want to say the first thought that came to her mind, that by just being there for her, he'd already helped. "This is on me," she finally said. "But thanks."

"You know you're not alone, right? Even if I look like an idiot with shit all over my face?"

"Yeah." She smiled at him. "And it's not shit, it's magic. You're going to have great skin when this is over. And you're the one who's supposed to be spilling your guts, remember? What's this I keep hearing about saving the resort? Can you save it?"

He gave her a bland look. "My mom again, I take it."

"She's worried about you guys. She's worried you're going to lose the place."

"There's a lot we can do before that happens." He blew out a sigh. "Might have to cut staff, but we're going to try really hard not to do that." He slid her a look. "That's extremely confidential information, by the way."

"Understood." She didn't mention Char had already told her that, not wanting to get her in trouble.

"My mom blames herself," he said. "She shouldn't. She didn't walk away from her family, leaving them powerless and broken."

Lily put her hand on his arm. "I knew you then. Knew all of you. I never saw you powerless or broken."

The corner of his mouth twitched in a grim smile and he shook his head. "You saw what I let you see, what I let everyone see. We were fucked up, Lily, and in some ways still are. But this place means everything to Gray, and he means everything to me. Jacob, Hudson, Kenna too. It keeps us together or mostly," he added. "And it's ours."

"*You've* earned it," she said.

He nodded. "And we'll find a way to keep it. We have to, if nothing else to prove that Richard Kincaid didn't take it away from us. He didn't win."

She got that *he* and the rest of the Kincaids had their self-worth, their very identity tied up in this place. Saving the place was so much more than just saving a family business to them.

So much more.

But she wished that Aidan could see that they had worth with or without the resort. "You work your butt off," she said. "No one can say you all didn't try hard enough. Have you thought about getting your dad to help, seeing as this is his mess?"

"Not happening," he said in a tight tone she'd rarely heard him use. A tone that said drop it.

She got it. He didn't want to go there. In any case, she believed they would save the resort, because she wanted it to be true, for him. And because she believed in him. She always had. That had never been the problem.

Their gazes locked and held.

"It killed me when you left," he said quietly. "Not as much as letting you put this ridiculous mud on my face, but close."

She stilled and stared at him, a little dizzy with the abrupt subject change.

Not to mention the frankness of the statement in spite of the infused humor.

It killed me when you left. "You…you never said."

"Didn't get a chance, but believe it. You going without a word devastated me. I kept imagining you trying to get over Ashley's and your dad's deaths on your own." He shook his head. "But you made it clear you weren't looking back. Even now it's like that. You're here for the job, but you still have one foot out the door, ready to bolt at a moment's notice when the next, better job comes along."

This was painfully accurate. "I had to go like that, had to cut the ties or I couldn't have done it," she said softly. "I just couldn't stay here and face…everything."

"That's my point, Lily. You didn't have to go it alone."

Said the guy who'd always had a pack of siblings to pull together for support. But she realized there was something more, something he hadn't said.

He'd felt abandoned by her, which was a very real issue for him since he'd been abandoned cruelly before. "Aidan—"

"No one but you blamed you," he said, clearly not intending to let this be about him. "Do I need to repeat that?"

"That's not quite true."

"Yes it is—"

"*No,*" she said. "I appreciate you saying that, really, I do, but at Ashley's funeral, my dad—" She broke off and closed her eyes, and just like that she was back there. Sitting in the front row next to her sobbing mother as she met the gaze of her dad, his eyes burning with fury.

At her.

And then in the next moment he was clutching his heart and falling to the ground.

He'd died there, mad at her.

She opened her eyes. "My dad blamed me."

Aidan shook his head and reached for her. "No—"

"He did, Aidan. I saw it in his eyes. And then he had the heart attack."

"I was there," he said, "at the funeral. He was devastated, yes. And angry at fate or whatever, but not you. Lily "

She quickly turned away to get a damp, warm cloth to clean him up— and to give herself a moment to fight the tears threatening to fall. She remembered Aidan trying to talk to her beforehand and her being unable to speak about what had happened. About the fact that she was leaving. About anything, really. She'd been consumed by the need to go. He'd seen that, and they'd had some angry words that night, and she knew now in hindsight that she'd hurt him badly. It was a wonder he talked to her these days at all, which was a visceral reminder that he wasn't a man to repeat his mistakes. No matter what she wished for in the deep, dark of the night, she knew he'd never trust her with his heart again.

"Even if you believed what happened to Ashley was your fault," he said behind her, with devastating gentleness, "even if your dad blamed you and you had to get out of town, you didn't have to stop what was happening between you and me."

Standing with her back still to him, she closed her eyes, her chest aching so that she could hardly speak. "That's the thing," she whispered, denying what her heart wanted to believe was true. "Nothing was happening be-tween you and me. Not really."

"Bullshit."

"It's true. There was nothing between us—"

His hands settled on her shoulders. He'd gotten up from the bed and turned her around to face him, making her gasp in surprise. "Aidan—"

He yanked her in and covered her mouth with his.

This was no soft, gentle, nice-to-be-kissing-you-again kiss. This was a no holds barred, hard body plastered to a much softer one, tongues clashing, hands fighting for pur-chase, and rough groans cutting the air.

When he pulled back, it was only an inch to speak. "Yeah," he said roughly. "You're right. There's nothing between us. Nothing but heat and fire and crazy need."

"And coconut and cucumber," she said, licking her lips.

He swore and took the cloth, turning to the mirror to wipe his face himself.

"Okay, maybe," she said softly to his broad back. "Maybe there's…something." Her entire body was hum-ming and throbbing with that something. "But it's still not going anywhere."

"Why the hell not?" he asked, sounding mystified. "I don't know about you, but this"—he gestured between them—"doesn't just happen for me."

She gave a rough laugh. "What are you talking about? It happens to you, always. All the time. Women love you, Aidan. And you love them back. Hell, it was happening with my—" She clamped her mouth shut, horrified it had almost run off without her brain's permission.

But Aidan hadn't gotten the memo. "With who?"

"Forget it."

"I don't think so," he said quietly. "Tell me."

She closed her eyes and went to war with herself. He'd shared something of himself with her, and she owed him the same in return. It was past time to face this. Face him. "Ashley."

When there was no immediate response, she opened her eyes and found him staring at her.

"You're wrong," he said flatly. "There was nothing between Ashley and me, not like you're thinking."

"She liked you. A lot."

He went very still. "I didn't know that."

Lily believed him. But that didn't change the fact that this was one thing she refused to take from Ashley, dead or alive. She backed away and opened the door because suddenly the room was way too small and intimate.

Aidan immediately closed it. "Lily," he said very quietly. "Tell me you didn't leave and then not talk to me for ten years because you thought I had something going on with your sister."

"That's not it."

"Then what?"

"We competed over everything, Aidan. And I usually won. The things she really wanted, I took from her. I won't take this."

He studied her expression for a long moment before opening his mouth to speak, but his phone buzzed. He pulled it from his pocket, eyed the ID, and blew out a breath. "It's Hud. He needs me."

This wasn't the first time she'd seen him drop everything for a Kincaid, and it also wasn't the first time that she took a beat to marvel at the closeness of his family.

And her lack thereof…

She'd always told herself it was best that way, but there was no denying that a little part of her no longer believed it.

Shoving his phone away, Aidan lifted his gaze to hers again. "This isn't over," he said.

She had no idea if that was a promise or a threat, but it didn't matter.

He gave a mirthless smile, shook his head—probably at both of them—and left her with nothing but her own unsettled thoughts and the taste of him still on her lips.

Chapter 16

Aidan drove straight to The Slippery Slope, which was where Hud had texted him from. He hit the bar and ran into Lenny staring into an empty glass.

"Hey," Aidan said.

Lenny lifted his head and met his gaze with bleary eyes. Shit. "Thought you stopped drinking," Aidan said.

Lenny shook his head. "Knew that was coming." He stood and tossed some money down before he met Aidan's gaze. "I've got two months plus left on my suspension. Seemed like a waste to quit drinking so soon."

"Lenny—"

"Save it, man." And then he was gone.

Aidan blew out a breath and searched out Hudson, finding his brother sitting at the other end of the bar nursing a beer and a bad 'tude, staring at his phone.

"Hey, Princess," Aidan said, taking the seat next to him.

"Call me that one more time and I'll—" Hudson looked

up from his beer and narrowed his eyes. "What's up with your face?"

Aidan put his hands to it. His face was most definitely still there. "Nothing, why?"

"Your skin looks...smooth."

Aidan stared at his brother.

Hudson stared back while taking another long pull on his beer. "Yeah, you smell like a chick, but your pores look fantastic."

"What are you—" Aidan whipped around and searched out the crowd. "Fuck you. Gray put you up to this, right?"

Hudson grinned and with one finger pushed his phone across the bartop, closer to Aidan.

A woman's tinny voice came out of it. "Aidan Scott Kincaid! I can't believe you talk to your baby brother that way!"

Aidan sighed and picked up the phone. "Mom, trust me, Princess here is nobody's baby anything." He eyed a smug-looking Hudson. "He's a huge six-foot-four gigantor. And I can't believe you got him to ask me about my pores."

"And I can't believe you tried to ruin my date with Marcus. Did you know that the man won't sleep with me yet because he says he's got to do right by my children?" She sputtered with outrage over this. "My children are idiots!"

"Mom." Aidan pinched the bridge of his nose to try to get rid of the image of his mother sleeping with Marcus. "You don't need to rush into anything—"

"So I should wait until what, I'm eighty-five and Marcus needs a little blue pill to make his penis work?"

Hudson was laughing his butt off, the jackass.

Jesus. "Okay," Aidan said to his mom. "I'm going to need you to never again say that word to me. *Never.*"

His mom sighed. "Give Hudson a kiss for me, okay? Tell him I sent his mama a box of her favorite candies and some of that tea she loves. I hope the ladies at her home make sure she gets it."

Aidan softened and glanced at Hudson again, whose expression was inscrutable now. It always was when it came to his mom, or anything to do with his past.

If Aidan and Gray thought they'd had a rough childhood, Hudson and Jacob's past made theirs look like a walk in the park. They'd grown up alone with their mother, who suffered from mental illness. She was on meds now and in special-needs housing, safe at least. "That's nice of you, Mom," he said. "So now that that's out of the way and all is well with my pores, we're going to have a truce, right?"

"Hmm," she said. "I'll consider it. Love you, baby." She disconnected.

Aidan stared at the phone. "Shit. We're not going to have a truce."

"Nope," Hudson agreed and took another long pull of his beer.

Aidan shook his head. "Can you imagine if she ever decided to use her powers for good? She'd obtain world peace in a few hours."

"There's no doubt," Hudson said.

The bartender came over. Shelly again. "Another one, handsome?" she asked Hudson, completely ignoring Aidan.

"Yeah," Hudson said with a warm smile. "Thanks, Shel."

"Suck-up," Aidan muttered to him beneath his breath.

Shelly graced Aidan with a long look. "Huh. Didn't figure you for the chemical peel type. Your skin looks annoyingly perfect."

Hudson grinned. "He just had a facial."

Aidan gave him a shove that nearly knocked him off his barstool.

Hud winked at Shelly. "He's had a rough day at the salon. Think you can bring him a beer?"

"Sure," she said sweetly.

"And you won't...do anything to it?" Aidan asked.

She smiled. "Of course not."

Uh-huh. "So you're not mad at me anymore?"

"Oh, I'm still mad. But the boss is here tonight." She nodded her head to the tall, dark, and tough guy at the other end of the bar. Mason. He and Aidan went way back. Mason ran a tight ship and had an extremely low tolerance for bullshit.

Shelly moved off and Aidan turned to Hudson. "So what's up?"

"Besides your skin resembling a newborn's ass?" Hudson grinned but it faded quick. "I did some digging."

"And what did you dig up?"

"Jacob."

Everything inside Aidan stilled as he tried to read into Hud's flat voice, but Hud was good at not giving anything away when he didn't want to.

Jacob had been gone for eight years now. No one knew why he'd left, or at least no one was talking. If Hud knew, he'd kept it close to the vest. But Jacob had left after finishing high school. He had joined the army.

And had never come back.

"Turns out he was injured," Hudson said now. "He stayed in Germany at a military hospital there and was released, but I can't get any specifics or his location."

"Any indication on how bad he was hurt?" Aidan asked.

"No." Hudson looked quiet and stoic, so when he slammed a fist down onto the bar it startled everyone within hearing distance. Except Aidan.

He put a hand on Hudson's forearm and leaned in close to speak, because the place had gone quiet. "Hey, let's go home and—"

"Don't. Don't do that."

"Do what?"

"Be the calm, rational older brother just because I'm losing it," Hudson said. "I hate when you're the calm, rational one. I'm not losing it."

"Whatever you say." Aidan squeezed Hud's shoulder. "Come on, man, let's go. We'll grab a pizza and—"

"Jesus, I don't need you to baby me. I'm fine."

"Fine? You've got fifty people staring at you right now wondering when the barstools are going to start flying. Not that I mind a good brawl now and then, but it's been awhile and I'm out of practice."

Not amused, not even close, Hudson met his gaze, his own hard. "If you're looking for someone to save, maybe you should look in your own damn mirror."

Aidan eased back. "What's that supposed to mean?"

"You're just as fucked up as me and you know it."

"About?"

"We're the middle brothers, man."

"You're a twin."

"I'm talking about all five of us, you idiot. But if you

want to get technical, I was born seven whole minutes ahead of Jacob," Hud said. "That makes me a middle brother, like you. And as such, we're the pleasers. The fixers."

"Fuck you, I'm not a pleaser," Aidan said. "Or a fixer, whatever the hell that means."

Hudson smiled grimly. "You know what it means, and you know what I'm getting at. You'll do anything for someone you love or care about. You'll help Gray save the resort, a place that, thanks to Dad, leaves a bad taste in your mouth. But you'll do it for Gray, because he's everything to you."

Aidan made a point of looking around. "What, are we filming a chick flick? What's with all the feels?"

But Hudson was on a roll, and once the guy had a bone he never let go. "And even though you think Jacob wants to be left alone, you'll help me find him for the sole reason that *I* need to. And then there's Kenna. You brought her here to Cedar Ridge when she crashed and burned even though she was afraid of being an imposition— which she was—but you never let her feel it."

"You done?" Aidan asked.

"No. Because then there's whatever it is you're shoving deep down and pretending isn't eating at you."

"That's a load of bullshit," Aidan said, even though he knew. Christ, he knew.

Lily.

Hud shook his head. "It's not, and you know it. So do me a favor and remember how screwed up you are too the next time you feel the urge to save me."

Aidan felt his temper rise, but he reminded himself that's what Hudson wanted. A diversion away from himself. He wasn't going to get it. "This isn't about saving you. It's about Jacob." Or it had been before he and Hud had provided the evening's entertainment for the bar patrons. "We'll find him and bring him home," Aidan promised.

Hudson's eyes darkened with his own temper that barely hid his grief. "And if we can't?"

"We will."

"What if we're too late?"

"We won't be," Aidan said grimly, and prayed to God that would be true as he pulled out cash to cover their bill.

"I still want to knock your ass into next week," Hudson said as he stood.

"Ditto," Aidan assured him.

It was noon a few days later when Lily took a break from waxes and facials and hairdos for a quick escape to the back room that was office, staff room, and kitchen all in one. Gray must have approved the renovations she'd requested. They'd picked out paint colors and she was getting new shelving in as well. She'd been working on a new layout and, over a sandwich, she played with it some more on the computer. Then she checked her phone and found exactly zero emails sigh and a missed call from her mom that brought panic. She and her mom talked about once a month—unless there was an emergency. And as there'd been a few of those—Ashley, her dad—Lily still felt her heart drop whenever her mom showed up on her phone screen.

"Lily!" her mom said in delight when Lily rang her back. "Is that you?"

"Hi, Mom, yes it's me. Are you all right?"

"Of course I am. Why do you ask me that every single time I call you?"

Lily let out a shaky breath and tried to calm her racing heart.

"Lily?"

"I don't know," she finally said, trying to channel Aidan and sound calm. "Force of habit?"

"Darling, it's been ten years," her mom said softly. "You've got to let it go. It's okay to let it go."

"I have," Lily said. *Lied.* "Totally and completely. "One hundred percent."

"Do you mean one hundred percent *minus* one hundred percent?"

Lily let out a low laugh. "Let's talk about you, okay? What are you up to?"

"Nice subject change. But because I'm in South Africa I'm going to allow it. Did you know they serve fried caterpillars and sheep heads here as a delicacy?"

"Yummy." Lily still wasn't used to the changes in her mom. Once upon a time, Donna Danville had been born and raised right here in Cedar Ridge, Colorado. She'd married and had two kids and worked just about 24/7 at Mt. Rose, never leaving the only town she knew and loved.

Until she'd lost half her family in the span of a single week from hell.

Lily and her mom had had many talks over the years about how Donna wanted Lily to let go of the past enough to move on. Lily always assured her she had, telling her she had a full and happy life in San Diego.

And most of the time Lily even believed her own lies.

Until she'd come back to Cedar Ridge.

Now she knew the truth. She hadn't let go of the past at all. She'd buried it deep, let it take root, and had even secretly harbored it. "It's good to talk to you, Mom."

"Oh, darling, so good." Over the air came the telltale sniff and Lily's heart dropped.

"Mom, don't cry."

"It's just so lovely to hear you." She paused. "I've sent you something that I had pulled out of storage, I hope it won't upset you. But it should arrive today and I wanted to give you a little heads-up about it so you aren't surprised."

"What is it?" Lily asked.

"A framed pic of you and Ashley on the mountain. And her favorite scarf. I thought you might want them there in Cedar Ridge. One to keep you warm on the outside, the other to keep you warm inside. In your heart."

It took Lily a moment to answer because her throat clogged with emotion. She knew the scarf well, she'd been the one to give the baby-blue length of cashmere to Ashley on her seventeenth birthday—her last. "That's sweet, Mom," she finally managed, meaning it. "I'll love them both, thank you."

"Just do me one favor," her mom said. "Promise me now that you're back home, you won't leave there until you forgive yourself."

Lily closed her eyes. "Mom—"

"Promise me, Lily Ann, or I swear to you, I'm on the next plane. I'll get all up in your grill and everything."

Lily managed a laugh. "All up in my grill?"

"Yes. That's what all the kids are saying now, right?"

Lily shook her head. "Fine, you win. But, Mom?"

"Yeah."

"Stop streaming MTV."

Lily was smiling when she disconnected and still smiling when a candy bar got waved beneath her nose.

Jonathan dropped it into her lap. "Nice to see you looking happy."

Lily picked up the candy bar and felt her mouth water. "A bribe?"

"You know me so well." Jonathan jerked his chin to the reception area. "Passing off another client to you."

No problem." She took a bite of the candy bar. "Omigod, so good. You know, at my old job these were considered the work of the devil and were banned. I've been making up for lost time so much my dress was tight this morning."

"Your old job sucked and so did your boss," Jonathan said.

True enough.

"And Lily Pad?"

"Yeah?"

"You look like hot stuff in that dress."

She finished her candy bar and hit the reception area. Waiting there were Danielle and Chelsea, two sixteen-year-old BFFs. They wanted matching updos for a rec center teen summer dance, so she took one and Rosa took the other.

"The dance sounds like fun," Lily said to the girls after they'd each been washed. They were sitting side by side at the stations. "Are you going with anyone?"

"It's stag," Chelsea said, the taller, more outspoken one of the two. "But I'm meeting someone there."

"Me too," Danielle said smugly as Lily began to do her hair. The girl had a smile that revealed dimples and more than a little trouble.

Over at Rosa's station, Chelsea's eyes narrowed in the mirror at Danielle. "Who? Who are you meeting there?"

"I promised not to tell."

"Why?" Chelsea demanded. "I'm your BFF. You have to tell me. It's in the manual."

"Can't," Danielle said. "Trevor doesn't want me to tell anyone so no one gets jealous." She slapped her hand over her own mouth at the inadvertent slip.

Chelsea pushed Rosa's hands out of her hair and stood up, hands on hips. "Trevor? You're meeting Trevor? *You?*"

Now Danielle's eyes narrowed. "What's that supposed to mean? You think I'm not good enough for him?"

"Not even close," Chelsea said. "And he's *my* date tonight. So back off, heifer. And you might want to back off the cheeseburgers too. Just sayin'."

Danielle leapt to her feet as well. "Who's going to make me, you skinny, skank cow?"

That's when they dove at each other and wrestled around on the floor, fighting like two cats.

Rosa stood there gaping. Jonathan ran in from the private client room, skidded to a halt, and looked horrified. Then he pointed at Lily.

Lily got the message. *Deal with this.* She pulled the handheld faucet from the hair-washing station and squirted both teens. Worked like a charm.

When they were gone and the mess was cleaned up, Jonathan shook his head. "I should give you a raise for most creative use of a station."

"You should," Lily agreed. Not that she'd hold her breath. Jonathan was so tight with his money he squeaked when he walked.

Her next client was a huge, thirty-something lumberjack with a Wild-Man-of-Borneo beard. He requested a shave.

Lily pulled out the clippers to trim the bushy beard but he stopped her.

"My head," he said.

She looked at his beautiful thick, luscious mane of hair. "You sure?"

He patted the top of his head. "Positive."

"But—"

"My wife has cancer," he said, and then he ran a hand over his face. "So yeah, I'm sure," he said hoarsely. "All of it goes."

Afterward he tried to pay her, but Lily refused to accept any money from him.

When he'd left, Jonathan came up to her, arms crossed.

"Don't worry," she said. "I'll pay for it out of my till."

He looked at her for a long beat. "You're pretty damn amazing, you know that? And you won't be paying out of your earnings. I've got it covered. Because for cancer, anything goes. Always."

It was six o'clock before Lily left the salon. It'd been a long day, made longer by the way she kept thinking about Aidan. *This isn't over*, he'd said. And then there'd been the conversation with her mom.

Forgive yourself.

Promise me.

Lily got into her car, but instead of going home, she parked in the empty clearing at the trailhead to the hiking trails. There she drew in a deep breath and looked at herself in the rearview mirror. "You're okay," she told herself.

Her reflection didn't look convinced.

"You just need to feel Ashley," she said, testing that theory out loud.

It was the truth. She desperately needed to feel her sister. The first problem with that was that she was still in her work clothes, a sundress and cropped sweater with wedge sandals. Alone in her car with no one nearby, she first looked around for security cameras. Not seeing any, she quickly stripped down to her sports bra and spandex shorts, and then dug into the duffel bag in the backseat for a T-shirt and running shoes.

She got to the exact same spot she'd made it to on her first day back in town before stopping for a break. She sucked in some wind and checked her phone.

No missed calls. And no texts from a certain firefighter...

She sighed. Without water and supplies she knew better than to go much farther. She might be a little unbalanced and a lot messed up, but she wasn't stupid.

So she went another half mile and then sat on a rock, taking in the view. If she'd been geared up, she'd have had several choices from here—the rest of the hike—another two miles up a near vertical. Or free-climbing down to the river.

She'd done both many times, a long, *long* time ago.

But it was the cliff that drew her. She walked to the edge and looked down.

A staggering three-hundred-sixty-degree vista of sharp, jagged mountain peaks and the blanket of green forestland that covered them, lined with rivers and tributaries, as far as the eye could see. This wasn't the exact spot where Ashley had died. That was up about a mile farther. But the view was the same, and in fact from here she could see the face where Ashley had climbed and then fallen to her death.

Lily stared across the chasm at it. She didn't know what she'd expected to find. A neatly wrapped box of forgiveness? Her sister's ghost?

She got nothing as she looked at the heart-stopping drop-off from the cliff to the winding river far below, nothing at all but the silent dare.

Climb me....

"Next time," she told it.

Chapter 17

After two straight days on a fire out on Eagle Flats, Aidan staggered out of the station when his shift was over, blinking at the bright morning sun.

He turned on his phone and found the usual myriad of messages, including one from a pissed-off Lenny who'd gone to court to fight his DUI to no avail. Aidan texted him back that his job would be waiting for him, no worries there. But Lenny texted back with a "whatever" and had Aidan shaking his head.

He couldn't give any energy to that right now.

Someone honked, and he turned to see Gray waiting at the curb in one of the utility vehicles that belonged to the resort.

Aidan ambled over to him, and Gray rolled down the window. "Kenna had to borrow your truck for a fucking interview, so I'm your ride."

"You need to figure out what she can do for the resort, man," Aidan said. "And quick."

"Yeah. But when I ask what she wants to do, she just shrugs. I don't have a lot of year-round positions open for a pissed-off-at-the-world twenty-four-year-old."

Yeah. Aidan knew this. He tossed his duffel bag in the back and slid into the shotgun position before laying his head back.

"Coffee's for you," Gray said, nodding to the steaming to-go cup in the console.

Aidan reached for it, sipped, and looked at Gray, eyes narrowed. "Sugar and milk?"

"Isn't that how you like it?"

"Yeah, but since when do you care how I like it?"

Gray didn't answer, just pulled away from the curb. Shit. Aidan set the cup down. "What's up?"

"Who says something's up?" Gray asked casually as he whipped a U-turn.

"When you're nice to me, something's always up."

Gray blew out a breath, and Aidan's bad feeling deepened. "Mom?"

"No, she's fine."

Aidan gave him an impatient go-ahead gesture.

"It's Dad," Gray said. "He finally caught up with some of Hudson's messages and called me back instead of him."

Aidan stared at his brother's profile, totally and instantly pissed off for Hudson's sake. "What the hell did he call you for?"

"Because he's an asshole who doesn't want to acknowledge Hud and Jacob exist."

"What kind of bullshit is that?"

"Hey, I agree, but it doesn't change the fact that he called me. He wanted to tell me why he wasn't coming back. Ever."

Aidan didn't show his relief, but he was glad he was sitting down.

"Don't you want to know why?" Gray asked.

"Don't give a shit, as long as he stays away."

Gray slid him a look that had Aidan's feeling going from bad to worse.

"So you're telling me you don't care that you are the reason why he doesn't want to come back or be a part of our lives?"

Fuck. "Pull over."

"I'm—"

"Pull the fuck over," Aidan snapped.

Gray yanked the truck to the side of the road. For as far as the eye could see there was the narrow two-lane road and trees. Miles and miles of trees. Aidan shoved out of the vehicle and started walking.

"Where the hell are you going?" Gray yelled after him.

Aidan kept moving.

"Goddammit." This was followed by the sounds of Gray's running footsteps as he tried to keep up with Aidan.

"You should've told me," Gray said breathlessly. "Back when it happened."

Aidan shook his head and kept moving. No, he couldn't have told Gray when it happened. And they weren't going to talk about it now either.

But Gray finally caught up with him and grabbed his arm, whipping him around. "He told me you caught him," Gray said, his hair blowing away from his face in the breeze. His eyes went hard. "And he also told me what happened after that."

Aidan doubted that. "No. No way he'd tell you."

"You'd walked in on him and his admin going at it at

the resort. You tried to run out, but he wouldn't let you."
Gray's voice was low and dangerously quiet now, the way
it got when he was *really* seriously ticked off and trying to
keep his shit together. "He said that he got so furious and
pissed off that he beat the shit out of you and then drank
himself into a stupor and passed out. When he woke up
you were gone."

Aidan tipped his head back and stared at the sky. Azure
blue. So bright it hurt. He kept staring at it.

"He beat the shit out of you?" Gray asked, sounding
raw and devastated.

There was only one cloud, a white puffy cloud in the
shape of an elephant, floating lazily across the sky.

"Say something," Gray begged.

Aidan pointed to the sky. "You see the elephant, or is
that just me?"

Gray blew out a breath. "He went looking for you," he
said. "Found you at home with Mom. He figured you'd
told her everything, but I know you better than that. You
keep your shit bottled tight."

Aidan closed his eyes, guilt squeezing his airway so
tight he couldn't breathe.

"But apparently Mom figured things out," Gray said,
"and that's when she went after him with a frying pan.
And the rest is history. But Jesus, Aidan. All this time I
had no idea you were there that night." He paused and
then said again, "You should've told me."

"No," Aidan said, eyes still closed.

"No? What the hell, man. He hit you, hurt you. I'm going to—"

Aidan opened his eyes and met Gray's gaze. "I meant
no, I didn't keep that shit locked up." Shame burned his

throat like he was trying to talk over shattered glass. "I did tell Mom. Not about what he'd done to me, I'd never lay that guilt on her, but about the affair. Even though he'd threatened me and told me that it would kill her, I did. I wanted her to leave him right then and there and she…" He shook his head. "I'd hidden my injuries with a baseball cap and hoodie. She took them off and saw that I had a black eye and my ribs…they weren't great. *That's* when she went apeshit on his ass."

"Good," Gray said grimly

"Don't you get it?" Aidan asked. "It's my fault she got hurt, my fault she got arrested. That's all on me."

"Are you fucking kidding me? You were just a kid, Aidan—"

"Doesn't matter, I should've protected her," he said. "Us."

"No," Gray said, his voice low and rough with emotion he rarely allowed to show. "You listen to me, A Dad should've protected us. And failing that, Mom should've—"

"Don't you blame her."

"I don't." Gray shook his head. "It was a seriously messed-up situation that no kid should've been caught in. And I originally thought he should have to fix this, but now—"

"He can't come here. Mom's doing good, she's happy. If he comes—"

"He won't," Gray said tightly. "If he does, I'll kill him."

"The resort is ours now. We're going to save it. He's not going to win, Gray." He started to move away, but Gray caught him and pulled him back around.

"One more thing," Gray said. "I'd give anything to be able to go back and protect you. I'm your big brother."

"I can out-bench-press you. I don't need protection."

"Too bad," Gray said. "I'm right here standing at your back and always will be. Got it?"

Aidan stared into Gray's very serious eyes and nodded.

"Good," Gray said. "So. We do this the way we've done everything. Without him."

The relief almost knocked Aidan on his ass. "Thanks."

"Don't thank me for that. We're a family. And speaking of that, I know you only stick around here for me."

This was way too deep to handle on utter exhaustion. "Well, and also to watch Penny boss you around," Aidan said, trying to lighten the mood.

Gray let out a rough laugh and dropped his head for a beat before lifting it and looking at Aidan. "I don't want you to stay just because you feel you have to."

"I don't," Aidan said. "I stay for you. And Mom. And Hud and Kenna. You guys mean something to me. I stay because I believe in us, dammit. We belong here. Together."

Gray started to step into Aidan, no doubt to hug him, but Aidan slapped a hand on his brother's chest. "What's with you and Hud and all the chick flick moments?"

"Suck it up," Gray said, and hauled him in anyway. And then for good measure he lifted Aidan off his feet and shook him like he used to do when they were kids, proving Gray could at least tie Aidan in a bench-press competition after all.

Aidan sighed. "We're right on the side of the road for chrissakes," he grumbled. "Anyone can see us."

Gray laughed and tightened his arms, refusing to let

him go until Aidan managed to give him a head noogie and they shoved clear of each other.

A few minutes later they were back on the road, their silence much more comfortable now. Aidan was the first to break it. "How much of a shot do we really have at handling this ourselves?"

"We have a year," Gray said. "And there's nothing us Kincaids are good at if it's not saving our own asses in the home stretch."

Aidan nodded and hoped that was really true. But he was too tired to give it much thought. He rested his head back and closed his eyes until Gray pulled up in front of their building, his gaze locking on the sight of Penny's car parked in the lot. "Nothing like coming home to a good woman."

They got out and Aidan stared at the building, wishing that he had even a half a percent chance at finding Lily in his bed waiting for him. "You're a lucky son of a bitch, having Penny decide on you way back in middle school, when you were actually decent-looking."

Gray laughed. "I know exactly how lucky I am. Especially given what an idiot I was."

"Was?" Aidan asked.

Gray wrapped an arm around Aidan's neck and returned the painful noogie.

Aidan gave Gray a push in front of him and then tripped his brother up the stairs.

Then they walked into the building together and went their separate ways. Aidan walked into his and Hud's place starving and exhausted. He wanted a huge breakfast spread that included eggs rancheros and a mountain of French toast and Lily in his bed.

Naked and willing.

None of the above was waiting for him. He opened his fridge and was staring at slim pickings when his phone rang.

"Problem," Hudson said.

Aidan closed his eyes. "Dude, I just got home and am on three hours of sleep. Solve your own problems."

"I'm at Gray's desk staring at a monitor and I've got Lily sitting on a north-facing rock staring down Dead Man's Cliff."

"*Shit*," Aidan said.

"Want me to go out there?"

"No." Aidan shoved his hand through his hair. "I've got her."

He drove up the hill and jogged the rest of the way, and was at the trailhead in under seven minutes. He tried calling Lily. He went straight to voice mail. Blowing out a breath, he hit the trail. It wasn't often he did this. In the winter, he often skied every part of this hill, but in the summer months if he ended up out here in any capacity, it was because he was looking for someone, or fighting a blaze.

He was halfway up when he heard Lily coming down. And sure enough around the next turn she nearly plowed right into him.

She was flat out running for her life.

So that she didn't take them over the edge he grabbed her arms and absorbed the impact.

With a gasp she stilled. Out of breath, damp with sweat, she stared up at him. "What are you doing here?"

"You first," he said.

She backed from him and gulped in air. "I'm running."

"From what?"

She stared at him for a beat and then laughed. She had to bend over and put her hands on her knees, and he took the moment to soak up the sight of her in a T-shirt and spandex shorts, both revealing lots of smooth, gorgeous skin and mouthwatering curves.

Finally she straightened.

"You going to tell me what's so funny?" he asked.

"You, thinking the only reason I'd be running is because something's chasing me." She smiled. "I've spent the past month eating my emotions. The only thing I'm running from is the calories I've consumed."

"Oh." He relaxed. "I thought maybe—"

"I needed rescuing?"

"Well…yeah," he said, and rubbed his jaw, watching her closely to see if she was going to fall apart.

He should've known better.

Her smile gone, she shook her head. "I don't need rescuing." Then she gnawed on her lip. "Okay, so not counting the snake and the tire, I don't need rescuing."

"No," he agreed. "You don't. You're one of the strongest women I know. You bury your shit deep. I know a little about that, Lily, and it never works out well. I can promise you that."

"And just what do you think I'm burying?" she asked.

"Just about everything…including your feelings for me," he said.

She stared at him. He waited for her to laugh and deny it, or throw the words back in his face, but she did neither.

"This is my battle to fight," she said. "Alone."

This was an alien concept for Aidan, who never felt alone. Hell, his siblings lived right on top of him. "But you're not alone."

"I need to be for this," she said stubbornly.

Independent to the end. And God forbid she accept help or support from anyone, especially him. "Lily, you've been on your own a long time, but you don't have to be—"

"The past is the past. It plays no part in the here and now."

"If that was really true, you wouldn't be harboring a mad at me," he said.

She crossed her arms over her chest. "I'm not mad at you."

"You sure about that?" he asked.

She held his gaze for only a beat before looking away.

"We're going to get to the bottom of this," he said.

"Oh, goodie," she said. "Sounds like fun." And then she took off down the trail on her own.

Chapter 18

Lily slept poorly that night, thinking of what Aidan had said. She *was* mad at him, she realized. Not because of Ashley. It wasn't his fault her sister had fallen for him. No, Lily was mad because he'd made *her* want him again, with no effort at all.

Also not his fault, a small part of her brain said.

She didn't care. She wanted him, quite badly as it turned out, and irrational or not, it made her mad. Being back in Cedar Ridge was hard. Being on the mountain was even harder. But she was working on all of that.

But to fall for Aidan and even consider sticking around as she did in the deep dark of the night?

Insanity.

And now she was getting somewhere, she had to admit. Her anger was a cover-up for the real emotion that was clogging her throat—fear. Fear for her, because she wasn't good at needing and wanting someone, and that made her vulnerable. She hated being vulnerable.

And in any case, she was much better at being independent and alone.

But that wasn't all she was afraid of. She was also
afraid for Aidan. It was his job to go up on the mountain
that had claimed half of her family, and he did it in the
worst, most dangerous situations possible, risking his life
to save others. It changed nothing.

She worked all day, and when she got home, tired and
out of sorts, it was to find her apartment the temperature
of a refrigerator.

She'd left the windows open.

Only a few hours earlier it'd been in the nineties and so
hot and dry the air had crackled and she'd given herself
electroshocks every time she touched anything. But this
was the Rockies, and often the temps dropped drastically
with the sun.

She blew out a breath and eyed the cute little framed
pic of her and Ashley that her mom had sent. Ashley was
smiling.

"Let me guess, it's because you don't have to load wood
anymore," Lily said, picking up the baby-blue cashmere
scarf that she'd left alongside the photo. She wrapped it
around her neck, feeling the incredible softness of it like
it was a hug from above. Lily buried her face in the cashmere, remembering the last time she'd seen Ashley wear it.
They'd been on bikes—racing each other, of course. Ashley had been in the lead and she'd glanced back at Lily,
laughing wildly, the blue cashmere flying out behind her.

For a long moment Lily stood there, lost in the memory. Then, needing to feel her fingertips and toes, she
kicked off her sandals and shoved her feet into her boots
and went outside and down the stairs to the woodpile.

She stood and stared at it, trying to will any snakes away.

A car drove up and stopped. The window rolled down.

It was Penny. She was beautiful, deceptively petite, even dainty, and though Lily didn't know Penny all that well, she did know that Gray's wife could kick some *serious* ass.

"Long time no see," she said to Lily. "Nice look."

They both eyed Lily's cute sundress and Uggs. "I'm freezing my parts off. I forgot how cold it gets at night here in Timbuktu."

"Yeah," Penny said. "But since it's so gorgeous here, I tend to forgive it."

"I'm working on that."

Penny's smile faded. "You doing okay?"

"Sure."

"I'm not just being polite," Penny said. "I really want to know. Are you doing okay being back? It's got to be hard—or so I'm guessing, since it took you ten years to do it."

Lily sighed. "Yeah. I'm sorry I didn't keep in touch."

"No apology necessary. You're making some changes at the salon, I hear. That facial you gave Aidan made his face look smoother than a baby's butt. If I come in, can you make my face look smoother than a baby's butt?"

"Absolutely," Lily said.

"And maybe while you work your magic, you'll tell me all about what's going on between you and my brother-in-law," Penny said in a casual tone that was in direct opposition to her obscene brow waggle.

Lily kept her cool. "That won't take long, since there's nothing going on."

Penny studied her a beat and then smiled. "Do you know what I do for a living these days?"

"No."

"I'm an investigator for an insurance company, and I happen to specialize in reading people. That's how I know you've told me two lies in two minutes."

"I..." Lily shifted her weight. "Well, not two *whole* lies."

"First lie," Penny said, holding up a finger. "You're not fine. And the second..." She added another finger to the first. "There *is* something going on between you and Aidan, some sort of relationship. I just don't know what."

Lily managed a laugh. "You know as well as I do, Aidan isn't all that interested in relationships."

"You're wrong there," Penny said. "He's actually extremely attached to the people in his life and protects his relationships with them like a dog with a bone." She let that sink in a beat. "I've got to go, but I'll come into the Mane Attraction this week. Maybe we can have drinks after and count the ways in which the Kincaids drive us crazy."

"You're married to one of them," Lily pointed out.

"Which makes me an expert on counting the ways..."

Lily laughed, and when Penny drove off she went back to the woodpile. All she needed were two, maybe three logs. That would warm the place up enough to get going. She carefully chose her logs, surprised at how heavy they were with last night's rain soaked in. Damn, maybe she needed to lift fewer cookies and more weights.

She stacked the logs in her arms and climbed the stairs. At the top, something dropped from her load and hit the landing. Then it ran over her feet and vanished.

She screamed, took a step back, and—

Fell backward down the stairs.

The logs went with her, hitting each stair with a thump, making the entire fall—which seemed to happen in slow motion—super noisy.

She landed in a heap at the bottom, stunned.

There were a few beats of utter silence during which the only thing she could hear was the thunder of her heartbeat in her ears. Then—

"Don't move!" A face swam into her focus. Lenny. "Jesus, are you all right?" he asked.

"Are you here for a haircut?" she asked a little woozily and a whole lot confused.

"No, I live in your building," he said. "Are you all right?"

The truth was, she had no idea. Her pride was cracked in half, and possibly her ass as well. She tried to sit up but he stopped her. "Wait," he said. "Give yourself a minute. That was a bad wipeout."

She groaned. Great.

"Anything feel broken?" he asked.

"No." She didn't care if that was a lie, she wanted to get up on her feet, preferably with no witnesses. Pushing Lenny's hands away, she sat up and looked down at herself.

Dirty but surprisingly very little blood. With various aches and pains already starting to make themselves known, she staggered to her feet.

"Hey, wait," Lenny said. "You're not supposed to move. If you broke your neck, your head could fall off."

She gave him a long look.

"I saw it on *CSI* once," he said.

"I didn't break my neck."

"Just let me call for help."

"Honestly, it's not necessary. I'm perfectly fine." If not completely mortified. She waved at him and then with him watching her, she forced herself not to limp back up the stairs and into her place.

In the privacy of her own apartment, she immediately sagged and whimpered as she slowly limped to her bed.

Her knees and palms were torn up, and she suspected her hind end had suffered a similar fate, but she wasn't ready to look. Nope. She was going back to bed and staying there until the day went away. And maybe tomorrow too. She stripped out of her dress and pulled a big T-shirt over her head.

She'd just crawled beneath the sheets when she heard her front door open. Normally she'd jump up, grab a baseball bat from beneath her bed, and kung-fu her way into the living room to kick some ass.

But she was too sore.

So instead of playing Superwoman, she tried to become invisible and pulled the covers over her head. She was still huddled there hoping she wasn't about to star in her very own horror flick when the covers were yanked down.

She squeaked and opened one eye.

Not Freddy Krueger.

It was Aidan, face impassive, gaze sharp as he ran it down her body.

And damn if her nipples didn't pretend to be cold.

"What are you doing?" she demanded, pushing herself up with a wrist, which sent an immediate bolt of fire up her arm. She gasped and fell back.

Aidan bent over the bed, a hand planted on either side of her body, effectively holding her down.

"Hey," she said indignantly, ignoring the tears burning her eyes.

So did he, which was a relief.

"Lenny called," he said. "Told me you need…"

"What? A rescue?" She laughed humorlessly, one part astonished and one part annoyed that he was doing it again and this thankfully chased her tears away. "In San Diego I could've fallen down my stairs and laid there dead for a year and no one would have even noticed."

"You're not in San Diego," he said.

"No kidding." She blew out a breath. "I'm starting to remember just how small this place is."

"Admit it, you just missed me. But you don't have to try so hard to get my attention, babe, you've already got it."

She rolled her eyes. "Good to know."

"How did you fall?" he asked.

"Backward. *Fast*," she quipped, not about to admit she'd been startled by a bunny. A *baby* bunny.

"Smart-ass." He began to check her over. As in he put his hands all over her and ran them over her body. "You're bleeding," he said.

"I'll buy you new sheets."

"Shut up." He frowned at her wrist and found another problem at her ankle, all while she attempted to keep her T-shirt covering as much of her as possible.

Then he pointed to her shirt. "Lose it."

"Bite me."

"Later," he said. "I want to see your ribs."

"How about my foot up your ass?"

He met her gaze, his own stubborn and unbending. "Me or a doctor, Lily."

He'd do it, too, she had no doubt. He'd drag her kicking and screaming out of here if need be. So she sighed and very carefully lifted the T-shirt to just beneath her breasts. "See? I'm fine—"

She broke off, the air backing up in her lungs when he ran his hands very lightly over her rib cage, stopping when she managed to suck in a breath.

"Bruised, not broken I don't think," he said, his voice quiet and calm and clinically dispassionate, in direct opposition to his eyes. "Turn over."

She bit out a harsh laugh. "Yeah, that's going to happen nev—"

He rolled her over and pinned her there with a hand low on her back.

She sputtered and fought him, but then went utterly still when he ran his fingers up the back of one thigh, scooping the edge of her boy-cut panties up a cheek.

"Also bruised," he said.

"That's where I landed. No worries, I'm padded nicely."

"Nicely is right," he said, and he removed his hands from her.

She leapt off the bed, tugged down her shirt, and had to tighten her lips not to whimper at the fast movement. "Okay, thanks. Be sure to lock the door on your way—"

"Did you hit your head or lose consciousness at any time?"

"No!" She didn't want to need his help, wanted to lick her wounds in private rather than get turned on by his gentle touch. But she was stupid light-headed from getting up too fast and knew she wasn't in the greatest shape.

And as much as she didn't want to like it, she did like how he always seemed to be there for her, even if her brain kept telling her heart she didn't want him to be.

He still wasn't leaving. "Tell me what really happened."

"I loaded up some wood and was making my way up the stairs when"—she broke off and grimaced—"something popped out of the wood. I nearly had heart failure and fell down the stairs. The end."

He never took his eyes off of her. "What popped out at you?"

"A spider," she said, because hey, that could've totally happened. Just because she'd freaked out over the baby bunny didn't mean that there wasn't also a spider. Maybe she'd been so busy falling down the stairs she just hadn't *seen* the spider.

"A spider made you fall down the stairs?" he asked in disbelief.

"A big one." She lifted her hands so that they were about a foot apart.

His lips twitched.

Her hands spread apart even wider. "It might have been a mutant spider."

"Or a baby bunny," he said.

She stared at him while he grinned wide.

"You knew the whole time," she accused.

"Yep. Lenny told me."

"Well isn't that just like a man," she said in disgust.

Aidan tipped his head back and laughed out loud.

"Fine. Whatever," she said. "I'm taking a shower. *Alone.*"

"Make it lukewarm, not hot," he said. "I'm going to the truck for my first-aid kit."

"Aidan, I'm so not in the mood to play doctor."

"Good," he said. "*I'll* play doctor and you play the nice, sweet, passive patient."

She opened her mouth to retort to this but he was gone. Argh. She limped/hobbled after him and hit the lock. Proud of herself, she limped/hobbled to the bathroom and locked that door as well.

And then she crawled into the shower, where she had herself a nice, private cry. When she was done, she turned off the water and stared at herself in the mirror. She was bruising from head to toe, her damn hands hurt, and her knees hurt and so did her butt. She was still staring at herself when someone clicked open the bathroom door and made her jump nearly right out of her towel.

Aidan.

"Hey, I locked my front door!"

He set a red duffel bag on the counter. It had a white cross on it and read: FIRST AID.

"*And* the bathroom door," she added.

He narrowed his eyes. "Were you crying?"

"No."

Looking pained, he let her have the lie as he gestured to the closed commode. "Sit."

She instantly put her hands to her backside. No way was she going to be sitting. Maybe not ever again.

He stared at her, clearly trying to decide whether to force her or not. And maybe also worried she'd start crying again. She was tempted.

Instead of waiting for him to figure it all out, she brushed past him, nose high. "I'm busy."

"Yeah, busy healing. Now if you won't sit, then lie down." He dropped his bag on the bed.

She decided to put up with his annoying boorish behavior, because she figured he had Band-Aids in his bag and she didn't have any.

So she very carefully sat on the bed, sucked in a breath at the pressure on her sore butt, and came to the conclusion that he was right. Lying down seemed like the way to go. She lay back.

Without another word, Aidan perched a hip on the bed and went to work, doctoring up both knees first.

She hissed out a breath when he sprayed antiseptic over the abraded skin. "Hurts."

He lifted his head and met her gaze. "You fell down the stairs without a peep, but this hurts?"

"I don't want to talk about it."

"How about the baby bunny?" he asked. "You want to talk about that?"

She crossed her arms over her chest.

"Fine," he said. "Let's talk about why you're mad at me."

"I'm not mad," she said. Lied. But there was no way she'd explain that the anger was really self-directed and came from wanting him again. And not just a silly crush want, either, but much, much more. She couldn't have that conversation because the wanting was mutual, she knew that much. Just as she knew it couldn't go anywhere. Aidan and his lifestyle—putting his neck out on the mountain daily—would kill her.

He shook his head, but he bent over and kissed the Band-Aids over her knees, one after the other.

She didn't say a word, couldn't because the breath had backed up in her throat again. How the hell was she supposed to hold on to her mad if he was going to be sweet?

Then he went to work on her palms. After he finished the first one he brought it up to his mouth and gently pressed his lips to the bandage there, too, and damn if she didn't feel all her defenses crumbling down. "What are you doing?" she asked, her voice annoyingly breathless.

"Kissing it and making it better." A wicked light came into his eyes and she began to realize that "sweet" might be the wrong adjective, and when he spoke, she knew it for sure.

"Now turn over," he said.

Chapter 19

Aidan watched Lily sputter with indignation and anger, and both looked good on her. A damn sight better than the misery and pain of a few minutes before.

Or the sadness from the other day. Yeah, that one had nearly killed him. He didn't know exactly when or where or how but one thing was clear—he was no longer guarding himself against her.

Not good.

But if he'd softened, Lily had actually seemed to go the opposite route. The closer they got, the more she pushed him away.

"I'm happy to have you kiss my ass," she said, eyes still flashing. "Theoretically."

"I prefer literally," he said.

She let out a low laugh and tipped her head up, staring at the ceiling. "What are you doing here, Aidan?"

"Told you. Lenny called me."

"And so you came running to the rescue."

"It's what I do," he said.

"Right. Your job."

"I'm sensing sarcasm," he said.

"And irritation," she said. "Don't forget that one."

"Look, I get that you don't like the idea of being just a job to me," he said, "but we both know you don't want to be anything more either."

At that, she rolled off the bed. Hugging her towel to herself, she limped to the closet. And though it was the size of a pea she shut herself in there.

Rustling sounds came from within and then a thump—an elbow hitting the wall?—and a muffled "Dammit!"

Picturing her in there, possibly dropping her towel, struggling naked in that small space, had his amusement fading, replaced by something far more difficult to ignore. "Tell me something," he said to the door. "Rescue aside, why are you mad at me?"

The rustling stopped.

Everything stopped. It seemed as if she was not even breathing in there. "Lily?"

The closet door opened slowly. She'd ditched the towel for a sundress, this one peach with a snug bodice and filmy, loose skirt that fell to midthigh. She strode toward him, her bandaged hands on her breasts holding the bodice in place.

He sucked in a breath, staring down at her as time switched to slow-mo. She licked her lips and they parted…and he couldn't believe it. She was coming at him, half dressed, her eyes soft, her mouth…God, that mouth. He wanted it on him. He wanted that more than he wanted anything in the world… And then that mouth started moving. She was talking, and he had to force himself to tune in to her words.

"—zip me."

The slow-mo screeched to a complete halt and then it was real time again. She'd turned her back and was looking at him over her shoulder like he was a half-wit.

He shook himself and zipped her, covering up the creamy, smooth skin of her back, which was the opposite of what he wanted to do. The dress still bared her shoulders, however, and he stared down at the delicate tat of an infinity sign, unable to stop himself from running his finger slowly over it.

She shivered and he turned her to face him. "Lily, I—"

"I want to be done talking now," she said.

Yeah, him too. But this was important. He felt like they were teetering on the edge, flirting with something deep. There were two choices here, two very different options—ignore what was happening and just sleep together, or take the plunge.

And *then* sleep together.

His body voted for whatever option got her naked the fastest, because damn she looked hot, and he knew with one kiss that she would melt for him.

But his brain…it wouldn't shut up. He needed to know what her problem was so that he could fix it, once and for all. "This is too important to ignore," he managed.

She dropped her head to his chest.

He lifted her chin. "You're too important. What we're working on here is too important."

Her gaze skittered away. "What we're working on?"

"Yeah," he said. "Us."

Now she met his gaze again, hers confused. "I wasn't even aware there was an us."

Yeah, he hadn't been sure until right about now, either, but he *was* sure. Shockingly so. "Feels like there's a big us," he said.

Lily shook her head, and just before she closed her eyes he saw the truth. "You're running from me again."

"You know that my being here is temporary," she said. "Soon as I get a job offer…"

No, that wasn't it. Well, it might be part of it, but geographical issues were just a matter of logistics. Then the real reason occurred to him and his gut hit his toes. "You don't feel like you deserve to be loved," he said.

More stillness from her. Hell, he wasn't even sure she was breathing. He stroked a hand up her back. "Lily—"

"I'm working on that," she said softly. "I am. But you make me feel things I'm not ready for. I've been really good at keeping myself isolated so I wouldn't engage my heart. So good that I'm not sure I can stop. I'm really talented at not feelings things anymore, Aidan."

"I don't buy it," he said. "You're warm and open and caring. You can't be those things without feeling something. You give so much to everyone—"

She shook her head.

"You do. Jonathan," he said. "Your clients…" He gently wrapped his hand up in her ponytail and tugged her head back to see her eyes. "Me."

She snorted. "I don't give to you. You give to me. Constantly rescuing me like one of your five-alarm calls."

"I care about you."

"You care about all your calls."

"I care for you differently," he said, narrowing his

eyes, wanting to force her to believe this. "With a fire call, I don't get a terrifying fear gripping me like I do whenever I hear that you're on the trail heading up to Dead Man's Cliff, or that you've fallen down a flight of stairs. You're not a job to me, Lily. Not even close. You're more. And I think I'm more to you too. You want to know what I think?"

"I'd say no, but I'm getting that it wouldn't stop you from telling me anyway."

He smiled grimly. "I think it's not that you don't feel anything, it's that you feel too much. I scare you."

"Your life scares me," she said, and seemed shocked that she'd admitted such a thing.

His heart squeezed, hard. He'd never really given any thought at all to what the people who cared about him went through while he was working. The anxiety and worry. And for someone like Lily, who'd lost her sister so tragically, it would be worse, so much worse. "I get that," he said quietly. "I do. And I can't promise I'll rein it in—it's my job. But I *can* promise you that safety is of the upmost importance to me and everyone working with me. Always. But I don't think that's what this is. I think the real issue is that you're afraid of loving someone and letting them love you."

The look on her face said he'd hit bingo. But he could also tell that she wasn't ready to go there, wasn't ready to admit her feelings yet at all.

But at least he could show her his. Especially since he was more of a show-don't-tell kind of guy anyway. "Come here," he said.

"I'm right here."

"Closer."

She walked into his arms. He pulled her in and kissed her. He kissed her until he knew he'd taken it as far as he could without tearing off that pretty sundress right then and there, and only then did he lift his head.

"Oh," she breathed, staggering back a step, clearly trying to play it cool—which might have worked if her eyes weren't dilated and the pulse at the base of her throat wasn't going apeshit crazy.

He gave a slow smile and pulled her back in, not hard for him to do, since she already had a grip on his shirt like he was her lifeline and she was going down for the count.

She cleared her throat. "So you showed up all Captain America to save the day, and now what? I jump into bed with you? Was that your plan?"

"Yeah," he said, "but in my version we didn't talk this much."

"A full-service rescue then," she said evenly.

He tried a cajoling smile. "I'm really good at full service."

"Do you really think this is a good idea?"

He laughed softly and let his mouth brush over her temple and then her ear, which caused her to shiver. "Of course it's not a good idea. Or we'd have gone for it already. But sometimes the bad ideas turn out to be the best ideas of all."

"Yeah?" she asked. "Name one."

"Bringing out your keys from the convenience store after the postcard display demolition."

She let out a soft laugh and fisted her hands in his hair. "So what now? We really going to try this out?"

Were they? He'd promised himself he wouldn't give her a chance to devastate him again. But somehow over the past few weeks he'd lost sight of keeping his heart safe and moved onto wanting to heal her heart. "I'm game."

She hesitated so long he took a step back from her and prepared himself to leave. But her hand came out and gripped his. "You're wearing too many clothes," she said softly.

Lily's breath caught when, eyes glued on hers, Aidan pulled off his shirt. He kicked off his shoes next and reached for the zipper on his pants.

"Wait!" she cried.

Aidan froze, shirtless, his thumbs hooked into the opened waistband of his pants, looking so incredibly hot that she started to sweat.

"We stopping here?" he asked, voice rough but in control.

He'd do whatever she wanted, she knew that. The question was what did she want—stop, or go on... Oh, who was she kidding. She'd had enough of the yearning and endless need. She wanted to go on. Bad. "Never mind. Carry on."

He raised a brow, a silent *You positive?*

And because he was being so patient, she suddenly found herself very, very positive. "I just needed a minute. I'm okay now," she said. His bare torso was rippled with strength and very lightly dusted with chest hair including a treasure trail that left her without a coherent thought in her brain.

"Be more than okay. Be sure," he said in a voice that made her go damp.

"I am." Or at least she was ninety-five percent sure. Maybe seventy-five... Because the real problem was that the light was on and she was going to have to lose her clothes too and she didn't look as good as he did. "So…" Mental knuckle cracking… "How are we going to do this?" she asked. *Please say in the dark…*

He just smiled. The kind of smile the Big Bad Wolf might have given Little Red Riding Hood. This caused a chain reaction of tremors inside her, the really good kind. "I mean *where*," she clarified. "Because the light's on and I'm having a fat week, so—"

He picked her up. Just scooped her into his arms like she didn't weigh a thing—even though she'd single-handedly wiped out her entire junk food collection the night before.

"I love your body," he said, carrying her across the room.

Her heart squished in her chest, but her wits weren't ready to give up the fight. "The light," she said, pointing to it as they passed by. "Let's turn off the—"

He set her very carefully on the bed and didn't turn off the light. "You still with me?"

"Yes, but—"

But nothing because he straightened and stripped the rest of the way.

Every inch of him visible.

While she stared in shock and admiration, trying to take in everything at once, from his broad shoulders to the ridged muscles of his abs—which, by the way, she wanted to lick—she forgot herself.

Until, that is, he sprawled out on his back on the bed and pulled her over to straddle him. "Watch yourself," he said. "Don't do anything to pull on your cuts."

What cuts? she thought, dazed. *Aroused.*

Pressing openmouthed kisses along her throat, he un-zipped her dress.

"Uh-oh," she whispered, holding her dress to her as she remembered.

"What?"

She felt herself flush. "I'm not wearing panties. They weren't in my closet where I got dressed so—"

He grinned. "You're commando."

"Yes."

"I love commando," he said, and then tugged the dress over her head with a gentleness that she knew was in rev-erence of her injuries even as he somehow also moved with absolute steely unwavering determination.

"Um." She started to cover herself. "The light—"

"God," he murmured huskily, holding her hands out, away from her body. "You're so beautiful, Lily."

She looked into his warm, soft brown eyes, saw he ab-solutely meant it, and…melted. Or maybe that was his hands making her melt as they cupped her breasts, then headed south as he slid one between her spread legs.

"Oh," she breathed, and then her hands were busy, too, trying to touch every part of him she could reach, and with him beneath her, sprawled out for her touching pleasure, she didn't hold back, wanting all of him. Every single inch.

And he had a *lot* of really great inches.

He said her name again, his voice low and rough, and then he very carefully rolled her beneath him and slid her hands above her head, pinning them lightly to the mat-tress.

He looked down at her as she squirmed. "Right where I want you," he said.

She squirmed some more, but not in nerves now. More like she couldn't *not* move. She needed him to touch, needed the feel of his mouth and hands on her. "Aidan—"

Lowering his head, he let his mouth brush over hers, hovering just enough to tease. She tried tugging her hands free, but he resisted with one of those wicked badass smiles tugging at the corner of his lips, nibbling her lower lip, sucking on it, running the tip of his tongue over it lightly.

Which had her ache intensifying. "*Aidan.*"

Letting go of her hands, he slid down her body. His eyes were darkened and focused on her. "I want to taste you."

"I—"

He started with her breasts, teasing her nipples before sliding down farther, kissing her sore ribs, then low on her quivering belly.

She opened her mouth to say God knew what, but he pressed his mouth to her hipbone and sucked in a breath.

He looked up at her, eyes hooded, before dropping his attention back to her body spread out beneath him. "Perfect," he murmured, brushing a knuckle over the skin just beneath her belly button. And then lower, over the core of her.

She bucked against his hand and he did it again, the motion too light so she thrust harder.

He resisted the pressure and eased back.

"That's just mean," she gasped.

With a smile that promised all sorts of naughty pleasures, he lowered his head and brushed the stubble of his jaw over her inner thighs.

"Oh," she breathed softly, going utterly still. "Oh, please."

"Patience," he murmured against her, the rumble of his voice sending another wave of pleasure through her as, with a featherlight touch, he rubbed the pad of his thumb right over ground zero.

She cried out and arched up, desperate to have him do it again, but he just held her down as his thumb rasped over her slowly, each stroke pure torture, lazily manipulating her into a panting frenzy. "Aidan!"

"More?" he asked politely.

"Yes!"

He slid a finger into her and then another, and she just about came undone.

Then he replaced his fingers with his lips, gently sucking her into his hot mouth, and her every single muscle clenched as she rocked up and came hard. He slowed but didn't stop, drawing out the intensity for longer than she could have imagined possible. When he finally released her, he pushed up with his hands and met her gaze, his own blazing. "You liked that."

She had to unpeel her fingers from the sheet beneath her. "A little bit," she admitted and thrilled to his rough laugh.

And she wasn't the only one who'd liked that. Aidan's body practically vibrated with tension now, some areas more than others. Reversing their positions, she slid down the bed and wrapped her hand around one of his parts in particular, the one quickly becoming her very favorite part.

He twitched under her touch and pushed his hips into her hand with a groan. "And you like that," she teased, throwing his words back at him. And then she bent over him and took him into her mouth.

He didn't let her have her way with him for long, and she knew that was in deference to her injuries. He rolled her to her back again, kissing her long and deep and hot before lifting his head and pinning her with his very serious gaze. "Don't move."

To her disappointment, he left the bed. Naked and apparently completely unconcerned with that fact, he searched the pockets of his cargoes and came back with a condom.

"How about now?" she murmured playfully when he'd protected them both. "Can I move now?" And then, without waiting for his response, she guided him home.

They both gasped as he slid deep.

Aidan braced himself on his forearms on either side of her face as their gazes locked, and then his mouth found hers as he began to move.

Threading her hand into his hair, she slanted her hips against his and met him thrust for thrust. Deliciously pinned, the fire built inside her again with shocking alacrity. She could hear herself whispering his name. She was close, so close...

When his hands gripped her hips hard and shifted her, changing the angle so that he could go even deeper, she burst into a thousand pieces.

He was right behind her.

They were both breathing hard as he braced his weight on his forearms above her and kissed her, tenderly now, lazily, and full of something she couldn't easily identify.

He simply stole her breath away.

After a minute he untangled himself from her and again left the bed. The loss of his weight was a huge gaping hole of desertion but she got it. He had a bazillion things to do, fires to put out, people to rescue, a resort to help his brother save.

But a small part of her wished the rest of the world would just go the hell away and let her have a few more minutes with him. Not in the cards, and that was probably for the best. She prepared to heave herself out of the bed, too, but then he was there, right there.

He pointed for her to lie back down, which she did, and then in the most surprising move of all he grabbed the covers and made to get back in with her with a questioning look, brow raised.

She scooted over, making room.

Taking the invite, he slid in and reached for her, hauling her into his arms. The first touch of his mouth along the column of her throat sent a jolt to her already overloaded system and she shuddered again.

"Okay?" he asked.

She was so far above okay she didn't even have words.

Aidan lifted his head to look into her face and smiled. "Yeah," he said. "You're okay."

"You can tell that just by my smile?"

"No. It's the dazed I've-had-my-business-thoroughly-taken-care-of expression that gives you away."

She laughed and closed her eyes, letting herself relax into him.

When she woke up, the light was finally off but morning had shown up. She replayed it all in her mind; the tenderness, the urgency, the passion… Still smiling she rolled over, but she was alone.

Chapter 20

Lily showered, dressed, and walked out into her living room only to stop in shock.

Wood was neatly stacked against the wall next to the woodstove. She stared at it as she pulled out her phone.

"I can load my own wood," she said when Aidan answered.

There was a beat of silence.

She grimaced. "I mean *thank you*. Really. But I don't expect preferential treatment just because we..." She trailed off, unwilling—and not to mention unable—to put a label on what they'd done.

"Did you forget already?" he asked mildly. "I can be there in seven minutes to remind you."

As if she'd ever forget, and he knew it, too, the cocky bastard. Through the silence she sensed he was smiling, remembering everything.

And then so was she, picturing how he'd moved over

her, his voice low and rough, his hands seductive, his body demanding and giving.

So giving…

Great, and now she was sweating a little bit. "I'm going to work now," she said, walking to the freezer and sticking her head in it.

"You sure?"

"Yes!" She glanced down at her hardened—and still hopeful—nipples. "I've got to go."

He laughed softly. "Have a good day, Lily. Think of me."

She wasn't sure she would do either of those things, but she ended up doing both.

"You okay?" Jonathan said when she'd walked into the staff room/kitchen twice, each time forgetting what she'd gone in there for.

"Yep," she said. "Why?"

"Because you fell down the stairs thanks to a bunny."

She sighed. "Hey, it was a very big, very scary bunny, okay?"

He laughed. "Whatever you say."

Damn straight what I say… She sighed and pulled out the bags of dirty towels, replacing them with clean ones just to keep her hands busy.

"Why are you doing that?" Jonathan asked. "Rosa does that."

"Rosa's on her cell in the bathroom sobbing to her sister, something about Devon being a dick."

"Devon *is* a dick," Jonathan agreed. "But he's a hot dick, and Rosa won't cut him loose. She prefers looks over substance. Not me. How about you?"

"I don't have *any* requirements right now," Lily said. "I'm not interested in your species. At all."

"Uh-huh. What about your own species then?" he asked. "Because there's nothing wrong with changing up teams for a little bit."

"I'm not interested in *any* team," she clarified.

"How do you know unless you try it?"

He was teasing her, and she teased back with, "Who says I haven't tried it?"

Jonathan nearly choked on his own tongue, but then he caught sight of something over her shoulder and his gaze went from amused to frank and appraising in a single beat.

Either Channing Tatum had just appeared out of thin air, or...

Yep. Aidan.

He stood there in his firefighter polo and work cargoes, radio on his hip, expression broadcasting a rough mood, looking hot enough to start a fire all on his own.

He nodded to Jonathan and met her gaze.

"Hey," she said, trying to look and sound cool. But apparently she failed, because he grinned. Behind her, Jonathan chuckled at her predicament, the rat-fink bastard.

Blowing out a sigh, she met Aidan's gaze. "Can we help you?"

Mercifully, he let it go and gestured to the stocked shelves of product. "My mom wanted me to come by and pick up some of that girlie gunk stuff you used on her hair."

"A man who's not afraid to stride into a salon and ask for girlie gunk," Jonathan said. "I like it. I'll leave it on the front counter for you. Now you kids take a minute to yourselves and don't do anything I wouldn't do." Then he waggled his brow at Lily and walked off.

She sighed. "How long were you standing there?"

Aidan smiled. "Long enough to know I want to hear your 'one time at band camp' story."

She blushed. "Never mind me. Are you really here for your mom?"

He shrugged. "She says she can't live without the stuff. She asked Gray to come get it, but he told her over his dead body. So she threatened to tell Penny, and then he finally agreed to get it for her."

"So why isn't Gray here?" she asked, fascinated by his family's crazy dynamics and how in spite of that they all remained close.

"Because he doesn't have a thing for the new, pretty cosmetologist."

Ridiculously, Lily's heart picked up speed, but she rolled her eyes.

He grinned at her. "It's true. Even if she did cut my hair uneven."

"I did no such thing," she said, straightening, completely indignant.

"Look." He shoved his fingers through his hair, making it stand up on end. "See? Crooked."

She gave him a nudge toward her empty chair. "There's no way. Sit."

"Don't you have to wash it first?"

She turned to look at him, but he didn't seem to be up to anything, so she led him to the wash station and cranked the hot water. She had just wet his head and run her fingers through his silky hair when the radio at his hip crackled.

"Is that you?" she asked.

He reached down and cranked up the volume, listened for a minute, and then shook his head. "No. Not my unit."

She let out a breath. She'd given thought to what his life as a firefighter meant to her—terror. But she'd not thought about what it meant for him, being on call, constantly at the ready to literally jump into the fire, carrying the burden of all the responsibilities that went with it, like saving lives.

On a good day she felt overwhelmed by her life. She couldn't even imagine carrying the weight he did. Reaching over him, she pumped some shampoo into her hand.

His gaze ran the length of her arm just over his head and then met her gaze.

His eyes were hot.

Ignoring both him and her reaction to him, she sudsed him up. His eyes drifted shut, and his entire body relaxed. As she gave him a scalp massage, he let out a low groan from deep in his throat.

"You have great hands," he said.

She should have known it. He had managed to con her into a skull massage. She held her tongue until she finished and brought him back to her station. Standing behind him, she ran her fingers through his wet hair. His *perfectly cut* wet hair that was so evenly matched on both sides she could have used it to set a ruler. Then, hands on hips, head tilted, she met his gaze in the mirror.

"Busted," he said, not looking the least bit embarrassed or sorry.

"You could have just asked for a wash," she said.

"Nah, this was way more fun."

She opened her mouth but his radio went off again, and though his eyes remained on her, he was clearly concentrating on the radio and the garbled words she could barely make out.

Then suddenly he stood, all joking and good humor gone from his gaze. "Gotta go," he said.

"You're still wet."

"No worries." He shook his head like a big dog and then, shoving his hand into his pocket, came up with cash.

Lily pushed his hand away. "No."

"I pay my debts."

"Not this time," she said.

His eyes landed on hers as one of his hands slid to the nape of her neck. "Think of me." Lowering his head he gave her one quick, hard kiss. "Later," he said against her mouth, and then he was gone.

"Good sweet baby Jesus," Jonathan said from the hall behind her.

She turned to find him fanning himself. "It's not what you think," she said.

"Are you sure?" he asked. "Because what I think is that man is sex on two legs. He wears that firefighter uniform like nobody's business. Well, except maybe his brother Hudson. Cuz Hudson looks pretty damn fine in his as well. I mean, when he strides toward me with that gun on his hip..." Jonathan gave a full body shiver.

"Going back to work now," she said with an eye roll, and did just as Aidan had suggested—thought of him.

That night, back at her place, Lily found herself on edge. Did Aidan's "later" mean tonight? She had no idea.

Normally her after-work routine consisted of a hot

shower and PJs, but she stayed up late in her sundress, makeup still on. No need to scare the man unnecessarily.

But Aidan didn't show, and this left her torn between relief and unease.

Unease won, and she called his mom. "I know it's late," Lily said quickly, "but I—"

"Oh, honey, I got the styling cream," Char said. "Thank you so much for that. I should've called you, I'm sorry."

"I'm not calling about that, I was wondering…" She grimaced. "Is everything okay?"

"Of course. My hair's so much better than okay, it's fantastic. Marcus can't keep his fingers out of it—"

"I meant with Aidan," Lily said. "He got called away today on a fire and he didn't get back. At least, I don't think he did."

"No, you're right, he's still out. I got a text from Gray." Char paused, softening her voice. "You should know he's often out for days without a word. We just have to trust him, Lily. He's the best at what he does."

"I'm not— I mean, I don't—" She blew out a breath. "It's not what you think," she said for the second time that day. And for the second time that day she got the same response.

"Are you sure?"

Chapter 21

The fire started out on a 10,000-acre horse ranch, which backed up to the base of Mt. Hennessy. This meant it threatened hundreds of thousands of acres of forestland if they couldn't contain it quickly.

By noon the following day Aidan, Mitch, and the rest of the crew *still* didn't have a handle on it thanks to an unseasonably hot day and forty-five-mile-an-hour winds. When the flames jumped the highway and started to climb the mountain, they called in reinforcements.

Aidan ran into Hudson at the incident command post. They'd arrested the arsonist, who was currently cooling her heels in county on a million-dollar bail.

Which isn't what Hudson wanted to discuss. Nope, he wanted to discuss their dad. Perfect. Just what Aidan wanted to do.

"He called Gray," Hud said, pissed. "He couldn't even bother to call *me*. What the hell?"

"Told you, we don't need him."

Hudson stared at him. "Is that what you told Gray when me and Jacob appeared in Cedar Ridge? That you didn't need us?"

"How is that anything close to the same thing?" Aidan asked.

"You're all about family unless it doesn't suit you. Hypocrite much?"

"Hud, he dumped you guys like you were a bad habit, just like he did us. How are you defending that?"

"I'm not. At all," Hudson said. "I just think he should have to come back and help us fix *his* mess."

"No," Aidan said flatly.

Hudson let out a long breath of frustration and stalked off. But he only went a few feet before he whipped back around. "You just picked a fight and let me walk."

"No, *you* picked the fight. If you want to pout and sulk, who am I to stop you?"

Hudson strode back, eyes narrowed, steam coming out of his ears. "You're misdirecting."

"Nice to see your night psych class is coming in handy."

"And now you're trying to piss me off." Hudson stood firm. "Tell me what I'm missing."

"Drop it," Aidan said.

"Can't. You're my brother," Hudson said simply.

"Shit." Aidan stared up at the sky and then dropped his head, rubbing the back of his neck with his hand. "Just let it go, all right?"

Hudson's eyes darkened with temper. "So you trust Gray but not me, is that it?"

"This has nothing to do with trust—"

"Yeah, right," Hudson said. "Thanks for the reminder

that you only do the things that suit you, Aidan." And this time when he stalked off, he kept going.

Aidan swore and went back to work, but the fight with his brother remained forefront in his mind. It was an unfortunate two whole days later before they got the fire contained. Finally released from duty, Aidan and Mitch drove back into town. Mitch drove while Aidan checked his phone.

"Problem?" Mitch asked when Aidan swore.

Aidan thumbed through his bazillion messages. Gray checking on him. Penny checking on him. His mom checking on him. Kenna checking on him.

Nothing from Hud. Which really fried his ass, because hell no, he wasn't a damn hypocrite. Family meant everything to him, and Hud damn well knew it. "No," he said a little too tightly. "No problem."

"Uh-huh. And you're full of shit. Is it Kenna?"

Aidan slid him a look. "Kenna?"

"Yeah, you know, your sister?"

"I'm aware of how we're related, thanks. What I'm unaware of is why my sister would pop into your brain, seeing as the two of you don't like each other."

"Who said that?" Mitch asked. "I like her plenty."

"You do?" Aidan asked.

"Yeah." And when Aidan slid him a look, Mitch squirmed. "Well, maybe not *plenty*," he said. "And some parts more than others."

Again Aidan looked at him.

And again Mitch squirmed. "Never mind," he muttered.

Good idea. Because Aidan didn't have the brainpower for whatever was going on in Mitch's head at the moment.

Whatever it was, it'd have to get in line. He brought up an empty text, typed Hudson's number in, and…stared at the blank screen. He hit CANCEL. Shit.

They drove in silence a few minutes, for which Aidan was grateful. He got the feeling Mitch was just as grateful.

"I'm glad I don't have a wife," Mitch eventually said, seemingly out of the blue. Aidan followed his logic.

"You mean because we just fought a four-day fire started by a pissed-off wife?" he asked.

"Man, she burned her husband's ranch to the ground." Mitch shook his head. "He had to evacuate his hundred horses and nearly killed himself doing it."

"She was his *ex*-wife," Aidan pointed out. "And she was pissed because he dumped her for a woman half her age and then had more kids while ignoring the ones he'd had with her."

Mitch slid him a look. "And now she's going to jail without passing Go. And you of all people know how that sucks."

Yeah, Aidan knew. Hell, he'd been there the night his mom had been arrested as well.

Protecting him.

"So tonight at The Slippery Slope?" Mitch asked when he pulled up in front of Aidan's place. "Ladies' night, two for one." Mitch waggled his brow. "I'm up for a two-for-one. How about you? And just to be clear, you'll have to get your own two-for-one. I don't plan on sharing."

"Good to know," Aidan said dryly.

"Meet you there?"

"Maybe. I've got some work to do at the office, Gray's been there twenty-four seven. This summer season has been our busiest yet. I need to give him a break so he can go spend time with Penny." Plus, Aidan needed to try to track down Hudson and…shit. That was another fight just waiting to happen.

"And you?" Mitch asked. "Don't you want company?"

"I'll be fine by myself."

"You know you can go blind from doing that," Mitch said.

Aidan rolled his eyes but as he opened the car door, they both saw the woman waiting there, watching their approach. Lily.

"Seems like you've got your company after all," Mitch said, smiling. "You two make sense."

"I have no idea what we're doing," Aidan admitted.

Mitch laughed ruefully. "Isn't that always the case with us? All in control and on the ready for whatever our job brings. But when it comes to our personal lives and the women in it, we're the ones who need rescuing."

"Fuck you. I don't need rescuing."

Mitch laughed.

Aidan got out and shut the door.

Lily rose to her feet and stared at him uncertainly.

He felt no such uncertainty. Not a single lick. He dropped his pack, took the bag she was holding and set it on top of his pack, and then he backed her to the front door and kissed her.

Lily moaned against his mouth, hot and sweet, and he curled his hand around the back of her neck and took what he'd been thinking of for four-plus straight days. He kissed her until they both ran out of air and then as he pulled back, he tugged her lower lip between his teeth for a beat, unable to let go.

She let out another soft sound of arousal in her throat and if he hadn't already been hard at just the sight of her, and then the taste, that would have done it.

So of course his phone went off with the tone of a five-alarm fire. "What the—" He pulled his phone from his pocket. The ID screen read: *Mom.* "I'm going to kill Mitch for constantly changing the ringtones on my phone," he muttered before answering. "Mom, not a good time."

"No? Well when would be a good time to call your mama and tell her you're alive?"

Still holding Lily flush to the door, Aidan thunked his head to the wood a few times next to hers. "I'm alive and well," he said, "and you know it because you called my captain—twice—and he told you so. And, by the way, he's not real thrilled that you stole his contact info from my phone. He wants you to lose his number."

"What? Are you kidding me? I used to babysit that man!" Char complained. "He wasn't potty trained until he was five. He sucked his thumb until second grade. He can answer my damn calls—he owes me."

"Mom."

"Okay, whatever, I'll 'lose' his number," she said. "But that means that in the future, I get to hear you're alive from you."

"Duly noted," Aidan said.

Lily snorted.

Aidan met her gaze. Clearly she could hear every word and just as clearly she was enjoying this. Her amusement—at his expense—looked great on her.

"Thank you," his mom said, sounding slightly mollified. "Now, about your fight with Hudson."

Oh, Christ. "Mom—"

"Don't you 'mom' me. Tell me."

"I didn't have a fight with Hudson," he said.

"He told Gray about it. So now you can tell me about it and also, while you're at it, why you would lie to your mama?"

Aidan grated his teeth. Sometimes Gray was such an old lady. "Mom, I really have to go—"

"Fine. Soon as you tell me one thing—you get any good packages lately?"

At her oddly innocent tone—and she was far from innocent—Aidan lifted his head and met Lily's eyes.

Her hands still fisted in his shirt, she bit her lower lip.

He sighed. "Mom, stop meddling."

"I will if you will," she said, and disconnected.

"So," Lily said. "Old and feeble and not exactly with it?"

"Yes, well, I'm adding *evil* to her list." Cupping Lily's face, he leaned in, feeling human for the first time in days. She was warm and soft and smelled like heaven, and he couldn't get enough of her. "So my mom's the reason you're here?"

"No."

"Good."

"Gray is," Lily said.

Damn.

Lily felt Aidan go still and then he lifted his head and met her gaze.

"I ran into him outside the salon," she said, hoping she sounded nonchalant. "He was on his way out with Penny and asked if I'd bring this to you."

"And you said yes…" He rasped his thumb over her

lower lip and she shivered. Maybe moaned. "Because you missed me," he said huskily.

"I'm here because of the package," she said firmly.

"Which you could have just left for me," he pointed out.

Very true story. "Right," she said, looking around. "But it didn't seem super safe to just leave it out in the open, so…" She shrugged and tried to look like seeing him hadn't been in her plans when it totally had. "Anyway, you have it now, so I should go."

She'd barely gotten two steps when Aidan caught her arm. "You haven't given me the package yet," he said.

She picked it up off his dropped duffel bag and offered it to him.

"Sorry," he told her. "My hands are full. Bring it in, could you?"

"I—"

But he'd grabbed his duffel bag and was unlocking his door. Then, leaving the door open, he walked inside, leaving her to follow or not.

And dammit. She had way too much curiosity not to. Which he damn well knew, because he didn't even turn around to check. He'd *known* she'd follow him.

Hopefully he had no idea just how far she'd do so.

In truth, she had no idea, either, but she suspected it was to another zip code entirely. One she'd never been to.

Aidan dropped the bag from his shoulder and walked through his living room, down a hall to his bedroom, and out a sliding glass door to what was a private deck.

Which she knew because she was still following him like a lamb to the slaughter.

Aidan hit a button on the hot tub and the jets started up

with a rumble. He pushed the cover aside and kicked off his shoes.

"What are you doing?" she asked.

He still didn't look back at her. Again, just as well, because she was pretty sure where this was going and her eyes—glued to him, naturally—would one hundred percent give her away.

"I'm going on four hours of sleep over the past few days and I'm sore as hell," he said. "I'm getting into the hot tub."

Yeah. That's what she'd thought. "But—" She broke off when he pulled off his shirt and dropped it to the deck.

Gah. He was just so damn beautifully made. Like heart-stopping, drool-inducing, cut with lean muscles and smooth, tanned, sleek skin, beautifully made. She wanted to lick him from the base of his throat to the dangerously low and sinking lower by the second waistband of his pants. And then maybe she also wanted to bite his—

He unbuttoned his cargoes and she stopped breathing.

With his back still to her, he dropped the cargoes.

He was commando. And it was official. She definitely wanted to bite his—

He turned around to face her and caught her gaping. He smiled and gave her the finger crook. The universal "Come here."

"Oh. Well…" His chest was hard, his abs were hard, his thighs were hard…*everything* was hard, and she felt herself staring, unable to tear her eyes off the hardest thing of all, which was pretty much standing up and waving hello at her.

She swallowed hard. "Um— You're—"

"Yeah, ignore him," Aidan said. "He's just happy to see you too."

Oh boy. Her feet moved her over there and once again Aidan took the bag from her and set it aside. Then he pulled off her sweater.

"Um," she said again, inanely.

He went brows up. "No?"

She hesitated, and he surprised her by backing right off. "It's okay," he said. "You can just watch if you want."

And if that wasn't an image that would fuel her fantasies for nights to come...

Unconcerned, he ambled over to the hot tub and got in, lowering his body into the hot water with a groan. Closing his eyes, he leaned his head back and let out a long breath.

"A rough one, huh?" she asked sympathetically. She could see a bruise across one of his shoulders and arm, and he rolled his neck like it ached.

"Yeah," he said without opening his eyes. "And you're still staring."

Without even realizing it, she'd moved closer. Giving in, she kicked off her sandals and sat on the very edge of the hot tub, hiking her skirt up to her thighs to stick her feet into the water.

And then realized Aidan was now watching her, eyes glittering with things that made her thighs tremble. "What," she said defensively. "You were making all those happy noises so I had to check it out. The water's nice."

"Happy noises?"

"Yeah, like when you—" She broke off as she felt her cheeks flame again and she clapped her hands to them when he tipped his head back and laughed.

"Stop it," she said.

"No, I want to hear this," he said. "I make the same happy noises when I what?"

"You know what."

"Tell me," he said, and pushed away from the edge he'd been leaning back on to wrap his arms around her calves and press his chest against her knees. With his face practically in her lap he smiled up at her. "Tell me a dirty story, Lily."

With all those hard, warm, wet muscles leaning on her, he looked like something right off one of Jonathan's favorite Tumblr pages.

"You're bad," she said, giving him a kick, which only made him laugh all the more.

"Yes," he agreed. "Very, very bad."

She leaned back to grab the bag she'd brought and handed it over to him. "Gray said you had to open this in front of me."

"Nice subject change."

She just thrust the bag beneath his nose.

He took it, looked inside, and blew out a breath. "Son of a bitch." He said this almost conversationally.

"What is it?" she asked.

"You didn't look?"

"No."

He pulled out a pair of men's briefs with little red hearts mixed with little red lips all over them.

She stared as Aidan dangled them from one finger. "Are those…yours?" she asked.

"No," he said, sounding disgusted.

"Gray's."

"They'd better not be."

"I don't understand," she said.

"Yeah, because you don't have any asshole brothers—a fact for which you should be eternally grateful."

She blinked. "I still don't get it."

"I have to wear these tomorrow no matter what my day looks like, and if Gray or Hudson show up, I have to drop trou and prove I'm wearing them."

She looked at him, horrified and yet trying not to laugh. "No matter what you're doing at the time?"

"No matter what I'm doing," he said grimly. "On Gray's last turn, Hudson delivered him a man thong the night before a management meeting. It was pretty good," he admitted reluctantly. "Especially when Gray had to do some exhibition mountain biking that same day. It was kinda fun watching him squirm past a wedgie all day long."

"And when it was Hudson's turn?"

He beamed with remembered pride. "That was my gig. I sent him a pair of women's bikini panties. Pink. Satin." He narrowed his eyes in on her as she burst out laughing. "You think this is funny?" he asked.

"I do."

"Hmm," he said, and before she could figure out what that *hmm* meant, he'd pulled her right into the water, clothes and all.

Chapter 22

Hauling Lily's laughing ass into the water with him felt great, and since the past four days had been one shit show after another, Aidan needed this. Needed a good time.

His plan had been to hit the sack and sleep away as much of the adrenaline and exhaustion as he could. But then he'd found a present waiting for him, a present in the form of this sweet, sexy, perfect-for-him woman, all wet and warm and...

Sputtering with outrage.

"You dunked me!" She gasped, swiping the water from her face.

"Yeah." He moved in closer. For years after she'd first left Cedar Ridge he'd felt an emptiness, and regrets. He'd wanted her, but she hadn't wanted him back. He couldn't have her and that was that.

He'd moved on.

He'd told himself so. He'd moved on and had done

okay for himself in the women department, unlike his brothers, remaining mostly unscathed by love and unattached by choice.

Then Lily had driven back into town and blasted right through his brick walls in a way no one else had ever managed.

That she'd done it so effortlessly terrified him.

He liked to be in control. Needed to be in control. It's how he and Gray had managed to keep it together, they'd stepped up to head of household, gathering in all the innocent pawns—their mom, Hudson and Jacob and *their* mom, and also Kenna—and they'd created a family. A fucked-up family, but blood nevertheless.

But being one of the two who'd held it together all these years also meant that the buck stopped with him and Gray. It meant staying tough, putting his own needs and feelings aside, and that was fine but also…lonely.

Gray had always had Penny.

But Aidan didn't have that kind of a connection, and yeah, that'd been by choice, but he'd been wrong about that. He knew it now. He was sick of being alone, and if he was being honest, he'd felt that way for a while now. The part that was new was that he wanted to not be alone with…Lily.

The question was, had he convinced her yet that she might be starting to feel the same way? He hoped so. Taking a chance, he slid his arms around her, hauling her into him.

She looked down at herself in shock. "I'm all wet."

"Just the way I like you."

With steam rising all around them, vanishing like tendrils of fog into the night above, she stared into his eyes and then at his mouth. "You're having fun at my expense?"

"It was my turn."

Her dress had suctioned itself to her skin. And being the palest of blues, it had also gone sheer. The effect was more erotic than if she'd been naked, and he couldn't tear his eyes off of her. "Christ, Lily, you're the hottest thing I've ever seen." He nudged a wet spaghetti strap off her shoulder.

"You *dunked* me," she repeated, apparently still stuck on that thought.

"Yeah. Felt good. *You* feel good." He encouraged her other strap to fall as well.

"What are you doing?"

"We obviously need to do this more often so you aren't confused," he said, still bent to his task of getting her naked.

She swiped water from her face. "What if my dress is dry clean only?"

"I'll apologize and buy you a new one." With her still in his arms he turned and pinned her against the tile. He knew he had her when her eyes ran down his chest and abs and then into the swirling water for the rest of him and her breathing changed. He fought the urge to crush his mouth to hers, needing her to want him as badly as he wanted her.

"I didn't think we'd be doing this again," she said.

"Why?"

"Because..." She paused and that's when he knew. She was most definitely feeling the same as he was, and she was still scared. They weren't just having fun, or exorcising ghosts. They weren't just scratching an itch. It was more, far more, and he wanted her to say it. "Because what?" he asked, pressing a thigh between hers.

"Because it wasn't just sex," she whispered, eyes heated. "Was it?"

Eyes on hers, he slowly shook his head, getting even harder when she rocked into him. "No, it wasn't."

"I'm not ready for what this is," she said breathlessly.

"What do you think this is?"

She opened her mouth and then closed it, either unable or unwilling to define it.

"Lily, whatever you think is happening between us, it's under control," he said, meaning to reassure her. But he knew that though he meant those words, the truth was he had no control over his feelings for her. He was in love, she was leaving, and he couldn't do a damn thing about that.

She stared at him for a long beat. "I won't want to stop," she whispered.

Thank Christ, he thought as a groan shuddered through him. He lowered his head, skimming his lips up her throat, along her jaw to her ear, wanting her to do that thing where she hissed out a breath and clutched at him like he was the only anchor in a spinning world.

And then she did exactly that.

When he finally kissed her, she arched her wet, warm body harder into him, her breathing already labored, her hands sliding along his shoulders. One of her hands curled around the back of his neck, sinking her fingers into his hair as she slowly deepened the kiss, giving into him with the sexiest sigh of acquiescence he'd ever heard.

And there in the moonlight, surrounded by a zillion

stars and a beautiful, wet, warm woman, he leaned in close and watched her eyes dilate. Then he nibbled the curve where her neck met her shoulder, tracing his tongue over the spot as he ran his hands under the water and down her body, beneath her dress, sliding his palms slowly along her thighs, bringing the material of her skirt up with them.

"Aidan—"

"Hold this," he murmured against her mouth when he had the dress up around her waist.

When her hands reached down and gripped the dress, holding it up for him, he kissed her again and encouraged the bodice of the sundress to slip.

She wasn't wearing a bra. Her eyes were wide on his, her mouth open a little, like maybe she needed it that way just to breathe. Her expression said she wasn't one hundred percent sure what he was up to.

Which was just as well, since what he was up to was no good. He cupped her breasts and bent his head to them.

She seemed to melt then, and he liked to think that if he didn't have such a grip on her she'd have glided into a boneless heap at the bottom of the hot tub.

But he did have her.

He knew he always would.

"What if someone comes?" she whispered.

"No one's coming but you." And then he slid his hand between her legs, finding her hot and slick and ready. "God, Lily."

"Aidan—"

"No one's home tonight," he promised. "By some miracle even Kenna's out at a movie."

When she closed her eyes, swallowed hard and then

moaned her pleasure, he knew he had her. He played his fingers over her and she sighed again, completely relaxing into his touch. Trusting. Pliant. "You want this," he murmured.

"I want you," she agreed. "Always have."

It wasn't a declaration of love, not even close, so why did it feel like one? He kissed her again, this kiss intense and lingering.

She whispered against his lips soundlessly, but he heard her. Felt her.

"Now. Please."

Yes. Now. He lifted her to the edge of the tub. Water splashed as he put hands on her thighs and gently nudged them wide, making himself at home in between.

The only light came from the stars and crescent moon but it was enough to see clearly. She looked beautiful. He wanted this to last all night, but all his good intentions slipped when she whispered his name again, husky, needy. Hungry.

Hungry for him, thank God.

He kissed a slow trail down her body, lingering over her breasts. He took his time, rasping his work-roughened fingers over her quivering flesh, then his mouth as her hips began to rock, silently asking him for more, which he gladly gave. For long moments the only sounds were the night crickets, the gentle slosh of the water, and her soft sighs of pleasure that drove him wild. Her teeth were gritted, her lips parted, her breath coming in little gasps. "Aidan— I'm going to—"

"Come," he said against her. "I want to watch you."

She shuddered around him, and his own body vibrated with the need to let go right along with her. Lifting her in his arms, he turned and sank into the water, sitting with his back to the tile.

Her face was pressed into the curve of his shoulder as she worked at catching her breath. He stroked her body, bringing her down slowly. When she stirred and kissed his throat, and then bit him lightly, he knew he was in trouble.

And sure enough she shifted, humming her pleasure deep in her throat at finding him hard as a rock. Raising her face to his she straddled him—but he stopped her.

"Not here," he said, his voice nearly unrecognizable in its gravely roughness, even to himself. He tried to hold her still, but that was an impossible feat and every single oscillation of those sexy hips threatened to get him off right then and there.

"Why not?" she asked, cupping his face, running her mouth over his jaw, his ear, back to his mouth, his throat, everywhere she could reach. "You did me. Now I want to do you."

Yeah, she was going to be the death of him. "Condom," he managed to grate out. "I don't have one out here."

Her eyes met his. "I'm on the pill. I tried to tell you last time, but I could barely think much less speak. You don't need a condom, Aidan. I've never not used one, but I trust you."

This last line was said just as the jets kicked off, so her words echoed louder than the others into the air and right into his heart.

I trust you.

How was he supposed to keep things light and easy and not scary for her when she said things like that to him? He had no idea what he'd done to inspire her trust, but he was grateful, and aroused as he'd ever been. He'd never had sex without a condom, either, had never even thought about it, but he didn't want a condom with Lily. He wanted nothing between them.

She kissed him this time as she raised up on her knees and sank down on him, taking him deep, so deep that his eyes nearly rolled back in his head.

Then she whimpered, her fingers digging into his biceps and he held her hips still. "Did I hurt you?"

"No— Please," she whispered, undulating with the need for more. "Aidan, please."

"I don't want to hurt you." He could barely get the words out, he was holding on by a thread.

"You're not... Don't stop. Oh, God, just don't stop." She made another little orbit with her hips and Aidan lost whatever little bit of restraint he had. Her arms were around his neck, tight enough to suffocate him, and he didn't care. Holding on, he began to move with her.

She gasped his name—he fucking *loved* that—and smiled at him. He loved that, too, and in less than two seconds he was breathing like a dying man. And he *was* dying. Of pleasure. He ran every day in full gear. He shouldn't be out of breath from having a woman ride him like a bronco.

But it wasn't the exertion.

It was all her. How many nights had he spent over the years fantasizing about this, with her, and he'd never once come close to the reality of being buried deep inside her.

They moved together like they'd been made for this, their bodies perfectly in sync. No awkwardness, no hoping that she was as far gone as he.

She wasn't only right there with him, she'd somehow climbed inside him.

Snugging her thighs to his hips, she held him close, her hands roaming his chest, arms and back, sometimes sliding up into his hair to grip him tight, her breathing quick and shallow, her cheeks flushed with desire as she met his gaze, never looking away.

He felt like he could see all the way into her, a glimpse of the woman she so often hid. And she was so damn beautiful she made his throat ache.

They stared at each other as they moved, and when he slid a hand between their bodies and touched her, just slid his thumb across her center, she whispered "*yes...*" and began to come, her head falling back, her body clenching around him as she cried out his name again.

She was lost in him, and knowing he'd gotten her there made him feel about ten feet tall. It also made him come right along with her, and he pulled her down over him so he could bury his face in the curve of her neck as he let go of everything but this.

When his sanity returned he knew he was doomed. Just as he knew the truth.

He didn't have one ounce of control over what was happening between them.

He knew eventually he'd be forced to move on when she left town, but he'd done it once. He could do it again. Probably.

From somewhere outside the hot tub he heard his phone beep. He hoped like hell it wasn't any sort of emergency because he didn't think he could get up to look. Fact was, he wasn't all that sure he still had legs. At least he wasn't on call tonight...

"Aidan." Lily stirred. "Your phone—"

"I'm not on call tonight. Ignore it."

"Hmm." She ran a finger down his chest, past his abs, and south. "Like I'm supposed to be ignoring this?" She wrapped her fingers around him and stroked.

"Jesus, Lily."

"Nope. Just me."

He choked out a laugh and managed to get them both out of the tub and lay her on his lounge chair, where he stopped to take one long look at her spread out all wet and gleaming and naked.

Then he made himself at home between her legs.

"Again?" she whispered hopefully.

"Again," he said, and followed through on the only promise she was ready for him to make.

Long before Lily's heart rate made its way back to normal, her purse began vibrating like it was having a seizure. "My cell phone," she said lazily.

"Let it go."

She bit her lower lip. She wasn't good at letting things go. It went against the grain. But she didn't make a move for her phone.

Aidan gave her a smile that said he was going to reward her and yanked her into him just as her phone went off again.

For a beat she just dropped her head to his chest, but then she imagined all that could be wrong if someone was calling twice in a row. Maybe her mom, with an emergency. With reluctance she pushed away from Aidan and climbed off the lounge.

When she bent for her purse, he let out a rough sound of pure male appreciation behind her.

"Nice view," he said.

She looked down at herself. Completely naked. She'd actually forgotten. She'd never forgotten before. She supposed that meant she was comfortable with him, shockingly so. Dripping water everywhere, she pawed through her purse and grabbed her phone. Jonathan. "Hey," she said into the phone.

"I need you at the salon. We have an emergency."

"An emergency?"

Aidan stood up, eyes sharp, reaching for his pants.

"What is it?" she asked Jonathan. "Did you call nine-one-one?"

"Not that kind of emergency. We've got a reality star up here. She sneaked away for the weekend to slum it in the Rockies with someone from her show. Unfortunately that someone isn't her husband. They were playing some waxing game and she messed up her hair."

"And you can't fix it?"

"Yeah, I'm not talking about the hair on her head," he said.

"Oh." She winced. "Okay, I'll be right there." She disconnected and looked at Aidan. "I've gotta go."

"What is it? I can call dispatch on our way."

"It's a hair emergency."

He stopped cold and looked completely baffled. "There's such a thing as a hair emergency?" he asked. "How about I claim to have a hair emergency too?"

"Actually it's more of a waxing emergency," she said.

He stared at her for a beat and then let out a rough laugh. "Okay, I can't compete with that." He moved to her and pulled her into his arms, burying his face in her hair and inhaling deep like he couldn't get enough of her.

It gave her a warm fuzzy all over.

"I'll take you," he said.

"You don't have to—"

"It's late, it's dark, I'll take you. You can text me when you're done and I'll come back for you." He kissed her when she started to protest. Then he pulled back, cupped her face, and looked into her eyes. "Thanks for tonight."

She laughed. "Are you thanking me for all the sex?"

"Yes," he said. "Although, as previously discussed, we both know it was more than just that, hot as it was."

She opened her mouth but he kissed her again, effectively shutting her up.

"I love you, Lily," he said easily against her lips.

She went still in utter shock, not at the words—though they were pretty shocking, but at the casual ease he had in saying them.

I love you, Lily.

Like he was just stating a fact, no big deal.

With a light smile—and no apparent expectations from her—he handed her a towel and then brought her some of his sweats to wear before taking her to work.

Chapter 23

Aidan got to the station at the usual seven a.m. Unlike usual, he was already tired. Probably because he hadn't gotten much sleep. At the thought of what—who—had kept him up, he was smiling when he clocked in.

He'd picked Lily up from the salon an hour after he'd dropped her off, and they'd spent the night at her place.

In her bed.

He'd known his words had thrown her. Hell, they'd thrown him. But he wouldn't take them back—after all, they were the truth—and he wouldn't hide from them either.

So he'd done his best to keep the rest of their hours together light and sexy and fun. No pressure.

Because no way was he going to rush her.

Ten seconds later, the first call of the shift came in, and he had to set aside his thoughts on what they'd done in her bed to each other.

The call was an accidental death, and they arrived first on scene to a screaming woman.

She'd found her husband in the garage, and he was indeed dead. He'd gone to get something out of the garage refrigerator in a robe and lightweight slippers. Near as they could tell, he'd inadvertently stepped into a puddle of water just as he'd opened the fridge and electrocuted himself.

Sheer, dumb bad luck.

An hour later Aidan and Mitch were still on-site, sitting in the rig working on the report, when a uniformed Hudson climbed up into the shotgun seat and met Aidan's gaze.

They hadn't spoken since several nights ago, when tempers had gotten hot and Hudson had called him a damn hypocrite.

"Need a minute," Hudson said.

"Later." Aidan tried to get around his brother, who swore beneath his breath and blocked Aidan's path.

"I shouldn't have called you a hypocrite," Hudson said quietly. "Or implied that you don't think of me and Jacob as family."

Shit. When Hudson got a stick up his ass to discuss something, he never cared who was listening. But Aidan was very aware of Mitch trying to eavesdrop, because the lot of them were like a bunch of schoolgirls. "Okay," he said. "Good talk, thanks."

Hudson didn't budge.

"We can do this later," Aidan said grimly.

Hudson dropped his head, swore again, and then looked up. "How about a peace offering?"

None was needed but Aidan was hungry. "Sure. A loaded breakfast burrito would do it."

"I've got something better. I'm not going to make

you drop trou and prove you're *not* wearing the latest delivery."

"Shit," Aidan said. "I completely forgot."

"—because you spent the night at Lily's."

Behind Aidan came Mitch's intake of breath.

"Okay," Aidan said, and he shoved Hudson out of the truck. "Turns out I do have a moment. A moment to kick your ass. What makes you think I spent the night with Lily?"

"Heard it," Hudson said smugly, all remorse gone.

"From who?" Aidan demanded. "Who's talking about what I do on my own damn time?"

Hudson flashed a grin. "Me. You didn't come home. And I saw your truck in front of her building when I did a drive-by last night."

Shit. "Oh," he said brilliantly.

"So I assume you've been working on letting her in, showing her by example?"

"Seriously," Aidan said. "You need to stop taking those night classes."

Hudson smiled, but the smile quickly faded. "Now that you're talking to me…let's hit on why I'm here."

"Oh, for chrissakes—"

"I need to know why you don't want me to contact Dad."

"Not this shit again—"

"I went to Gray," Hud said.

Aidan tensed. "What?"

"Yeah. And he told me it's your story to tell, not his."

Aidan relaxed marginally.

"But," Hudson went on. "This isn't a damn monarchy. You can't just lay down the law like I'm some little kid.

I'm asking you for just one reason. And when you give it, I'll be on your side no matter what."

Aidan closed his eyes. "I don't want to do this."

"Because he hurt your mom, right?" Hudson asked quietly. "Is that it? He hurt Char and…also you?"

Aidan's eyes flew open. "Why? Did he ever lay his hands on *you*?"

Hudson's entire demeanor changed. He tensed and his eyes went dark with fury. "Shit. So he did," he breathed. "He beat you. And you never said a word."

When Aidan didn't respond, Hudson's hands fisted. "Because you were protecting us. Goddammit, Aidan." He let out a purposeful breath. "Okay. Okay." He nodded. "So we keep him clear of here at all costs."

"Not for me," Aidan managed to say. "But for my mom. She…" He shook his head. "I don't want him within a thousand miles of her."

"Ten-four on that," Hudson said tightly. He nodded, his eyes still hot but also softer now, with an understanding Aidan had hoped to never see. "I'll let you get back to it," he said quietly, but didn't move.

"If you try to hug me…," Aidan started.

"Hell no," Hud said. "We're on the street in broad daylight." He paused. "But we're okay, right?"

"Aren't we always?" And then to lighten the mood he said, "And maybe I was at Lily's last night for a late dinner. You ever think of that?"

Hud went brows up. "At three a.m.?"

"Fine," Aidan said. "You caught me. I'm a grown-ass man sleeping with a grown-ass woman."

Hudson grinned. "Does Char know?"

"No. And we're going to keep it that way, you hear

me?" Aidan asked warningly. "If she found out, she'd probably start planning some big, fancy wedding and then I'd have to kill you dead. You get me?"

Hudson laughed.

"*What?*"

"You just said *wedding* without getting hives," Hud said.

"I'm not allergic to weddings, you dumbass."

"No, you're allergic to letting someone love you," Hudson said.

This stunned Aidan into momentary silence. "You don't know shit," he finally said. "I'm perfectly willing to let Lily love me." He made a point of looking at himself in the sideview mirror of the truck. "Look, Ma, no hives. Now don't go away mad, just go away."

"Not yet," Hudson said, studying Aidan. "Because there's something else bugging you, I can feel it. And I'm not leaving until you tell me. I'll never make that mistake again."

Aidan took in the tension lining Hudson's mouth and felt like a complete asshole. Hudson blamed himself for Jacob's vanishing act, thinking if he'd only gotten Jacob to open up, he might have been able to stop him from leaving.

Which was complete bullshit, but the Kincaids never had been much on common sense. Still, he wasn't going to let Hudson feel responsible for anyone else in this family, ever. "It's about Lily. It's not important right now."

"Humor me."

Aidan sighed. "I'm just not sure she's ever going to let herself…"

"What?"

"Be loved. She's been independent and on her own all this time and she's gotten good at it. She doesn't see herself as worthy of letting anyone in."

Hudson nodded and then, proving he wasn't just a pretty face, came up with a shockingly simply and brilliant solution. "So show her otherwise."

Lily rushed toward the salon at ten minutes past nine, gulping down some desperately needed caffeine to wake herself up after not enough sleep. This was directly related to how she'd spent the rest of the night, and not the waxing emergency.

Aidan hadn't said "I love you" again, and she hadn't said anything at all, but as magical as his place had been, her bed was just as good. Her bed, her shower, her kitchen counter…

A few feet from the door of the salon she fumbled with her purse to put away her sunglasses and ran right into a hard chest that belonged to—

"Aidan," she gasped as he easily caught her, steadying her coffee as he did.

He felt amazing, but when she lifted her face to see his, she frowned at the tension she saw there. "What's wrong?"

For a beat he looked startled, like he hadn't realized that she could read him so well. Then he cleared his face of all expression.

"Aidan," she said softly. "You okay?"

"Yeah. Just been a long morning already."

She'd sought comfort from him before. She'd sought his help as well. But he'd never asked her for either of those things. He'd never asked her for anything at all and probably never would. So she stepped into him, into his warm, hard body.

He hesitated before moving into her, wrapping his arms around her waist and burying his face in her neck.

"What's going on?" she asked softly, stroking a hand up his back, past the nape of his neck, tunneling her fingers into his hair.

"It's nothing," he said, and then paused like he was struggling with whether or not to share.

"Nothing." He paused. "Hud and I've been fighting about our dad," he finally said. "He wanted to bring him here, make him help us clean up the mess he left."

Lily didn't know much about Richard Kincaid, other than he was deadbeat dad of the century for starting and deserting not one but *three* families. "And you don't want him to come," she guessed.

"I don't want him anywhere near my mom. He screwed her over when he left."

"And you," she said quietly.

"No, I wanted him gone." He tightened his grip, keeping his face hidden. "I wanted him dead."

"I'm sorry, Aidan."

"Don't be. You didn't do anything."

"I'm sorry for your bad memories."

"Yeah, well, we both have those."

Yes, but she had a feeling his were even darker than hers. She held him tighter.

He gave her another long moment, and then he pulled back and looked into her face. "You were in a hurry."

"Yeah, I'm running a little late." She watched the small smile flirt at the corners of his mouth and felt her face heat. "Listen, I'm not so great with this whole morning-after-quickie stuff, so I'm just going to…" She gestured to the door, but he slid a hand to her waist to stop her.

"We talked about this," he said. "It's more than a quickie."

On some level she knew he was right. It just wasn't a level she could fully access right now. "Aidan—"

"Yeah, and you know it," he said, and took her mouth. Tender, soft, his lips coaxed more than a kiss from her, until she felt open to him and willing to give him everything she had. Somewhere in the dim recesses of her mind she heard her purse fall to the ground, but she didn't care. This had sneaked up on her. *He'd* sneaked up on her. Quiet and strong, he wanted her to believe things she'd never been able to believe before.

Believe and trust…

"You're stronger than you think," he said softly, making her realize she'd spoken out loud. "You've always been stronger than you think."

She stared up into his fathomless gaze, hoping that was true. He looked so sure as he met her gaze. She could use some of that confidence. "What do you want from me?" she blurted out.

He picked up her purse and handed it over. "Worried?"

"A little." She paused. "Or, you know, a lot."

His smile was warm and made her throat tighten. "This," he said, and put a hand over her heart. "I want this."

Oh. Well, if that was all…

He kissed her once more and then opened the door to the salon for her, giving her a little nudge in. "Have a good one," he said, and he was gone.

Just like that, as if he hadn't only a second ago made

a bid for her heart. She shook her head to clear it and walked through the salon, taking a big sip of her coffee.

Jonathan spoke without looking up from his laptop. "You're ten minutes late. There's only two acceptable excuses for being late. A life-or-death situation, or morning sex."

Lily choked on her coffee.

Jonathan looked up. "Holy shit," he said. "Ding-dong, we have a winner at door number two. You got morning sex, you lucky bitch."

Lily stopped and inspected herself in one of the mirrors. "No way could you tell that by just looking at me."

"Yes, way," he said. "And I want to hear every single detail, including size and expertise, but for now get the towels out and start up the register."

"I thought that was Rosa's job."

Rosa popped her head out from the back. "Nope. The person who gets morning sex has to do the shit jobs so the rest of us feel better about our sexless lives."

Jonathan nodded. "It's in the employee handbook."

Lily shook her head. "Fine," she said, heading to the back. "But no one's getting any details out of me."

"Where's the fun in that?" Lenny asked.

Lily hadn't noticed him in her hurry, but he was standing right there. In his T-shirt and jeans low slung thanks to his tool belt, he had sawdust in his hair and all over her floor. "What are you doing?" she asked.

"Just put in some new shelves. Gray said I could handle your list of requested renovations as a side job."

She looked the shelves over and nodded approvingly. "They look great. Let me grab a broom and sweep up the sawdust before any clients get here."

"No worries," he said. "I'll clean up after myself. I'm a full-service contractor. So about that promise…"

Baffled, she shook her head. "What promise?"

"You said you'd think about going out with me."

No, she hadn't. She'd been careful not to lead him on. "Lenny—"

He smiled. "You going to break my heart, sugar?"

She rolled her eyes. "We both know I couldn't do that."

"Don't underestimate yourself."

There was something different about him today from the last time she'd seen him. His cheeks had a lot of color, and his eyes were glassy. She might have thought he was sick except for one thing—she could smell liquor on him. "Have you been drinking?"

"Is that against the law?" he asked.

"It's not even nine thirty."

"But it's five o'clock somewhere."

"You're on the job," she said quietly.

His smile was a bit tight now. "You going to rat me out, Lily? Wouldn't be the first time you told on someone, would it?"

She narrowed her eyes at the reference to what had happened at her last job. "Maybe you should just go."

"Because that would be easier than admitting to my face that you never had any intention of going out with me. Is that it?"

"I never had any intention of leading you on or going out with you," she said. "I'm sorry if you thought otherwise."

"Because you're fucking Aidan?"

Their gazes met and held. She couldn't be surprised he knew about Aidan. Cedar Ridge was a small town, and the people in it enjoyed talking. A lot.

"I've seen you with him," he said. "Funny thing about body language. It's always honest."

"This conversation is over," she said.

"Look at that, you even talk like him. I get it, you know," he said. "He's a Kincaid. Owns the resort. Of course you picked him."

"Out," she said. "Now."

He jerkily packed up his tools and left.

Jonathan came close. "Heard the tail end of that, which didn't go well."

"Seeing as the alternative was me kicking him in the nads, I think it went really well."

"Oh, I most definitely agree there," Jonathan said. "I just meant that in my experiences, dickheads like that don't go quietly into the night. And Lily? You need to let Aidan and Gray know what happened here. If you don't feel comfortable saying anything, I'll be happy to do it."

She blew out a sigh. "I'll handle it."

"Sure?"

"Yeah. I clean up my own messes."

The door opened again, and in came Penny.

Lily let out a breath and managed a smile. "Hey."

"Hey. I want the baby-butt skin you gave Aidan," she said.

"Baby-butt skin coming up," Lily said.

Penny stared at her. "And also I want that glow you're wearing. What's that from?"

An all-nighter with your brother-in-law... "Um, I think I'm sunburned."

Jonathan choked and spilled his coffee. "Dammit."

Penny was still staring at Lily. "You slept with him."

"What is it with you people?" Lily asked the room.

"Jealousy," Jonathan said.

His client, an eighty-five-year-old woman, nodded. "Sure is, honey," she said in a three-pack-a-day voice. "None of *us* are getting any."

"Hey," Penny said. "*I'm* getting some."

"Yes, but that's *married* sex," Jonathan said. "Married sex doesn't count."

"Hmph," Penny said.

The rest of the day spun by pretty quickly with the exception of several people asking Lily if she was going to finally be the one to tie down the elusive Aidan Kincaid.

"It's a compliment," Jonathan told her as they were cleaning up at the end of the day. "People are fascinated by the Kincaids. They're all wild as hell—though marriage has tamed Gray—somewhat. People are wondering about the woman who's looking like she might snag another brother. Really, the gossip and questioning are inevitable."

"It's ridiculous," Lily said. "Love is a private business."

"Whoa." Jonathan went brows up. "I didn't say anything about love. But since you went there—"

"Sorry," she said, grabbing her purse. "Gotta go."

"Fine, but Lily Pad?"

She looked back.

"Tell Aidan about Lenny."

She nodded and hightailed it out of there. She didn't look forward to that conversation. The last thing she wanted to do was bring trouble on anyone, even Lenny.

Not to mention once again spilling the beans out of turn...

Back at her place, she changed her clothes and grabbed Ashley's scarf and went up the mountain. Not even close to being in the right mind-set to attack Dead Man's Cliff, she hiked Heaven's Peak instead, visiting some of her favorite haunts, looking to prove to herself she could start and finish *something* at least.

She stopped for pictures when the mood struck, sat on a rock outcropping and drank her water when she got tired, and when her second wind hit, she headed home.

Inside her apartment, she walked straight to the framed pic of herself and Ashley that her mom had sent. Removing the scarf from around her neck, she set it next to the frame. "I went hiking again today," she told her sister, and had to draw in a deep breath. "I'm not climbing. It's not fear, I want you to know that. It's not regrets either. I just…I had to grow up, you know?" She paused and had to swallow the lump in her throat. "I really thought we'd be doing that together, growing up," she whispered. "I really did."

A stupid tear slipped out, and she swiped it away. "I hiked Heaven's Peak," she went on. "And it felt good. Actually, it felt great. I forgot how much I missed being out on the mountain. But I promise you, Ash, I've never forgotten how much I miss you."

She had to swipe another damn tear, but that was the last one. "I won't ever forget you," she whispered to her sister's happy face as she ran a finger along the cashmere. "But I think I need to forgive myself. I'm having problems with that," she admitted softly. "I've been trying and can't seem to do it on my own." She paused again. "Maybe you could help me there."

Oh, how Ashley would have loved that, Lily needing

her help. And at just the thought Lily was suddenly able to smile through her tears.

"See," she managed. "You're helping already."

Aidan was in the main office, playing Ruler of the Universe for Gray, who was out on the mountain overseeing a biking event.

After working all night at the fire station, Aidan was tired and feeling out of sorts because he hadn't had a chance to see Lily again. He'd been thinking of her though, plenty, as he flipped through the files, like how he felt when she smiled at him. How soft her skin was. How she tasted…

Lenny stuck his head in the door. "Finished the shelving unit at the salon yesterday," he said. "Thank Gray for me for getting me some work."

"Glad it worked out," Aidan said. "Invoice the resort so you can get paid."

"You sure? Because I heard the bills aren't getting paid right now."

"What are you talking about?"

"I get that you're keeping this tight. You never did do failure well. But come on. Since when do your friends get left out of the loop?"

Aidan felt his temper stir. Standing up, he closed the office door before turning back to Lenny.

"Right," Lenny said, before Aidan could speak. "Wouldn't want anyone else to hear this."

"Actually, I don't want anyone to see me kick your ass," Aidan said, definitely pissed off now. "The only thing that's ever come before my friends is my family."

"Then explain Lily."

Aidan narrowed his eyes. "What's your problem today?"

"I'm practically one of the Kincaids. Or I was, until you got too busy for me. Still, the rumor is that you're losing the resort. You could've told me yourself that you're going to have to cut employees next quarter to save yourselves."

Aidan let out a long breath. "Okay, I want you to listen to me very carefully. We're not losing the resort. And any employee layoffs have not been decided on."

"Got it," Lenny said snidely. "So as long as you Kincaids stick together all is good, right?"

"What the hell are you talking about?"

"I got the four-one-one at the salon. People talk about all sorts of things there, including you and your daddy's money issues."

Aidan stilled at that. There were damn few people who knew about his relationship with Richard and how it affected the future of the resort. Gray, Hudson, Kenna...but they'd never say a word. They just wouldn't.

Lily knows, too, a small voice said—which he ignored. Or tried to.

"Something else the salon has," Lenny said. "Nice view, your latest hot piece working there."

He narrowed his eyes. "I know you're not talking about Lily like that."

Lenny smiled grimly. "She grew up nice, yeah? I mean she has a smart-ass mouth on her, but she's still sexy as hell. I heard things were getting hot and heavy between you two, but apparently not that hot and heavy if she's still open to chatting it up with other guys."

Aidan stared at him. "Why don't you just come right out and tell me what it is you really want me to know."

"All right," Lenny said. "You give me work. You let me tag along with you when you're feeling generous. You throw me a lot of bones, we both know that. But this time, it's my turn to win."

"I wasn't aware we were in a competition," Aidan said as mildly as he could.

"Bullshit."

"What exactly is it that you think you're going to win?" Aidan asked.

"Maybe your girl."

And that's when Aidan's radio went off with a fire call.

Aidan swore, then grabbed the radio and headed to the door. As he passed Lenny, he stopped and sniffed. "Have you been drinking?"

Lenny tried to brush past him, but Aidan put a hand on his chest. "I can smell it on you."

Lenny knocked Aidan's hands away. "I'm out of here."

"Good," Aidan said. "And you're wrong about—"

"Lily?" Lenny stopped in the doorway. "You sure about that?"

Aidan wasn't sure about much when it came to Lily, but he was sure she'd never hurt him purposely. "About practically being a Kincaid," he said. "Kincaids don't turn on each other. Ever. You're done here at the resort, Lenny, and not because we're losing it. You're done because I no longer trust you."

"Maybe Gray feels differently."

"Gray wanted to let you go a long time ago. Your job here was a favor to me. Favor revoked. Get your stuff and get the hell out."

Chapter 24

Lily took a quick break between appointments and checked her email. Still no responses to any of her resumes.

None.

Zip.

Zilch.

She waited for the usual ball of panic to kick in, knowing that this left her still stranded here in Cedar Ridge.

But the panic didn't hit.

Instead she got a brand-new feeling. A warm fuzzy. It confused her at first, until she realized that it meant she was okay with being stuck here indefinitely.

Maybe even permanently.

"Liking that smile," Jonathan said. "Did you get a response on a resume?"

"No." She turned to look at him. "The opposite actually."

Jonathan looked confused. "And this is making you happy because…?"

"Because maybe I'm not in a huge hurry to leave anymore."

He grinned. "Well of course not. Not when you're getting all the orgasms."

Outside the shop, a man got out of a truck and walked toward the salon.

"And look!" Jonathan said. "It's the orgasm donor in the flesh."

Aidan walked in wearing his firefighter polo, cargoes, dark lenses, and no smile at all.

Jonathan's faded. "Hey. You okay?"

"Need a moment with Lily," Aidan said.

"Take as many as you need." Jonathan moved toward the front of the shop, turning to Lily behind Aidan's back to fan himself.

"Hey," she said to Aidan as evenly as she could, which wasn't all that evenly, because being this close to him still made her pulse leap and her heart kick.

He walked past her without touching her. Unusual because one, lately he always took any opportunity to touch her, and two, the space was small and he was as broad as a mountain. In the back room he turned to face her, arms crossed over his chest as he leaned back on one of the counters.

"Everything okay?" she asked, shutting the door to give them some privacy. Or as much dubious privacy as one could get in a hair salon.

"You seeing Lenny, Lily?"

She blinked. "Um, I'm pretty sure I'm seeing you."

He didn't crack a smile. "I don't care if you're seeing other people, I'd just like to know where we stand."

"You don't care?" she repeated, doing her best to hide her shock and failing utterly.

He made a dismissive gesture, like this wasn't the important part. "Did you tell him about the resort possibly having to lay off employees?"

She felt the shock reverberate through her.

"Did you tell him about my dad?" he asked.

She found her voice. "You really think I would?"

"Why do you keep answering my questions with a question?" he asked.

The hurt welled up so fast she couldn't breathe. "Okay," she said, moving back to the door. "We're done here." She yanked open the door and gave him her best PMS bitch look.

He blew out a breath. "Listen, I had to ask."

"You had to—" She broke off. "Whatever you told me in confidence stayed in my confidence. Hell, *everything* you've told me stayed in my confidence. I keep my word, Aidan. And I thought you knew that about me." Far too close to tears, she made to leave, but he caught her with one hand and held the door closed with the other.

"Don't," she said, trying to pull free, but he held her in an inexorable grip of steel.

"I'm sorry," he said, effortlessly holding her, bending at the knees a little to look into her eyes. "I just needed to know."

"Fine," she grated out, furious with herself for the small part of her that was enjoying being held so tight against him. "Now you know. We both know. We know I'm an idiot for believing you when you said that this thing between us was more than it is. I should have known better.

It's never more than I think it is, and in fact, it's usually far less. Dammit, let me go!"

"Lily—"

"I've got work," she said, and tore free. She rushed out and into the front room, ignoring Jonathan's worried look, calling her next client to the wash station.

Aidan followed. "Lily—"

"Working," she said.

"I need to talk to you."

Yes, but she did *not* need to talk to him. She'd been an idiot, she'd get over it. It's not like she'd just lost a family member tragically. "Busy," she said, settling her client into the wash chair.

Tessa was a teacher in her late twenties. She was goggle-eyed at Aidan in his uniform.

Not Lily. She just wanted to kick him. Especially when he came to stand on the other side of Tessa, looking straight across her at Lily herself.

"Sorry," she said. "If you want to book an appointment with me, go ahead. I know you've been too busy to manscape yourself. I could give you that bro-zilian we talked about, I have time right after Tessa."

Tessa let out a choking sound of horror.

Jonathan let his gaze slide down Aidan's body to his crotch area and went brows up.

Aidan didn't react, just looked Lily right in the eyes. "I'm sorry," he said quietly. Firmly.

"Oh, it's okay," she said. "It's not your fault you're so hairy."

Tessa choked again.

And this time Lily detected the slightest bunching of Aidan's jaw muscle.

"Lily," he said again, with rather remarkable calm given that the entire salon had gone quiet to listen in on this exchange about his manscaping prowess—or lack thereof. "I really need to finish talking to you. In private."

"Busy washing and then coloring Tessa," she said.

"You can talk over me," Tessa said quickly. "I don't mind."

"Oh, that's sweet," Lily said. "You hear that, Aidan? She doesn't mind us talking about how you think I'm sleeping around on you while I do her hair."

Jonathan gasped. "What the hell?"

"I don't think that," Aidan said to him, to everyone, and then he looked at Lily. "I don't."

At this point, you could've heard a pin drop in the salon.

Lily just kept washing Tessa.

Aidan's jaw was bunching good now as he reached in and turned off her water. He snagged a clean towel, pulled Tessa up to sit, and wrapped her hair in the towel himself—doing a damn fine job of it while he was at it, actually.

Then he led Tessa to Lily's hair station, handed her a magazine from the rack—a *Cosmo* that promised to teach its readers how to blow their guy's mind in ten moves or less. "Lily'll be right with you," he said.

"Take your time," Tessa murmured, watching his ass in the mirror as he strode around the chair toward Lily, eyes dark with determination.

Before Lily could make her escape or so much as squeak, he'd hauled her into the back room again, slammed the door, locked it, and then glared at her. "Bro-zilian?"

She crossed her arms and said nothing.

"*Hairy?*" he asked.

She looked pointedly at the clock on the wall.

He dropped his head, rubbed the back of his neck, and said, "This isn't going well, is it?"

"Well, how did you think it would go?" she broke her silence to ask, beyond pissed. No, make that beyond *hurt*. She opened the door. "I have to finish Tessa."

Which she did in an hour and a half, and then looked up her next client.

It was Aidan.

"He waited," Jonathan whispered in her ear. "He must want to talk to you *bad*."

She turned to Aidan, who was not in one of their comfortable waiting chairs, but instead standing by the door, arms crossed over his chest.

"Ready?" she asked coolly.

"Not for a bro-zilian," he said.

"What then?"

He looked resigned. "Anything else."

She tried to think of something especially good. "A brow wax it is."

He rolled his eyes up as if he could see his own brows. "What's wrong with them?"

"Bushy." They weren't, of course. He was perfect.

"How about another haircut?" he asked.

Oh, hell no. He just wanted another scalp massage. "It's the wax or nothing," she said. "Yes or no?"

He chewed on that a minute. "Yes," he ground out.

She wasn't cruel enough to hurt him, or even give him a bad wax. But still, she didn't realize her mistake until she had him in the private client room and was forced to lean over him very closely to apply the wax to his eyebrows. There was something incredibly intimate about the process, which she'd never given a thought to before.

His eyes never left hers. "Listen, Lenny was at the offices and he knew about the resort's financial problems. I assumed—" He shook his head.

She stared at him, her heart heavy with hurt. She would have rather felt fury, because hadn't she already done this? Fallen for a guy she thought she could trust? And then found out the truth? Why hadn't she learned her damn lesson? "You what?" she asked. "You assumed that not only did I betray your trust but that I also slept with him? Are you kidding me?"

"There you go with the question on top of a question thing again," he said.

She applied the strip and carefully ripped it from his skin.

"Son of a—" He blew out a breath.

"Another," she warned, and did his other eyebrow.

"You know what's crazy?" he asked after carefully sucking in a breath. "You women *willingly* do this to yourselves."

"Hold still," she said, and got the last stragglers.

"I'm sweating," Aidan said in disbelief. He sat up, making his abs crunch in a very sexy guy way behind his shirt, the bastard. "Holy shit. I'm seriously sweating."

"So did you figure it was me because of what happened at my last job?" she asked. "Where I got fired for revealing secrets?"

"No, I—"

She decided she didn't care and started to walk out, but he snagged her wrist. "Lily—"

"Nope, sorry, that's all the time I have," she said stiffly. "Enjoy your brow wax."

"We're not done here."

"Oh, we so are. And I have another client."

Thankfully this was true. She had a quick haircut and afterward started to go into the back because she badly needed a break from work.

Actually, she needed a break from her life.

This wasn't in the cards for her. Halfway to the back, Jonathan called out for her. "You've got another one, Lily Pad. A blow out."

Later she would marvel at Jonathan's straight face. She moved to the front and came face-to-face with Aidan.

"Oh, for the love of—" She shook her head. "You don't need a damn blow out—"

"The client is always right," Jonathan said.

She turned to glare at him. "Whose side are you on?"

"Yours," he said, which slightly mollified her. "Always. But I think we— I mean *you* should listen to him. I mean maybe he has a really good reason for being a bag of dicks." He looked at Aidan hopefully.

Aidan turned and walked to the hair-wash station.

Lily followed. She was tempted to use icy-cold water but she couldn't bring herself to act any more unprofessionally than she already had.

"So," Aidan said while she waited for warm water. "Where were we?"

"With you accusing me of sleeping with Lenny and also saying something I didn't. Because of what happened in San Diego."

"No," he said. "This had nothing to do with Lenny. Or San Diego—at all. San Diego was the last thing on my mind, actually. It was about my family and how hard I've had to fight to keep them from falling apart. And sometimes it makes me go stupid. Seriously, I'm a complete dumbass, okay? I shouldn't have come in here hot like I did. I'm sorry, Lily."

She felt herself soften a little bit in spite of herself. But only because she got it about his family. "I don't know much about being a part of a family unit anymore," she said, "but I can still understand that part." With the water warm now, she went to work washing his hair. He sighed and closed his eyes, like he couldn't help himself.

Which made two of them because she couldn't help but run her fingers through his hair for far longer than required.

Which changed nothing. She'd long ago learned there were things she could control and things she couldn't, and whatever Aidan thought of her, that fell into the latter. She had to let go of the things she couldn't control. It hurt too much otherwise. When she finished washing his hair, she moved him to her workstation and met his gaze in the mirror.

He opened his mouth to speak and she turned on the blow-dryer. She really did get that he hadn't meant to hurt her. She even got that he felt bad about it.

But though she could forgive, she couldn't quite forget. Not this.

"I'll book you for another hour to keep you talking to me," he said, as soon as she was done blow-drying his hair. "Hell, I'll go along with whatever torture you're dealing out, even a"—he shuddered—"bro-zilian."

He was teasing, but she couldn't turn it off like that. Maybe she couldn't make him take this seriously, but she was serious—she couldn't forget. Not this. "It doesn't matter anymore."

"What does that mean?"

"I'm done," she said very quietly. And with that, she walked away, heading to the back.

He got there first, placing one of his big hands flat on the door above her. She dropped her forehead to the wood.

"You're done?"

"As in stick a fork in me," she said tightly. "Are you going to go or should I?"

He turned her to face him and looked down into her eyes. "Let me get this straight. I have a question, I come to you, you get pissed about it, and you what, just walk away again? Is that it? Is that how this is going to work, Lily?"

"Yes, and speaking of work," she said past a burning throat. "I have to go. Or am I fired?"

He stared at her. "I'm not your boss. And I'd never fire you. Lily—" His radio beeped. He turned it down but she could tell by the look on his face that he was up.

"You'd better go," she said, weary from the fight. Weary and surprised at how sad she felt that something she couldn't even name was truly over. She headed back to the front.

Rosa was waiting for her. They'd arranged for Lily to cut her hair when she had a break. "You okay?" Rosa whispered when Aidan had left, her gaze searching.

"Never better," Lily said with a calmness she absolutely didn't feel.

Rosa reached out and patted Lily's hand. "Men can be so stupid, but in his defense I don't think he meant to be stupid."

Lily choked out a laugh. Better than crying.

"No, really," Rosa said. "I mean honestly, they think with their wrong head when they think at all, but he looked pretty devastated. What happened?"

"He asked me if I was sleeping with someone else. And he also thought maybe I'd said some private stuff about him."

Rosa bit her lower lip.

"What?"

"Well, I'm not an expert on the good guys," she said. "But I am somewhat of an expert on the rotten ones. And they never ask. They tell, or worse yet, they don't ever call or text. They take what they want and then they vanish. No talking at all. Seems to me if Aidan was asking, that's better than nothing, right? Maybe he wanted to make sure. Or maybe he just wanted to hear how you feel about him. I mean, I know we *think* we're obvious with our feelings, but we're not." She chewed on her lower lip. "Please don't give me a bad haircut."

"Lily Pad," Jonathan said. "You did tell him about Lenny being here intoxicated like I asked you to, right? And the way he spoke to you? You told Aidan all that?"

"No. I didn't want to be the rat fink." But she stared at them as their words sank in, especially Rosa's. Because Rosa had been right. Aidan had never made it a secret how he felt for her. He'd been open and frank. Always.

And in return she'd…been neither of those things. "Oh, my God," she said.

"What?" Alarmed, Rosa looked around. "What's wrong?"

"It's me," Lily said, turning to look at Jonathan. "It's all me," she said to him.

"Finally."

"This doesn't change the fact that he was an ass," Lily said to the room at large.

"Absolutely not," Jonathan's client said. "But just so you know, they *all* have their asshat days." She smiled at Jonathan. "Present company excluded, of course."

"Of course," he said demurely.

Chapter 25

Aidan got stuck on a ranch fire that went long into the night. By the time he got back to the station, he was losing his shit and not in the mood for anyone. Especially not Gray, who stopped by at six in the morning with some papers for him to sign before Gray went in to the office.

At least he remembered that he had something to make Gray as grumpy as he was.

"While you're here...," Aidan said, and went to his locker to pull out a brown bag, which he tossed to Gray.

"Shit," his brother said. "What is it?"

"Plain black boxers."

"Really?"

"No," Aidan said.

Gray peeked into the bag with trepidation. "*Shit,*" he said again, and gingerly pulled out a small neon-yellow package. "What the hell?"

"It's called a Man Sack," Aidan said. "Pretty self-explanatory."

Gray swore colorfully and shook his head. "Penny's going to love this."

"I thought she didn't know."

"Turns out she knows everything about everything."

"Just don't show her then," Aidan said.

"I save my secrets for the important stuff."

"Like when you come down to our place to eat our junk food?"

"Whatever, man. At least one of us is getting laid every night." Gray met his gaze, and his prissiness vanished. "What's wrong?"

This was the problem with having a brother who noticed every little thing, every single last detail, not to mention the fact that he knew Aidan like the back of his own hand. "Nothing."

"Try again," Gray said.

"I've got gear to clean."

"So talk while you do it."

"You've got a bunch of shit to do too," Aidan said. "Go be someone else's pain in the ass."

"Is this about you getting dumped after you accused Lily of giving out secrets like she did at her last job?"

Aidan narrowed his eyes.

"Hey, you're the one who picked a fight in a damn hair salon," Gray said. "You might as well have posted it to Facebook."

"Jesus," Aidan said, and shoved his fingers into his hair.

"Listen," Gray said. "Lenny's a dick and was wrong to approach her at all knowing that you had interest in her. And because I'm your brother, I'm going to assume she was wrong as well. That's just loyalty. So that makes you right."

"And?"

"And," Gray said slowly, like he was speaking to an idiot. "The question now is, do you want to be right, or do you want to be happy?"

"Shit." Aidan liked being right. Hell, let's face it, he *loved* being right.

But he couldn't remember being happier than he had since Lily's return. Aidan knew that his brother and Penny had their ups and downs like most couples. When they fought, the whole building shook with it. But then there was the good stuff. The other night Aidan had been standing in his kitchen grabbing a late night snack and he'd looked out the window to see his thirty-one-year-old brother and sister-in-law running around outside in their pajamas and bare feet with water pistols, soaking each other and laughing so loud their joy permeated the entire place.

Aidan realized he'd wasted a lot of time waiting for the perfect woman, when all he really wanted was someone to laugh with him for the rest of his life.

So yeah, if it came down to a choice between happy and right, the truth was that he knew exactly which one he wanted. "Okay, I pick happy," he said to Gray. "But how do you do that when you've already fucked everything up?"

Gray clapped him on the shoulder. "You drop to your knees and grovel your ass off."

Just then the alarm went off, and Gray tightened his grip on Aidan, his knowing smile gone. "Shake it off for now. You need to go into this call with a clear head, you got me?"

"I got you."

Aidan hit the engine at the same time as the rest of his crew, including Mitch. The fire was in Old Town, where the conditions of the row houses were mixed. All of them were old. Some looked it, and some had been remodeled, but they tended to go up like matchsticks.

They were built using balloon construction, meaning there were no fire-stops in the walls. So when flames got into the walls of one of these places, they traveled unimpeded from the basement to the attic, which sucked donkey balls.

Complicating the situation, being row houses meant each had a house attached on either side, so not only could the fire go vertical in a blink, it could go horizontal just as fast. And a multihouse fire was always a nightmare.

In less than five minutes from when they'd first received the call, they arrived on scene. Thick smoke curled in the air. The captain got on the radio telling dispatch to drop another full alarm, which would give them more engines and manpower.

It was going to be needed.

The good thing about Old Town was that it had a hydrant on every block, which meant that the second unit would have no problem getting a water supply. Their engine carried 500 gallons of water—about five minutes of pump action—so water supply was always a huge concern. Their saying "There's no feeling worse than having your hose go limp in the middle of heated action" came from experience, and not the good kind.

"Shit," Mitch muttered as they pulled up.

Yeah. Shit. A crowd stood out around watching smoke billow out of the eaves and windows. No visible flames though.

First things first. They verified all occupants were out of the house. Then they went to work ventilating the structure to allow gases to escape, preventing a flashover or backdraft. It also allowed for better visibility and got everyone off their hands and knees, where they'd been crawling around bumping into shit looking for a glow.

With their SCBAs—self-contained breathing apparatuses—in place, they combed through the smoke-filled house pulling hose as they went farther into the blackness.

The captain radioed them that the homeowners had reported they'd not seen any flames on the main level or second floor.

Which meant that the fire was more than likely in the basement.

The second unit arrived on scene and found the stairwell leading down to the basement, but the heat was too intense to make entry.

The second unit was assigned to open the basement windows from the outside to relieve that heat. And sure enough, a few minutes later they reported they had water on the fire and it would be extinguished shortly.

Aidan and Mitch were sent up to the attic to check there. It felt like a hundred and fifty degrees in the small, cramped, overstuffed-with-crap room but it was indeed fire-free.

When the captain ordered them to change out their oxygen bottles, Aidan and Mitch headed through the escape hatch to the main level of the house. Mitch stopped to open a window and Aidan walked across the floor and...

Fell through it.

As he fell, he heard the captain reporting on the "sponginess of the flooring" and warning them to use "extreme caution and stay to the edges."

Too late, he thought, and landed with a jarring thunk that knocked the air out of him.

The first thing he heard after landing was his own radio. Mitch was calling for the medic unit to stay on scene. Then the second unit radioed Aidan's captain, alerting him that one of his crew had decided to drop in and visit them in the basement.

Everyone was a damn comic.

Mitch got to him first, which meant that he was either magic or he'd flown down the stairs. "What the hell," he said, running his hands over Aidan's limbs.

Aidan shoved him away and sat up. "I'm fine."

No one believed him, so he was forced to cool his heels and let the medic give him a once-over, which only made him all the more pissed off at himself. "If this went out wide on the radio—"

"Oh, it did," Mitch said, looking amused, the bastard.

"Then text my mom before she calls the captain and gets me fired."

"Already done," Mitch said, and he held his phone up to take a pic of Aidan. "She insisted," he said.

Aidan rolled his eyes.

Mitch was reading his texts. "Oh, and she says you're an idiot to let Lily walk." He looked up. "You let Lily walk?"

An hour later the house had been confirmed condemned and a structural engineer had been called in. Official cause of fire—malfunctioning furnace.

"Hey, that's kinda like you," Mitch said to Aidan. "Official cause of breakup with Lily—*malfunctioning brain*."

By the time they got back to their station—with Aidan being mocked by his entire unit, both for his fall and for losing Lily—their shift was over.

In a hurry to get out of Dodge, Aidan showered quickly. Even more quickly when he saw the six-inch gash across his side. He slapped some gauze on it, called it good and left the station. In his truck, he pulled out his phone, which was loaded as usual. He flipped through the texts. The first two were from Gray. *Tell Kenna hell no.* And: *Just trust me on this.*

DELETE and DELETE.

Kenna had texted him as well: *Thinking about going to Argentina to ski the rest of their season.*

Aidan hit REPLY and typed: *Sure.*

He was no idiot. If he told his sister hell no, as Gray had suggested, his sister would be gone before anyone could blink. But if he agreed with her, she'd chill and hopefully move on to some other whim.

But just to be sure, he sent Gray a solution: *Sneak into her room, find her passport, and put it in the safe.*

Then there was Hud's text: *Heard what happened with Lily. You're a fidiot. Do I need to spell that out for you? F-u-c-k-i-n-g I-d-i-o-t.*

DELETE.

Aidan shifted, his side beginning to ache as he accessed the next text. It was a pic of two people kissing, a ridiculously close-up selfie, and he turned his head sideways trying to figure out what the hell he was seeing. When it clicked into place for him, he threw the phone to the passenger seat and stared at it like it was a coiled cobra.

It was his mom, making out with Marcus.

Jesus. He scrubbed a hand down his face and gingerly picked up the phone and thumbed to the next message, half terrified it'd be another pic. It was a text: *Sorry, darling, I meant to send that to myself and ended up sending it to my entire contact list.*

That had been sent twelve hours ago, and when he hadn't answered she'd sent another one: *I'm guessing by the silent treatment that you don't approve. Well, I don't need your approval, Aidan Scott Kincaid, and I don't want you getting mad at Lily for fixing my hair for my third date with Marcus, either, you hear me? And speaking of Lily, there's something you should know.*

He hit her number immediately. "What about Lily?"

"Honey, hi! You okay?"

"Yes." He rubbed the spot between his eyes where a headache was forming. "Lily," he grated out.

She sighed. "Okay, but you're not going to like this."

"I hate stories that start like that," he muttered. "Is she okay?"

"Yes. Or as okay as she can be after what happened with *you*."

He pinched the bridge of his nose. "Mom—"

"It's all my fault, Aidan."

He blinked. "What?"

"She didn't tell Lenny anything. I'm the one who's been talking to anyone who would listen, commiserating on how much we hope the worst doesn't happen, you know?"

"Mom—"

"I didn't realize Lenny was a bigmouth." She sniffed and sounding watery said, "I'm so sorry, Aidan."

Aw, shit. He blew out a sigh. "Please don't cry—"

"But I made a mess of things and you fired Lenny and yelled at Lily, and then she dumped you, and—"

"Lenny was fired because he'd had his three strikes, Mom. Not your fault. And I didn't yell at Lily. I'd never yell at Lily."

But he'd hurt her feelings, and that was all on him.

Char sniffed again. "I'll go talk to her for you and—"

"No." Aidan had to force himself to soften his voice. "Don't do anything, Mom. This is between me and Lily."

"But honey, you'll just make things worse."

Very likely, and again he had to rub the stress spot between his eyes. "I need you to stay out of it. Promise me," he said.

She hesitated.

"Mom."

"Fine," she finally said. "But you almost had a lovely thing going with her, Aidan. Don't blow it for the second time."

"The second time?"

"Well, yeah. You let her leave town all those years ago without a fight, remember?"

He let out a low laugh and resisted thunking his head against the steering wheel. Yeah. He vaguely remembered. "Gotta go, Mom. I've got a meeting."

"But—"

"Love you," he said, and hit END. This time he tossed his phone into the backseat, so he wouldn't be tempted to access any more texts, and drove home. Except his body must have disconnected from his brain because he didn't go home at all.

He went to Lily's. He needed to talk to her. And/or grovel.

He knocked on her door and then leaned on it because damn, his side hurt and he was suddenly so bone tired he could barely stand. She wasn't going to answer, and why should she? He was a complete dumbass.

When the door opened, he nearly fell inside.

Lily gasped and wrapped her arms around him. "Aidan?"

Chapter 26

Lily was as surprised and shocked to see Aidan as she was to find herself wrapped up in him. She hadn't heard from him. Not that she'd expected to after their last conversation, but she'd been having more than a few regrets on how she'd left things. In fact, she'd been about to go hunt him down and tell him so.

"I know you said you didn't want to see me anymore," he muttered. "But my truck drove me here." He buried his face in her hair. "God, Lily, you always smell so good. So fuckin' good..."

Something was off, and she tried to pull back to get a good look at him, but he tightened his grip. And more than that, he was *really* leaning over her.

"Sorry," he said when they almost toppled to their asses together in her doorway. "I'm really tired."

"You've been fighting fires," she said, smelling it on him. "How long have you been without sleep?"

"Two days," he said, and straightened. "I've never

resented the job before, but all I wanted was to get here. To you."

Not wanting to read anything into that, she refused to react. "Why?"

"Because I was a dick, Lily. I overreacted. I was pissed off at Lenny because he's been in my life a damn long time and I thought—" He shook his head and scrubbed a hand down his face. "Shit. I was wrong about him and I didn't take that very well. I thought I could trust him."

She knew a little something about that. "Not your fault," she whispered.

"Maybe not, but that I accused you of talking out of turn most definitely is my fault. Christ, Lily, I'm an idiot. A damned sorry idiot. My mom came clean and told me what happened, that it was her doing the talking—which I think you know."

She bit her lower lip, not about to throw Char under the bus.

Aidan gently stroked his thumb over her lip. "But even when I threw it in your face," he said softly, "you never said anything. You protected her."

"She's your mom," Lily said, just as quietly. "She's so worried about you guys, and she didn't mean to let loose state secrets."

He nodded. "I know. But that you knew it and never repeated it, not even to me, speaks volumes about who you are. So you think about that, Lily, the next time you tell me you don't know what to do with family. Because you know exactly. It's about loyalty and kindness and unconditional love, and you are more than capable of all that."

She remembered what Rosa had told her. *Seems to me if Aidan was asking, that's better than nothing, right? Maybe he wanted to make sure. Or maybe he just wanted to hear how you feel about him. I mean, I know we think we're obvious with our feelings, but we're not.*

"Neither of us is all that good with trust," she said now. "I get that."

Aidan shook his head. "Don't let me off the hook so easily here, Lily. I don't deserve it. I came into the salon furious, and I took it out on you because—"

"Because we're both head cases?" she asked.

He let out a short laugh. "Yeah, but I hurt you." His voice softened. "I'm so sorry for that, Lily."

"Well, I had it coming from you," she said, backing away from him, needing some space.

He leaned back against the door like he was too tired to stand on his own. "And how do you figure that?"

"When I ran out of here ten years ago, I hurt you." She took another step back.

"Sorry," he said, mistaking her movement. "I did shower." He sniffed himself. "Sometimes it takes two or three showers to really get rid of the smell, but I was in a hurry to get out of the station."

And he'd come straight here.

"I don't mind it," she said quietly, and she didn't. He worked his ass off, putting himself on the line, in danger, and he did it without hesitation.

He was one of the bravest men she'd ever met.

And that terrified her. But he already knew that. He wasn't quite as emotionally stunted as she, who managed to keep everything bottled up inside, locked down tight, never to be let out and shared. It was a special talent of hers, one she was someday going to learn to fix if it killed her.

But probably not today.

"You busy?" he asked, looking around.

"Yes." She had a date with a box of cookies and *Supernatural* season eight, but that was on a need-to-know basis.

"All right, I'll make this quick." He met her gaze. "About us."

"I didn't sleep with Lenny," she said. "I was sleeping with you."

"I know—" He broke off. "Was?"

Oh, yeah, it was *very* past tense in her book, no matter the fact that even now her eyes were soaking him up, wondering how fast she could get him naked.

Bad eyes.

"Lily—"

"No," she said, and held up a hand to hold him off, because she was weak when it came to him, very weak. So she spoke fast. "I need you to know that I can't sleep with two guys at the same time. I just..." She shook her head. "I'm not equipped for it. Hell, I'm barely equipped for one man at a time."

"That's not what I—" He blew out a breath. "I know you didn't sleep with Lenny. I know you didn't talk about the resort's business. I had a seriously dumbass moment and I'm here to ask you to forgive me for being that dumbass." He reached out and pulled her into him, still leaning against the wall. He set his hands on her hips and dipped his head to press his face to her throat, which was really freaking unfair because she loved when he did that.

"I do forgive you," she agreed, struggling to think. Not easy, since he'd slid his mouth to the underside of her jaw now and was nibbling his way to her ear, which set off a whole bunch of reactions. "But this still doesn't change anything," she managed, her hands on his shoulder, her fingers digging in. "You actually thought I could sleep with someone else when I was sleeping with you." And just saying it out loud made her mad all over again.

"I said I was a dumbass, right?" he asked. "*Complete* dumbass. One hundred percent dumbass. Ask any one of my siblings, they'll vouch for that."

His mouth was at her ear now, his breath warm against her skin, and her eyes drifted shut as her hands clung to him. "It's not that simple, Aidan."

He pulled back and looked at her. "So you've forgiven but…not forgotten? Is that it?"

"Look, it's not like you're the only dumbass in the room," she said, and grimaced. "I have a lot of dumbass tendencies when it comes to you as well."

"Like?" he asked, eyes locked on hers.

She wanted nothing more than to burrow into him, but he'd made that impossible. Or maybe she'd made it so. "Like I don't think I can do this," she whispered. "Regardless of how I feel about you."

"And how do you feel about me? You've kept that pretty tight to the vest."

She met his gaze with difficulty. "I did start this story with the fact that I'm a dumbass too," she reminded him, dropping her head to his chest. Panic gripped her. She knew she needed to do the whole talking through her feelings thing, but that was a lot easier said than done.

"Hey," Aidan said, and when she didn't look at him, he wound his hand in her hair and gently tugged until she lifted her face.

"What?" she asked, more than a little defensively.

His eyes had softened—when did that happen?—and he kissed her softly. "You take your time," he whispered.

Stunned, she stood there.

Not Aidan. He went back to nuzzling now, making a low, very male sound deep in his throat, like maybe she was the best thing that had happened to him all day.

And then there were his hands. Big and somehow both rough and incredibly tender at the same time, slipping down her back to squeeze her ass—which elicited another of those sexy growls from him, damn him—and then up and beneath her shirt.

He was hot, too hot, body heat radiating off him, and that feeling she'd had that something was off came back. He was leaning on her again and breathing fast. Too fast.

All hard to focus on when his hands cupped her breasts. He groaned, maybe because she wasn't wearing a bra. She might have asked him, but his work-roughened fingers rasped over her nipples and she couldn't form a sentence.

"You smell good," he murmured. "And you feel good. So fuckin' good, Lily."

Giving in, she ran her hands over him, too, unzipping his sweatshirt, peeling it off, letting it fall to the floor. This left him in his dark blue firefighter polo. "Aidan, why's your shirt wet?"

"It's not."

"Yes," she said. "It is—" She pulled back and her heart stopped. Just stopped. "Oh, my God, you're covered in blood."

"No, I'm not."

"Yes you are!" She carefully tugged up his shirt and gasped. "You're got a huge gash across your side."

He looked down. "Huh. Look at that."

She gaped at him. Then went hands on hips. "Strip," she demanded.

His mouth quirked, but there was a tightness to it and a grimness to the set of his face, making her realize that he was in real pain. And he'd hidden it. "I mean it," she said firmly. "*Strip*."

"Not even going to buy me dinner first?" he asked, but kicked off his boots and then unbuttoned and unzipped his pants. He tried to pull his shirt over his head and hissed in a breath. "No go," he said, and tore it off instead.

She gave a completely inappropriate shiver of sheer lust before taking in the bruises and cuts on his torso, and her heart squeezed again. All her fears coming to life right before her.

He's still breathing, she reminded herself, trying to calm her racing pulse. And joking around. He was going to be okay but God…his poor body. "Oh, Aidan."

"That's 'Oh, Aidan, I want to fuck you right now,' right?" he asked with a male's eternal optimism.

"Lie down," she said, and pointed to the bed.

"Great idea," he said, and flopped backward onto the bed. "I'm done in. Maybe you wouldn't mind doing all the work on this round. I'll take up the slack on round two."

"Don't move," she commanded.

He flashed another brief smile. "Love it when you go all dominatrix on me." He closed his eyes. "I'm all yours…"

She snatched his keys and his phone and ran out to his truck, thumbing through his contacts until she found Hudson.

"Yo," he answered. "You're alive. Thanks for answering your texts, asshat."

"It's not Aidan," she said. "It's Lily."

"He all right?" Hudson immediately asked, going from pissed to emergency calm in zero point two.

"I think he needs stitches, but he won't even admit he's bleeding."

"Of course not, he's an idiot. Where is he?"

"My place. It's—"

She was talking to dead air. "Damn Kincaids and their phone etiquette." She unlocked Aidan's truck and found his first-aid bag. She locked up the truck, turned back to her building, and plowed right into Hudson.

She put a hand to her heart. "You both need bells around your neck," she said.

He took the duffel bag from her, shouldered it, and took her hand, pulling her along at his pace, which meant she was nearly running.

"He's not bleeding out," she promised.

"Of course not. He's too ornery for that." Inside, he headed straight for her bed and sat on the mattress at Aidan's side. He looked over his brother's injuries, swore, then strode into the bathroom, where she could hear him washing his hands. When he came back, he started digging into the bag.

"I'm fine," Aidan muttered.

"You're a dumbass," Hudson responded.

Aidan opened his eyes and slitted Lily a look of amusement, which vanished quickly when Hudson squirted something over Aidan's raw chest.

Aidan swore the air blue.

"Suck it up," Hudson said, and tore open a pack that looked suspiciously like a suture kit.

"What are you doing?" Lily gasped, when Hudson began stitching up Aidan, who lay there perfectly still, his hands fisted in the bedding beneath him.

"Don't worry," Hudson said without looking up from what he was doing, which, near as she could tell, was torturing Aidan, given the seriously profane muttering still coming from his mouth.

Don't worry? Was he kidding? She felt bells clanging in her head, and her vision got cobwebby. "You've...done this before?"

"I became a pro on Jacob, although I think this one puts Aidan in a dead tie."

She made a sound that was pure anxiety, and Hudson spared her a look, narrowing his eyes. "You going to faint?"

"No!" *Maybe...*

He held her gaze, his own steady. "I need a cold, damp washcloth or something and a glass of ice water. *Lily*," he said firmly, when she just stared at him. "Go."

She ran to the kitchenette and came back with both, which she held while she stared at the scene before her.

Aidan was gritting his teeth and staring up at the ceiling, his face damp with sweat. Her heart squeezed, and she moved to his other side and put her hand over his.

He flicked her a quick gaze of surprise and managed a smile for her.

She rolled her eyes at him and sat at his side. "And we didn't get him to the hospital why?" she asked Hudson.

"Hello, have you met him?" Hudson asked. "He's got more rocks in his head than actual brains."

"Fuck. You," Aidan said between his gritted teeth. "Last time I stitched you up, you cried for your mama."

Lily divided a horrified look between the two of them. "You two play doctor a lot?"

Hudson shrugged. "Shit happens." He glanced up from his hands to Aidan's face, smirked, and then went back to work. "Hate to crack his image for ya, but he's really just a big baby, emphasis on big."

Apparently, Aidan only had enough energy to spare for a growl. Then he went on with his steady stream of swearing, directing it at Hudson.

Hudson just kept calmly stitching. "You know safety means everything to him, right? That he rarely gets hurt and if he does it's only because he's put someone else's safety first?"

Lily realized he was talking to her, and she stared at him.

"And he's never out there alone, doing something he shouldn't be doing," he said. "He's got Mitch or me at his back. We won't let anything happen to him."

She swallowed hard at the realization of what he was trying to tell her, that Aidan wasn't going to do anything like climb Dead Man's Cliff on his own without ropes and fall to his death.

She nodded, and Hud gave her a reassuring smile and went back to stitching, and then finally, after what seemed like hours but was really only twenty minutes, tied off the last stitch. Leaning over Aidan, he very gently added some ointment, and then carefully covered the entire injury with gauze and wrapping. His hands moved efficiently and professionally, and yet there was an affection and care very clear in every single touch.

When he was done, he kept a steadying hand on Aidan and said his name quietly.

Aidan opened his eyes and looked at him.

"Where to?" Hudson asked. "Because I'm about to

drug you, and you're going to stay horizontal for twelve hours."

"I'm going to kick your ass."

"Maybe tomorrow." Hudson twisted to Lily, took the ice water and cool washcloth, and turned back to Aidan. He ran the cool cloth over Aidan's face before tossing it aside and handing his brother the glass.

Aidan downed it in what seemed like two gulps.

"More?" Hudson asked quietly.

"I'm good."

Hudson rolled his eyes and turned to Lily. "He's good."

She gave a small smile.

"He staying here with you?" Hudson asked her.

She glanced at Aidan, who was watching her from those melting brown eyes. "Yes."

"He thinks he's 'good,'" Hudson warned. "But he's full of shit. He's dehydrated from working the fire, so keep him in fluids."

"And his injury?"

"He's had worse. Just keep him down as long as you can. And good luck with that, by the way." Hudson headed to the door.

Lily followed him. "Are you sure he's going to be okay?"

"Physically, yeah. He's running a pint low, but sleep is all he really needs."

"What about…not physically?"

At the front door, Hudson paused and turned to look at her. "Not physically?"

"Yeah." She spoke low enough for only him to hear. "You know, *mentally*."

Hudson studied her a moment and then spoke just as quietly. "I think you've got him all twisted up. Again."

"Again?" she repeated.

"Look, you left Cedar Ridge for some damn good reasons. I get it. You needed off the mountain. But you left a hole in him, Lily, one he's never quite closed."

"My leaving here had nothing to do with him," she said.

He lifted a hand to stop her from saying anything more, not that she would have. "Like I said, I get it," he said. "But I also get that you're only here until something else comes along. For his sake, I hope that's soon. Because the longer you stay, Lily, the harder it will be on him when you go again."

She stared at him, so intense, so protective of his older brother, and she missed that bond she'd once had with Ashley like she'd miss a limb if it got cut off. "You're making a lot of assumptions," she said.

"Maybe," he said. "Maybe not. Just don't hurt him again, Lily."

"I don't intend to."

Hudson searched her gaze and, not looking relieved in the slightest, he nodded at her and left.

Lily locked up, got another glass of water and a plate of cheese and crackers—look at her playing nurse—and headed back to the bed where she stopped to eyeball her patient.

He was in the exact same position as when they'd left him a few moments ago, flat on his back, arms stretched above his head.

Fast asleep.

Chapter 27

One minute Aidan was dreaming about Lily falling off the mountain the same way Ashley had, and the next he was wide awake. Heart pumping, he looked around. Given the darkness of the room it was the middle of the night. Unsettled, still shaken, he lay on his back in a bed that wasn't his with a woman who wasn't his snuggled in at his side. Lily had thrown one of her legs over his, her hand low on his belly.

And damn, in that moment it sure felt like she was his.

He'd been here with her for more than twenty-four hours. He had an arm around her, an arm that was half numb, his hand settled all possessively over her ass.

He really wished he could feel that hand.

Willing the blood back into his extremity, he squeezed experimentally and Lily shifted with a soft sigh.

Then went utterly still. Slowly, she lifted up to look down into his face. "How are you doing?" she asked.

He thought about it. His side ached, but not bad, considering. He owed Hud. "Never better."

She bit her lower lip. "I'm all over you," she said. "I'm sorry—"

"I like it."

She snorted. "You like everything."

Hard to argue with the truth. "I especially like having you back in Cedar Ridge," he murmured, watching the emotions his words caused play across her face.

Pleasure. Arousal…and uncertainty. It was hard for him to know she didn't believe or trust in emotions. Hers.

His.

But he understood. He'd set them back. "Are we okay, Lily?"

She met his gaze, her own uncertain.

"Huh," he said. "I was sure me nearly bleeding out was going to change your mind."

"I just need some time, I think. Not because of our fight, just because of me. I'm not used to this. To…being an us."

He could understand that. He was surrounded by family who drove him crazy and lived to torment him, but they'd lay their lives down for him.

Lily didn't have any of that and hadn't for a long time. He did his best to be quiet, to just feel the relief that she was no longer pushing him away. That she was trying in the only way she knew how.

"I like being back," she finally said softly. "I like being in this world again."

"It's your world too."

She shrugged, and he lifted her chin to look into her eyes. There was no way to go back and comfort the devastated, grief-stricken girl she'd been. But he had the grown woman right here in his arms. "You belong here as much as anyone."

He could tell that made her feel good but was also far too serious for her, because she changed the subject. "I still can't believe Hudson stitched you up like that. Let me see your chest."

Her holier-than-thou tone had him flipping her beneath him on the bed. "You've been the boss of me for going on two days now," he said, making himself at home between her legs. "My turn."

She stared up at his mouth like she wanted it on hers. He intended to oblige her. "Doesn't seem quite fair," she said, "since you've been a pretty big dud."

He felt his brows rise. "A big dud?"

"*And* a bad patient," she said.

Her hands were trapped between them. He entwined their fingers and slid her arms up over her head, holding them there while he lowered his body over hers and met her gaze. She was looking a little apprehensive and a whole lot aroused.

It was a good combo, he decided. "So you have complaints."

"Well," she said, hedging, clearly fighting a smile. "It'd be rude of me to insult your manhood when you're down."

He nudged his hips into hers, and he could tell by the way her breath caught that she could feel he wasn't down at all, but up. Very, very up.

"Consider me corrected," she whispered.

He kissed her neck, nudging the strap of her cami from her shoulder.

She moaned as his hand made its way beneath the soft material and skimmed lightly across her nipple, her entire body trembling under his touch. "Your injury…"

"Shh." Slowly he eased her top over her head and sent it sailing. Leaning over her, he kissed her sexy mouth and then flashed her a smile before dragging hot, open-mouthed kisses down her breasts, her ribs, a hipbone… She was making the sexiest little whimpers he'd ever heard as he got to her panties. He kissed her over them and then pulled the cotton away from her, sliding them down her legs, where they took the same flight as her top had. "Can't get enough of you," he whispered, and lowered his mouth to her wet center.

She sucked in a breath, and then another. "Aidan—"

"Shh," he said, and continued on with his plan to drive her crazy with lust.

It took a very gratifyingly short amount of time. When she cried out and began to shudder, he stayed with her to the end.

Panting, still quivering, she tried to roll, giving him a push to indicate he needed to go with her. Letting her have her way, he ended up flat on his back with her on top.

"Does this hurt?"

"You're killing me," he said. "But you're not hurting me."

She smiled and ran her hands down his chest, lightly over his bandage. His eyes nearly drifted shut in sheer passion at the sensation of all those smooth, soft curves lying against him. God, she felt so damn good. But her hands were headed south, her eyes on her own movements as she wrapped her fingers around him.

"Don't let me hurt you," she said.

Too late, he thought as she slid down his body. The

feel of her mouth around him shattered any control he'd been managing to hold on to. He managed a single shallow breath before she began to suck in rhythm. His heart rate doubled and then tripled, and his hands slid into her hair. "Lily—"

She didn't stop, not even when he was gasping and choked out her name. Not wanting to hurt her, he forced his hands from her hair and ended up fisting the sheets instead. She took him all the way to the edge before he managed to sit up and pull her in so that she straddled him.

She licked her lips like she was savoring the taste of him and then sank down on him so that he slid in deep.

"Aidan?" she whispered against his mouth.

"Yeah?"

"Can't get enough of you either."

He stilled and stared up at her. "Good," he said in a fierce voice that had nothing to do with lust and everything to do with emotion. Gut-wrenching, heartbreaking, to-the-soul emotion.

"I..." Her gaze dipped to his chest and then back to his eyes. "I do feel things for you," she whispered. "Big things. I just..."

He pushed her hair from her face. "You'll get there when you get there. There's no rush, Lily."

Her eyes were big on his. Uncertain. Wary. "I'm just..."

"I know. And I'm not going anywhere," he promised. "And neither are my feelings for you."

Her eyes went a little misty but she nodded. And then she began to move. And oh, Lord, how she moved. He sank one hand into her hair and wrapped his other arm around her, low on her hips, to keep her in tight as he moved with her.

Her eyes were closed now, her head back, her breathing shallow. He kept his own eyes open with great effort, watching as she tumbled over, coming hard against him, shuddering in his arms, his name on her lips.

This sealed his fate. He couldn't hold back, didn't even try as he tightened his grip and came right after her.

It took all his strength to roll to his side and pull her in close to him as he concentrated on getting his heart rate back into normal range. "You don't even want to know how many times I've fantasized about your mouth on me," he said.

"But you didn't let me finish."

"Needed to be inside you when I came." He met her gaze. "You ever fantasize about me?"

She blushed but didn't look away. "Yes."

"Tell me."

"You really want to know?"

"Hell yeah," he said.

"Okay." She grimaced. "But it's just a fantasy, okay? I don't have a rescue complex or anything, it's just that the way you look in your gear when you're out there on the mountain getting ready to rescue someone, with the ropes and harness and that fierce look of intense determination you get..." She broke off and bit her lip.

"You want me to rescue you," he said, and smiled.

"Not a *real* rescue," she said quickly. "I don't want to ever need a real rescue."

"Just pretend," he said, liking where this was going. "In my gear."

Her eyes lit with arousal and amusement. "Yes, and..."

"My ropes," he said.

"You think I'm terrible," she said. "Right?"

"I think you're the best thing ever." And then he proved it to her.

When Lily stirred next, dawn still hadn't hit, but she was violently aroused.

Aidan was over her in the dark, stroking her body, making her feel like she could go up in flames.

"You sure you're up for this?" she asked, her hands against his chest.

Instead of answering, he rocked into her.

Yep, there was no doubt that he was indeed "up" for this as his mouth nestled along her throat.

Her sweet spot.

She stroked her hands over him, the two of them exchanging lazy kisses and nibbles until Aidan suddenly got serious, rolling so that he was flat on his back. Warm strong hands skimmed her thighs, settling them on either side of his hips.

"You okay?" she asked.

"Getting there." And with that, he lifted her and thrust inside deep. "Yeah," he said on a rough groan that gave her one of those really great body shivers. "Definitely getting there." His hands skimmed down her arms to hers, entwining their fingers. Then he tugged so that she fell forward onto his chest. His face only inches from hers, he held her gaze, his own open and unguarded. He was aroused, but there was also affection shining from those warm brown eyes.

And more.

In fact, she could see anything and everything in those eyes.

A groan coupled with a thrust from Aidan had her

clutching at him as he continued to move beneath her. Not wanting to hurt him by squeezing too hard on his ribs with her knees, she clasped his hands and pushed herself upright, crying out as this seated him even deeper inside her.

"Okay?" he asked, sounding breathless.

She could only let out a short laugh. "So okay."

Aidan smiled and, hands still entwined with hers, locked his arms. Held suspended above him now, she rocked her hips, riding him, meeting him thrust for thrust.

"Oh, fuck," he murmured. "You should see yourself, Lily. You're the hottest thing I've ever seen."

He was one to talk. The sight of him sprawled beneath her, the muscles in his arms corded with the effort of keeping her balanced, the unadulterated hunger and desire etched on his face...

And just like that, the pressure inside her built and then exploded. As he followed her over she fell forward onto his chest again, burrowing into him. Murmuring her name in that husky voice she loved, he hugged her in close and they drifted back to sleep together.

Lily woke up with a smile on her face. It'd been a week since Aidan had shown up at her place injured, and she'd woken up with a smile every single day since.

She was alone in her bed now, but Aidan hadn't been gone all that long, and he'd left her boneless and satisfied as always.

She stretched, feeling her muscles ache in the best of ways after the night before, when he'd brought her fantasy to life showing up with ropes and some very... naughty uses of them.

And then he'd made her write a list of more fantasies, which had brought out that wicked, badass smile of his and a promise to make every one of them come true.

She reached for her charging phone on the nightstand and checked her email out of habit. But the truth was, she'd stopped worrying about the lack of hits on her re-sume awhile ago. She was actually loving being back in Cedar Ridge. She wasn't exactly sure what that meant, but it led her to the reason she felt happy.

Aidan.

In spite of her initial hesitancy, she'd taken him into her bed and it had forever changed what he meant to her.

Whatever *that* was.

But it wasn't a mystery how he felt about her. She thought of how he looked at her, how he always seemed to be looking at her as if he couldn't help himself. How he was there whenever she needed him.

And then there'd been the "I love you." Hard to dis-count that. Aidan never said something he didn't mean.

Never.

Her heart rolled over in her chest, exposing its tender underside as it tended to do in all matters Aidan, leaving her…vulnerable.

And both giddy and terrified at the same time.

She needed to relax. Some people did that with yoga, or meditation, or even a trip to the spa. Lily was starting to learn, or maybe it was her remembering, that she felt most at peace on the mountain. She put on her hiking clothes and, as she had every day since getting the pack-age, added Ashley's scarf. Today there was a wind that made her glad for the added protection.

Two hours later, she stopped at what had become her

favorite place atop the mountain, where she could see everything and feel closest to Ashley. And the fact that it was getting easier each time to get there made her feel good. This was her haven now.

Not the place she had to fear.

She let out a deep breath and a lot of tension. The wind kicked in and pushed at the trees high above her, making them sway and dance. The staccato sounds of the branches hitting each other along with the chatter of the squirrels as they ran for cover was comforting because it sounded like...

Her childhood.

There was only one thing missing, of course.

Ashley.

"Hey, sis," she whispered, fingering the scarf. "I'm back." She let out a low laugh. "Turns out I can't stay away. I feel you here, Ash."

She drew a deep breath and looked across the chasm at Dead Man's Cliff. "I'm so sorry. I'm sorry I ever climbed that stupid cliff. And I'm sorry you did too. Most of all, I'm sorry you can't be here now." Her breath hitched, constricted by tears. "I miss you so much."

When she'd first come back to Cedar Ridge, she'd honestly believed that she needed to get to the mountain and stare down the face where Ashley died. *Actually*, she'd thought that until this very second, but the truth was she didn't need to. If anything, what happened to Ashley there had taught her that there were some things that weren't meant to be conquered at all.

She knew the truth now. In losing Ashley, she'd also lost too much of herself. Lily needed to come back to Cedar Ridge to remember how to live.

Yes, being here was a visceral reminder of a terrible tragedy.

But it was also home.

She let that knowledge settle in, warming her from the inside out. It didn't take away her losses, but gathering Ashley's scarf closer, she understood something else.

It wasn't supposed to.

Ashley would always be a part of her, maybe one of the best parts, and she didn't have to let that go. She just had to be able to live the life she was supposed to live.

"Thanks, Ash," she whispered.

The wind caressed her, and she turned her face into it. It felt like Ashley's spirit telling her it was okay to carry on, to keep chasing adventure. That's who she was, and this was where she belonged.

Aidan was in the middle of an S&R training exercise with his team, hanging off the side of Heaven's Peak when they were radioed about a weather change.

They ended the exercise and were still packing up when Aidan's phone beeped. Seeing Gray's name pop up on the screen when he knew where Aidan was and what he was doing made Aidan pick up the call. "What's wrong?"

"She's back at it," Gray said.

Aidan grimaced. "Look, man, I've told you, whatever bedroom games you and Penny decide to play, just leave me the hell out of it—"

"Not Penny, you idiot."

"Kenna?" was Aidan's next guess. "You gotta give her a job, man, or—"

"I gave her a damn job, I gave her the ski school. Now

stop talking and listen to me. It's Lily. She's back on the mountain. She just passed out of our range, heading north. Which isn't exactly the way back."

No, north from there would take her straight to Dead Man's Cliff.

"And there's a hell of a surprise storm brewing," Gray said. "This morning we had a zero percent chance of precip. Now we're at one hundred percent, expecting high winds and flash floods in the basin."

"She's still trying to get up to where Ashley—"

"She goes up there as often as she can," Aidan said. "I'm sure she's fine."

"The storm—"

"She'll be okay. She's strong and more importantly, smart."

"Your call," Gray said, and disconnected.

Half an hour later Aidan was back from Heaven's Peak. He'd decided to call Lily and meet her up on the trail. For company, not because he doubted her abilities. If she wanted to face the cliff, they would do it together.

But before he could, a rescue call came in—a report of a climber stuck on a ledge of Dead Man's Cliff over the river. That was it, that was all the info they got, no exact location, no ID of the caller or the climber, nothing.

And Aidan's heart stopped.

What if Lily had gotten to the top, been caught up in the moment, and gone climbing on the face? He called her cell but was sent right to her voice mail. In the meantime, Search and Rescue mobilized and set up an incident command center back at the clearing where Aidan and the others had left their vehicles, doing so in fifty-plus-mile-per-hour winds and an oncoming storm.

There were four places on Dead Man's Cliff where a ledge overlooked the river, not a single one of them a safe place in a storm. A two-part plan was put into place. First, a Zodiac raft with a two-person crew would attempt to pinpoint exactly which ledge from far below. Second, Aidan, Mitch, and the rest of the team would come in from the park entrance, holing up at Dead Man's Cliff's trailhead until they got word from the Zodiac crew on which direction to go.

The wait wasn't easy.

"We don't know it's her," Mitch reminded him.

True. And it didn't matter. Either way, they were going to get that person down safely. But God, he hoped like hell it wasn't Lily. They had a high success rate with rescues overall, but Dead Man's Cliff had earned its name the hard way, and all too often a rescue turned into a recovery.

As in a body recovery.

Aidan slammed the door on that thought and forced himself into work mode. The four overhangs were spread out over a few miles along the river. Within half an hour, the Zodiac crew called with the news that they'd found the lost hiker on outcropping number two, about four and a half miles from where Aidan and his crew stood.

They drove the mile and a half of fire road they had, and then had to hike the other three miles to the location.

It was a long-ass walk, hauling all their rope and gear in the wind. By this time the Zodiac had reported in with more details on their victim. The stuck climber was in a sweatshirt, hoodie up, and leggings, so no age or sex could be determined. It could be anyone out there.

But not Lily, he told himself. And yet a small doubt

remained, messing with Aidan's head. He locked that shit down and kept moving as the Zodiac made contact with the stuck climber. Sign language communication only, since they couldn't hear each other over the roar of the wind barreling through the canyon and the water rushing along the canyon.

The climber was stuck. They couldn't—or wouldn't— go back up, and down wasn't an option.

With each step Aidan's fear grew that it was going to be Lily and he wouldn't be able to get to her before the storm swept her off the ledge.

Chapter 28

Lily got back home frozen and desperate for a hot shower. She was shocked to find Gray coming out of her place with a grim set to his jaw.

"Lily," he said, looking shocked as hell to see her.

Who else was he expecting?

But before she could ask, he had his cell phone to his ear. A few seconds later he said, "Fuck!" and stared at her. "You're not up at Dead Man's Cliff."

"No," she said slowly. "I never planned to be. I got to the three-quarter mark and turned around. The storm—"

"Fuck," he said again, and hit the stairs, running down them toward his truck.

"Wait!" she yelled after him. He didn't, so she took the stairs at a dead run as well but didn't catch up to him until he was just about to peel out of the lot.

"I don't have time for this, Lily," he warned when she stood at his driver's window. "Aidan's on a rescue up there and he's distracted, thinking it could be you. I've got to at least get to Incident Command and radio him, let him know you're safe so he gets his head in the game."

She stared at him for a single beat and then rounded his truck—in the front, so he couldn't leave without running her over. She climbed into his passenger seat.

"No," Gray said.

"You're wasting time." She hooked up her seat belt. "Go."

"I'm not bringing you up there."

"Save your breath and hit it."

Gray gritted his teeth and hit it.

"Tell me everything," she said. "Including why either of you could think I'd be stupid enough to climb Dead Man's Cliff alone, ever."

He drove fast through the driving rain but utterly in control as he laughed low under his breath.

"What?" she demanded. "What's so damn funny?"

"You're as stubborn as he is," Gray said. "You two deserve each other." He spared her a quick glance. "I hope you stick this time."

She met his gaze, though it was difficult.

He went brows up. A silent but demanding *Well?* if she'd ever heard one. Pretending not to read Eyebrow Speak, she turned to the passenger window, watching as they flew through the storm. "What is going on, why were you at my place, and why were you surprised to find me there?"

He didn't answer.

"I swear to God, Gray—"

"I saw you on the monitors," he said. "And per protocol, I called Aidan—"

"Per protocol?"

He grimaced. "Shit. You're going to get pissed."

"Already there," she said tightly.

Another grimace. "Okay, you're not supposed to know this, none of you are supposed to know this. We've had a Penny Protocol in place since the beginning. And now we have a Lily Protocol."

"Which means?" she asked in a deceptively quiet voice that sounded way calmer than she might have imagined she could come up with.

He didn't answer.

"Gray," she said.

That muscle ticked in his jaw again. "Look, it's about keeping our people safe, okay? He watches out for Penny when I can't, and I..."

"You what?" she asked, eyes narrowed.

"I watch out for you when he can't. Hudson does too."

She stared at him, stunned. "I watch out for myself," she said.

"Yes and you usually do a damn fine job of it. Except I saw you presumably heading toward DMC and that's code red."

"Code red," she repeated.

"You might've been in trouble."

"I've been out here hiking for weeks and I'm *still* not mental enough to attempt free-climbing that damn, cursed mountain," she said. Maybe even yelled.

He winced. "Not *physically* in trouble."

"So you thought, what, that I might fling myself off the edge and you called Aidan to run in and save the day?"

"Better to be safe and apologize later," he said. "Except a rescue call came in. A climber was reportedly stuck on a ledge above the river. Aidan's S&R team caught the call, and everyone thought it might be you."

"Except that I'm not actually climbing anymore," she said again, this time through her teeth." A thought occurred to her, and she narrowed her eyes. "So if you thought I was out there being stupid, why were you at my place?"

"Because maybe I knew that you and your smart-ass mouth aren't really all that stupid."

This actually slightly mollified her.

Gray used his Bluetooth to try calling Aidan again. No go. He made another call and then Penny's voice filled the air.

"Hey," she said. "I thought we were meeting for a quickie on your break—"

"You're on speaker," Gray said quickly. "And I didn't give you the safe word!"

Penny laughed. "Sorry. Whose ears did I burn? Tell me it's Aidan. I love messing with his head."

"It's me," Lily said.

"Hey you! We still need to grab that drink."

"Later," Gray said tersely. "Baby, where are you?"

"In your office, where *you're* supposed to be."

"I'm going to be late," Gray said. "We're heading up the mountain. Aidan's on an S&R. I'll be at Incident Command. Call if you need me."

"Is he okay?" Penny asked, all serious now.

"Yes, but he thinks they're looking for Lily and I've got her right here."

"I can read between the lines on that one," she said. "You're worried his head isn't in the game. And it's one hell of a storm coming too. Go take care of our boy, I'll handle things here."

*   *   *

On scene at the top, Aidan and Mitch peered over the edge and found the victim curled into the fetal position as the wind beat at her, her head and face covered by the hood of her thigh-length sweatshirt.

Aidan's gut tightened. "Don't move!" he yelled down, not at all sure she could hear them. "We're coming! Keep your head covered!"

There was some discussion with Incident Command on whether the wind was too strong for a rappel and rescue. If so, they would have to pull back and wait out the storm.

Aidan was vibrating with impatience. Mitch put a hand on his shoulder and met his gaze. "I'm going down there either way," Aidan told him.

"Of course we are," Mitch said.

Incident Command gave the go-ahead for the rescue— with the stipulation that they would be called back at a moment's notice if the wind worsened, or at the first sign of lightning. Lightning would stop everything cold, as the guys up on the top, out in the open with the gear, would be in the direct line of danger.

Not that it would stop Aidan, if it came to getting Lily off the face.

From the top of the cliff to the outcropping was a good forty feet. And down to the river was a hundred feet more. The Zodiac couldn't get in close due to the huge boulders at the river's shore, but they'd stick around in the event anyone hit the water.

With the crew setting up the rigging, Aidan and Mitch pulled on their full-body harnesses in preparation to go over. They checked each other's gear and checked the rigging setup to make sure the anchor points—in this case three tall, sturdy cedars—were strong enough for the three ropes they needed.

Aidan was in a huge hurry to get down there, but he still took the extra minute to double- and triple-check that all of the knots were properly tied and everything was correctly attached and tightened. Then he peered over the edge again, unable to take his sights off the all-too-still figure curled forty feet below, not moving. The distance was just enough to not be able to see clearly enough to identify or even catalog injuries, and that was the worst part. His heart kicked hard, and though he was trained to stay calm and alert and steady, his training threatened to go out the window.

Given the go-ahead, Aidan and Mitch went over the edge together, Mitch on the left of the climber and Aidan on the right. They made excellent time descending, aided by the blistering wind trying to tear them from the mountain.

They each landed lithely on their feet in the very small space on either side of their stuck climber, who was still curled up on her side. Aidan immediately crouched low, put a hand on her shoulder and she rolled to her back and opened her eyes.

Only it wasn't a she at all. He was a kid, maybe twenty years old, lean and lanky.

Mitch, crouched on the other side of the kid, met Aidan's gaze.

Not Lily. Not even close.

"Easy," Aidan said when the kid jerked in shock in the very tight space. "We've got you, but no sudden movements. What's your name?"

"Aaron Roberts."

Mitch grabbed his radio. "Victim is Aaron Roberts, male, early twenties—"

"Nineteen," Aaron said.

"Nineteen," Mitch corrected. "No visible injuries."

"Copy that," came the reply from the incident commander.

"What happened?" Mitch asked Aaron.

The story that tumbled out had Aidan grinding his teeth. Aaron and his friend Gil had taken two girls up the mountain to show off and hopefully get laid. The girls had dared them to climb down the face. To sweeten the pot they'd promised something "really special" if the boys could climb down the rock face on the left side, traverse the rock face itself, and reappear on the right side.

Mitch shook his head and gave Aidan a look that said, *Can you believe these dumbfucks?*

Another time Aidan might have laughed, but the weather was going south as they stood there and worse, he still had no idea where Lily was, or if she needed help.

She doesn't, he told himself. She was smart, she had more mountain experience than most, and surely she'd seen the storm moving in.

"Where are your friends?" Aidan asked Aaron.

"I think they went for help."

A third harness had been lowered for Aaron. Aidan was still fuming, so Mitch explained to the Horn Dog what the plan was. All Aaron needed to do was slip into the harness. That was it, the big extent of his efforts needed.

But Aaron paled at the thought of moving around on the narrow ledge and shook his head. Granted, their space was extremely limited, and, with the three of them there, they had precious little room to move around. But there were only two ways off the ledge: either a hundred-foot drop to the wild river below, or up.

"Can't you call a helicopter?" Aaron asked hopefully, squinting into the sky, which was now dark and turbulent, whipped into a frenzy by the winds. "Cuz that would be great."

"A helicopter," Mitch repeated, and looked at Aidan in disbelief. "And would you like fucking lunch to go with that?" he asked Aaron.

"Dude," Aaron said, looking hopeful. "Do they serve meals?"

A bolt of lightning had Mitch and Aidan looking at each other. One one-thousand. Two one-thousand. Three one-thousand—

Thunder boomed so viciously that the ledge beneath their feet shuddered.

"Two minutes," came the warning on the radio.

Shit.

"Listen to me," Mitch said hurriedly. "Here's what we're going to do. You're going to put on the harness, nice and slow, and then we'll check it. And then you're going to get your ass off this rock before we all blow off, and you can go home and get your own damn meal, and we can go rescue someone else. And you're going to do all of this *fast*. You hear me?"

Aaron nodded, eyes wide.

But it wasn't that easy. Hell, nothing was ever that easy, and Aidan should have known.

The skies opened up right then, dumping water like the heavens had sprung a leak, making the going even more treacherous as the rock beneath their feet was now slicker than ever.

Aidan stood along with Aaron, making sure to block him from falling as the kid got the harness on, the wind shrieking like a mob of banshees.

Then came another shocking boom of thunder.

Aaron startled. Aidan snagged him, steadied him, but as he did, his own footing slipped on the wet rock. He immediately let go of Aaron so as not to take them both out. Thanks to the rope he didn't go on a free fall into the rocky river far below. And also thanks to the rope, he swung under the momentum of his own weight face-first into the rock face of the mountain.

Chapter 29

Aidan hit the rock face hard enough to see stars. Normally he reserved seeing stars for the occasional drinkfest or orgasms. So it really sucked when these stars were immediately followed by pain. He bounced off another rock before he managed to regain his footing back on the ledge.

Mitch called an immediate halt to the rescue and everyone froze.

"You okay?" Mitch demanded.

Aidan took inventory. He was pretty sure he'd torn his rotator cuff again—the first time had been in a football game years ago, and that had been a lot more fun. He'd also sliced open an elbow and a knee, and as a bonus his face hurt like a son of a bitch, but luckily he couldn't see it. "I'm fine."

"Uh-huh, that's because you haven't yet met a rock that's harder than your head." Mitch's voice was light, but his eyes were anything but. "Look at me."

Aidan met his gaze, and Mitch gave him a sharp once-over. "Fine my ass," he said.

The rain had kicked up a notch, though none of them could possibly get wetter. "Let's just get this done," Aidan said through gritted teeth, and so, with his elbow and knee bleeding, his shoulder burning, and the impression of the rock presumably still on his face, he put the rescue back on track.

They got Horn Dog into his harness, made sure he was buttoned up nice and tight, and the ground crew above them began pulling him up using a handheld winch system that allowed for easy ascent of injured—or stupid—people, whichever the case may be.

"Gotta speed this up," came the order from Incident Command via radio. "This storm's escalating and the guys above you are sitting ducks. Any second we're going to have to make them retreat back to our location to avoid becoming lightning rods."

Just as he said it, more thunder rumbled, louder now. Definitely closer. Aidan met Mitch's grim gaze. Neither of them wanted to be left on this ledge while the crew above was forced to leave and wait out the storm.

While their victim continued to be pulled up from above, Mitch started fussing over Aidan's injuries, which were now bleeding in rivulets along with all the rainwater. The gash in his knee was three inches long and deep. His pants leg was soaked through with blood. Same with his elbow. And his face. Shit happened.

"Bad week to be you," Mitch said mildly.

"Shut up."

"Don't worry, next week it'll be my turn to get the boo-boos."

"Yeah?"

"Hell no. I'm just that good," Mitch said, chortling, impressed with himself, the asshole.

Aidan pushed him away. His elbow was just a scrape. His face felt bruised, but he didn't think it was anything to be too concerned about. He could see straight and could feel all his extremities. Horn Dog had made it to the top, and now it was their turn. "Okay, let's do this—"

Before he could finish the sentence, a lightning bolt flashed so bright he and Mitch jerked back, coming up against the rock wall of the ledge. The following boom of thunder nearly split their eardrums.

"Jesus," Mitch gasped. "Jesus Christ, my life just flashed before my eyes. Aidan?"

"Still here," Aidan managed, blinking hard but still seeing only white. "Too close."

There was a radio call to verify that Aidan and Mitch were still breathing, but as was feared, the lightning strikes made it way too unsafe to bring them up. It was even more unsafe for the topside crew to stay out in the open with all the gear laid out and the trees surrounding them.

Leaving the rescue lines attached to the anchor points with the ropes slackened enough that Aidan and Mitch could sit on the ledge as close to the rock face as possible, their crew pulled back to seek out refuge.

"Sucks to be us," Mitch said. But the truth was, they were in a better position there on the ledge than the guys on top had been. They sat with their backs to the rock and watched the storm rail.

"Nice view," Mitch said, after a few violently noisy but awe-inspiring minutes. "It'd be better with a few hot chicks and some popcorn."

Aidan set his head back to the rock and laughed softly. His muscles were quaking good now as the adrenaline wore off and the pain set in. Around them the thunder and lightning continued to rage, leaving them no choice but to play the waiting game.

Lily held on to the dash as Gray's truck tossed them both around on the drive up the mountain's fire roads. The storm had come out of nowhere, as it often did on late summer afternoons. They blew in, dumped, and then blew out.

But this one looked like it planned to stick around awhile, and it was violent. With the way the trees were bending in protest, she figured the winds were close to seventy-five miles an hour. Every few seconds lightning flashed—or rather cracked viciously   and thunder rolled.

"I can't believe they're out there in this," she murmured. "It's crazy."

"He's been in worse," Gray said, and peeled into a clearing with a bunch of other trucks and rigs.

"Incident Command," he explained. "We're three miles out from Aidan's position. Stay here." Shoving the truck into park, he exited the vehicle. Lily followed suit and ran around the front of the truck, head down because of the rain.

Which was how she ran headfirst into Gray.

He caught her and she couldn't hear his sigh over the weather but she felt it.

"What part of stay here didn't you understand?" he asked.

"All of it."

"Lily—"

Hudson pulled up in a county SUV. Looking serious in his uniform, he exited the vehicle, his gaze going straight to his brother.

"What?" Gray asked him.

"You don't have your radio on?"

"It's busted."

"Aidan and Mitch rescued some idiot off the face, but the unit had to pull back in a big hurry when lightning hit."

The look that crossed Gray's face told Lily this was bad. "So where's Aidan?" she asked.

Hudson and Gray exchanged another look.

"Someone better speak before I go batshit crazy on your asses," she said tightly.

Hudson met her gaze. "He and Mitch are still on the rescue site."

"You mean on the face of Dead Man's Cliff?"

Another glance between brothers. "They're a few miles up the trail on a rock outcropping forty feet down from the top," Hud said.

"*What?*" she asked on a gasp of horror. "Out in the open with this lightning? They could get hit like those climbers did last year. Why aren't they getting them off the face?"

When Hudson hesitated, she started to storm off toward the trail, but Gray grabbed her hand.

"Let go," she said, heart in her throat because all she could think was that she'd lost Ashley on a day just like this. "I'll go pull him up myself, dammit. What's wrong with all of you? You can't leave him there!"

"What we can't do is have you out here in the open in a lightning storm," Gray said. "Get back in the truck."

She understood what he was saying, but she was picturing Aidan and Mitch on a tiny ledge, huddled in this crazy-ass storm. She tried to move forward, but Hudson caught her against him.

"Listen to me," he said, low and calm, his arms bands of steel. He brushed her wet, clinging hair from her face so he could look into her eyes. "If I could, I'd be out there on that mountain right now, rescuing them myself."

She stared into his fierce gaze, saw the worry there, and realized that if it wasn't safe for him, it sure as hell wasn't safe for her.

"He's going to be okay," Hud told her. "He's on a rope and so is Mitch. Trust me, they're not going to let each other fall. But more importantly, they're safer than we are. Get back in the truck. I'll go get a radio and bring it to you. You can talk to him yourself and see. Okay?"

"He's on a rope?"

"Yes."

She gave the cliff one last stare.

"Lily."

"Okay, yeah." She let Gray pull her from Hudson's arms and guide her back to his truck.

He shut her in the passenger side and beeped the locks as he walked around the hood.

She smiled grimly. He didn't trust her. She didn't blame him.

When he got in, he relocked the doors, hitting the child lock while he was at it.

"Oh, for God's sake," she said.

He said nothing at all, just cranked the heater, pointing the vents at her.

They sat in silence for the few minutes it took Hudson to get back to them. He slid into the backseat and shook like a dog.

"Goddammit, Hud," Gray bitched.

Hud smiled at Lily, and she knew he was trying to make her feel better. She held out her hand for the radio.

He hesitated. "Okay, but first I need to tell you something. He's a little injured—"

"Oh, God." She sucked in a breath and felt her vision go wonky.

Hudson reached forward and slid his hand to the nape of her neck. "Push back against my hand," he ordered. "Deep breaths, Lily."

"We've got you," Gray said quickly at her side.

Most of her brain felt consumed by panic, but Gray's voice and Hudson's hand on her neck anchored her. They were turned toward her, concentrating on her, gauging her reactions. Probably they were worried she was a flight risk, and they'd be right on that score, but she saw genuine concern in their eyes.

"It's going to be okay," Hudson promised.

"You don't know that." She felt the hysteria come at her again. "Things aren't always okay. Things go south." *People die...*

"It's going to be okay," Hud repeated firmly. "Because I won't let it be anything other than okay."

She turned and looked into his eyes, dark with determination. Then she looked at Gray. Matching.

"He's out there because of me," she whispered, letting out her biggest fear. "He thought it was me." Which made her responsible. Again.

"It doesn't matter who he thought it was," Gray said.

"He'd have gone up there for anyone and you know it. Don't put this on yourself."

And then he slid his arm around her and squeezed.

Because they were Aidan's family and they took care of their own. She'd almost forgotten what that felt like until this very moment, surrounded by two of Aidan's brothers who'd clearly dropped everything to be here for him. It nearly brought her to tears. It'd been a long time since she'd been part of a family unit. And yeah, she and Ashley had fought like cats and had competed in every little aspect of their lives, but they'd had each other's backs, always. She missed that. God, she missed that. She purposely hadn't allowed herself to think about it, but she'd missed this. Belonging to someone. Having someone at her back, unconditionally, no matter what.

And yes, she still had her mom, but that was more peripherally. She had Jonathan, too, and now her clients, all of whom meant something to her, but this...this right here, she'd forgotten how good it felt to be a part of a family.

She might have even gotten all mushy on both Gray and Hudson if she weren't still so terrified for Aidan.

"He knows what he's doing," Hudson reminded her. "You've got to believe that. If nothing else, believe in the fact that he's the most stubborn bastard I know. He isn't going anywhere. Because I'll kill him myself if he does. Got it?"

"Got it," she whispered.

Gray spared his brother a look over his shoulder. "What the hell is wrong with you, dumbass? You don't tell a woman that you're going to kill the guy she's in love with."

Wait, what? *In love with...* The fuzziness returned and,

from what felt like a long distance, Lily heard Hudson laugh.

"You're the dumbass," Hud told Gray. "Telling her she loves him before she even knows she loves him. Good going, man. You're going to fuck it all up for him before he even knows what's happening."

Lily decided one emergency at a time and shoved Gray's arm away, swiveling in the seat to stare at Hud. "What's going on out there?"

"Some kid was trying to impress a girl. The idiot got stuck on the ledge—couldn't go up or down. At least they cited him. Not for climbing while stupid, which should be an actual citation, but for climbing in a no-climbing zone. Aidan and Mitch got him up to the top just as the storm moved in, but before they could do the same, Incident Command ordered the crew on the top to pull back. The threat of getting hit by lightning with all the equipment was just too big."

"You said he was hurt, what's his injury?"

"He slipped and swung into the rock face-first."

"Oh, my God." She closed her eyes. *I love you, Lily...* She'd let him tell her his feelings, she'd let them wash over her and heal her and make her happy. And what had she done in return? She'd held back, hoarded her feelings, keeping them to herself.

She'd always thought of herself as so brave. She'd gone out on her own at age eighteen, dependent on no one but herself, and she'd survived.

But it turned out she wasn't brave at all. She'd locked her heart up tight when it had gotten hurt, and she'd kept it isolated and alone ever since.

Which made her the opposite of brave.

But not Aidan. He didn't have any walls. Everything he felt or thought was all over him for the world to see.

This made him the bravest person she'd ever known.

And he loved her.

You love him too... She closed her eyes. "I need him," she whispered.

"We all do," Hudson said..

Gray grabbed the radio. "Aidan, you copy? It's Gray. Need verification that you're breathing. Over."

The radio crackled and then Aidan's voice filled the cab. "Last I checked," he said. "Does someone have eyes on Lily? Is she safe? Over."

As his unbearably familiar voice washed over her, Lily slapped a hand over her mouth to keep in the relieved sob. He was on the edge, literally a tiny, narrow edge, hanging by nothing but a rope in a thunderstorm that had been deemed so dangerous the other rescuers had retreated, and he wanted to know if she was okay. "I need to talk to him."

Gray shook his head no.

But she was a woman on a mission and she snatched the radio from his hand. "Aidan," she said into it, her voice not nearly as calm as his or his brothers'. She blamed the estrogen. "I'm here, I'm fine." She paused. "Over," she said awkwardly.

Gray smiled at her like she was cute.

"Define here," Aidan said, not sounding like he found her cute at all, his voice tight now. "On the mountain? Over."

"I'm safe. I'm in Gray's truck." Needing to get it all out before she choked on it, she sucked in some air. "I'm sorry, I'm so sorry I've been too scared to do this right.

I was afraid of what might happen, how I could get hurt, how you could get hurt. But that's not the way to live. Things happen. I can't control everything and I can't live a half life."

"Lily—"

"No, listen. I'm not going to hold back anymore." She gulped in a breath, needing to hear him say it was all going to be okay.

Radio silence.

She gulped, but she had to finish, she had to put it all out there, like he'd done for her. He deserved that much. "Aidan—"

"No," he said, cutting her off. "Not here. Not now, not like this. Not because you think I'm in danger."

"But you *are* in danger."

"Gray," Aidan said. "Get her out of here."

Gray took the radio from her numb fingers. "No can do, man," he said into the radio. "She's not going anywhere, and neither are me and Hud."

"You're all sitting ducks out there," Aidan said. "Take her home or I'll—"

Gray turned the radio off.

Lily gaped at him.

"He needed a moment to collect himself," Gray said.

"We're not leaving," Lily said.

"We're not leaving," Gray confirmed.

"This storm better not go all night," Hudson muttered, hunkering down in the backseat. "It's effing cold back here. Hey, Lily, were you going to give him the L-word?"

Lily huddled into herself and went mute. Had she just yearned for family? Because maybe she could do without brothers…

Hudson laughed softly. "You two were made for each other."

A month ago Lily would have denied that. Hell, even a few days ago she might have squirmed uncomfortably over the notion.

Not now.

Because she knew it to be true. They *were* made for each other. Aidan had given her back everything that had been missing from her life. Excitement, thrill, warmth, laughter, heat, heart...

Everything. He gave her everything.

She just hoped she hadn't realized it too late.

Chapter 30

The storm warred directly overhead for three solid hours. Aidan knew this because he counted off every single minute.

And through it all he and Mitch had sat with their backs to the rock, their hoods up, heads down. Their gear was the best of the best, but the storm was crazy wild and no match for any gear.

Rain and seventy-five-mile-an hour winds beat at them until sometime around midnight.

Then suddenly there was a lessening. And a promising gap without lightning.

And then *finally* came the radio call that he and Mitch had been waiting for—it was time to get out of this shit.

Aidan couldn't agree more.

Twenty minutes later, Aidan rounded the top of the cliff, where he was immediately tackled by a bundle in a bright red jacket that was scented like Lily but looked like a wild woman.

They both toppled to the ground.

He sucked in a breath because, son of a bitch, he hurt from the tips of his hair to his toes and everything in between. But the pain faded when Lily clutched him, wrapping herself around him like a monkey.

She was shaking so hard she vibrated. "Guys," he said to the crew who'd surrounded them. "Give us a minute."

"No way in hell," Mitch said. "Let's get this show on the road. You two lovebirds can kiss and make up later, after we make the hike back to Incident Command."

"A minute," Aidan repeated.

"Fine." Mitch tossed up his hands. "It's your face that's going to be permanently swelled up like the Goodyear blimp."

Aidan ignored that and the two medics trying to get at him. "Lily."

"Right here." She very gently cupped his face. "Don't be mad, we left Incident Command to be here once they gave the clear."

"Tell me now," he demanded.

"You're bleeding." She looked at someone at his other side, but Aidan didn't take his eyes off of her. "He's bleeding," she said.

"I know," Mitch told her. "It's his stubborn head. But apparently none of us are going anywhere until you two have this out. So maybe you could speed things up a little bit, yeah?"

Again the medics tried to move in, but Aidan grated out through his teeth, "*Wait.*"

No one backed away, but no one dragged him off, either, which he took to mean he could have his damn minute. "Lily. Tell me now."

She was still hugging him like it was her job, but she pulled back and stared into his eyes. Hers filled. "I love you."

Yeah. That was what he needed. His entire body relaxed, and suddenly he could breathe as the knot in his chest loosened. The night was pitch black, and one eye had swollen shut, but he had no trouble seeing the shadow of the men hovering over him, trying to move in. He held on to her tight. "Again," he said.

Her entire demeanor softened, and she bent over him to kiss him softly. "I love you. Always have. Always will."

He felt the stupid smile split his face and his already split lip. "*Shit.*"

She let out a breath. "Okay, so now you're going to stop growling at your team and let them take care of you," she said firmly.

Mitch laughed, cutting it off only when Aidan glared at him.

Lily ignored the exchange and scooted back just enough to let the medics take over.

"I'm fine," he insisted, and got to his feet, holding his arm across his chest funny.

"Damn," Gray said on a heavily blown-out breath. "You tore the fucker again, didn't you?"

"Yep," Mitch answered for him. "Rotator cuff," he explained to a shocked Lily. "It happened when he kissed the rock."

"Fuck you," Aidan said, and dropped back to his knees. "Aw, hell."

"Aidan!" Lily cried, dropping to her knees, too, facing him.

"I'm okay." He locked eyes with her and held the eye contact as the medics fussed over him, dabbing at the cuts on his face, carefully restraining his arm and shoulder from movement.

"We're taking him to General," one of the medics said to Gray.

"No, I'm fine," Aidan said again.

"You're going to the hospital," Lily said.

"Going to be fun to watch you two butt heads," Gray said, and Aidan realized both his brothers were leaning over them, shamelessly eavesdropping. "Even more fun will be giving Mom a new couple to obsess over and bug for grandchildren."

They began the hike back to Incident Command before he could try to kill Gray. Once there, he was taken into the ambulance.

"Let's get his shirt off," one of the medics said.

"Women are always saying that to me," Aidan murmured.

And then the truck was gone, off into the night.

Lily stared at it until it disappeared and still she stood there unmoving.

Well, that wasn't exactly true. Her heart was moving. In fact, it was cracking. Because though Aidan had listened to her very carefully and taken in everything she'd said, he hadn't responded in kind.

Nothing less than she deserved after doing the same thing to him. And if it had hurt him half as much as it hurt her, she didn't know how she could ever make it up to him.

Hudson grabbed Lily's hand. Gray took her other side. They led her back to their truck.

"We're going to the hospital," she said.

Neither man answered her.

"We *are* going to the hospital," she said.

"You're shaking and frozen. You need a shower and dry clothes," Gray told her. "And rest."

"Is that what you would do if Penny was hurt?" she asked. "You'd go home to rest?"

He grimaced.

"Exactly," she said grimly. "Hospital it is."

Aidan always marveled over the fact that he could be dead asleep one second and in the next completely awake, a brand-new day. As he shifted into awareness, everything flooded back to him. The rescue. Slamming himself into the wall like a novice. The long hours on the ledge while the storm beat at him and Mitch.

Lily.

The beeping and antiseptic smell told him he was still in the hospital, but the scent of Lily's shampoo told him he wasn't alone.

He opened his eyes and homed in on her like a beacon.

She leapt out of a chair and came to his side. "Hey," she said, in her throaty morning voice that he loved so much. "You're awake."

Which was more than he could say for Hudson, who had his long body sprawled out in another chair, head back, mouth open, snoring lightly.

"He had a rough night, worrying about you," she said.

Her gaze said she'd had the same rough night, and he shook his head, knowing how hard it must have been reliving the nightmare of Dead Man's Cliff, where she'd lost Ashley. "You okay?" he asked.

"That was my question to you," she said.

"I meant about what happened, and where," he said.

"There's going to always be risky rescues, dangerous fire conditions—"

"I know," she said softly.

"I don't know how to ask you to be with someone who—"

"You're not asking," she said. "It's my decision. I want to be with you, Aidan, just as you are, whatever your job is, whatever you do. I just hate that you got hurt—"

"I'm okay."

Her fingers ran lightly over the splint holding his arm to his chest while her gaze settled on the side of his face, currently burning like fire. Didn't need a mirror to know what he must look like.

"Are you?" she breathed. "Okay?"

"One hundred percent."

She arched a brow and he couldn't help it, he smiled, and…split his lip again. "Dammit," he said, and brought his fingers up to it.

She caught his hand. "If you're fine, and I'm fine…are *we* fine?"

"You still love me?" he asked.

"So you do remember," she breathed.

"Did you think I wouldn't?"

"I wasn't sure," she admitted, and he realized she was tense with nerves.

With some serious effort he lifted the covers in silent invitation.

She bit her lip. "It's a hospital bed, I can't—"

"Come here."

She glanced at Hudson, found him still snoring, and then kicked off her shoes. "Are you sure I won't hurt you?"

"He's fine," Hudson muttered, eyes still closed, body

not moving a muscle. "But you're killing me. Shut the hell up, the both of you. No talking until…" He opened one eye, looked at his watch, groaned, and said "until much later than seven a.m."

They both ignored him.

"I remember everything," Aidan told Lily, tucking her into him. "But you should tell me again just to be sure."

She smiled. "Well, for starters, I love what happens to you in the morning." She wriggled against the part of him that did seem to enjoy mornings more than any other part of him.

"Christ," Hudson muttered. "Get a room."

"We're in a room," Aidan said, sliding his one good arm around Lily. "You were saying?" he asked her. "Something about my good parts?"

"Oh, for God's sake." Hudson pushed to his feet, glared at them, and strode out of the room.

"Thought he'd never leave," Aidan said with a grin.

"He was worried about you," Lily said. "We all worried about you. Aidan, I'm sorry I was so slow about things. But I meant every word I said to you last night. I want to stay in Cedar Ridge. I want to give us a real shot. I want to love you."

He nodded, serious now. "For how long?"

"As long as you'll have me."

"Every day for the rest of my life," he said immediately. "Does that work for you?"

Her eyes misted. "Works perfectly."

Epilogue

Three months later...

A little out of breath—more from nerves than exertion, Lily staggered to the top of Dead Man's Cliff and went still.

"I did it," she whispered. "I got here."

Two warm, strong hands settled on her hips as Aidan pressed in behind her. "And you beat me while you were at it."

She leaned back into him, staring out at the vista before her. Rugged mountain peaks in all their fall glory, a volatile blanket of green laced with blue ribbons of rivers and tributaries.

Closer, in fact directly beneath her, lay the jagged rocky cliffs where all too many had found their end.

Her heart squeezed. Ashley had been one of them. She pulled the scarf from around her neck, hugged it to her heart, and then tossed it into the chasm. The wind caught it, held it aloft for a few heartbeats, and then it vanished from view.

Lily closed her eyes a moment, letting the emotion wash over her. *Good-bye, Ashley, I'll never forget you...*

She let the sun warm her face, let the mountain air fill her lungs. Let the ever-steady, amazing man at her back make her feel strong. "Thanks for helping me get here."

"I didn't help you," he said, his voice a low, warm rumble in her ear. "But I enjoyed the hike, and the company."

She smiled. She always did with him.

"Can you feel it?" he asked.

"What?"

"Winter on the air. You did this just in time, babe. Snow's coming."

"Haven't seen snow here in a long time," she said, feeling a nostalgic yearning to do just that, to watch it come down in snowflakes the size of dinner plates, watch as it accumulated into twenty-foot drifts, covering everything, making the trees appear as two-hundred-foot-tall ghosts.

And since Cassandra had decided not to come back to work after having her baby, Lily had a job at the salon for as long as she wanted it. Jonathan had given her carte blanche to continue to fix the place up, especially since it wasn't coming out of his bank account.

Aidan's arms came around her, warm and sure. "You're okay?" he asked.

She took one last look at the view that had dogged her memories and dreams for a decade and then turned in the circle of Aidan's arms to face him. "More than okay. I'm...at peace. Excited for whatever comes next." Going up on tiptoes, she kissed him softly before pulling back to look at him.

Aidan hadn't had it easy in the past few months. Jacob was still out there, injured and hopefully recovering, but he'd made no contact with his brothers, which was pretty much killing them. As for the resort, there'd been no magic solution to save it, but none of them had given up that fight. They still had nine months. The toll of that worry was dragging on him, on all of them, but she liked to think that she helped him. "And you, Aidan? You okay?"

He lowered his head and kissed her. Not softly. They were both breathing unevenly when he pulled back and met her gaze. "Depends."

"On what?" she wanted to know.

"What happens next. With us."

Her breath caught. "What do you want to happen next?"

"Me? That's easy. I want to fall asleep with you at night and wake up wrapped up in you in the mornings." He smiled and lifted a shoulder. "Anything else is just icing, babe. A ring. A white picket fence. Babies. Whatever you want."

She stared at him. "Whatever I want? You can't just offer me whatever I want."

"Of course I can." His eyes were intense now. Serious, smile gone. "Just name it."

"There's really only one thing," she said.

He waited with characteristic patience.

"I just need you to love me," she whispered.

"For the rest of my life," he promised.

Return to Cedar Ridge in Jill Shalvis's next
delightfully addictive novel

My Kind of Wonderful

Read on for an exclusive extract...

Coming soon from

headline
ETERNAL

Chapter 1

The wind whistled through the high mountain peaks, stirring up a dusting of snow as light as the powdered sugar on the donut that Hudson Kincaid was stuffing into his face as he rode the ski lift.

Breakfast of champions, and in three minutes when he hit the top of Cedar Ridge, he'd have the adrenaline rush to go with it. He only had time for one run before this morning's board meeting, aka fight with his siblings, and he was going to make it Devil's Face, the most challenging on the mountain.

Go big or go home, that was the Kincaid way.

Danger, excitement, and adrenaline rushes were par for the course for all of them and Hud, head of Ski Patrol at Cedar Ridge Resort, was no exception. The antics that happened on their Colorado mountain, combined with all he saw as a cop in the off-season...well, it was safe to say that not much surprised him anymore.

Just yesterday, two hormone-driven twenty-year-olds

had decided to have sex on one of the ski lifts. Because they were also idiots, they had the safety bar up so that when a gust of wind came along, it swept the poor pants-less girl off the lift, down thirty feet to a—luckily—soft berm of snow. She'd lived, though she'd do so with frost-bite in some pretty private places. Her boyfriend, of course, hadn't fallen, had retained *his* pants, and had reportedly dumped her in the hospital due to the humilia-tion.

The story made the news, but sex on a ski lift, stupid as it was, continued to happen at least once a season. And that wasn't even close to the most dangerous thing to have happened this week. Yesterday he'd caught a shift at the station, covering for a fellow officer who'd been out with the flu. A burglary call had come in. An eighty-year-old man said someone was in his kitchen eating his brand new raspberry tarts. And he'd been right. There'd been someone in his kitchen eating his raspberry tarts—a 350-pound bear, roughly the size of a VW Bug, had been sitting at the guy's bar calm as you please.

Call him jaded, but Hud usually operated from the place where he was pretty sure nothing could surprise him.

So when he skied off the lift and found a girl sitting just off-center at the top, her skis haphazardly stuck into the snow at her side, he didn't even blink.

Or at least he assumed she was a girl. Her down jacket was sunshine yellow, her helmet cherry red. She sat with her legs pulled up to her chest, her chin on her knees, her ski boots as neon green as neon green could get, staring contemplatively at the admittedly heart-stopping view in front of her.

Hud stopped a few feet away.

She didn't budge.

He looked around. Sharp, majestic snow-covered peaks in a three-hundred-and-sixty-degree vista. They were on top of the world.

And quite alone.

Not smart on her part. The weather had been particularly volatile lately. Right now it was clear as a bell and thirty degrees, but that could change in a blink. High winds were forecasted, as was another foot of snow by midnight. But even if a storm wasn't due to move in, no one should ski alone. And especially no one should ski alone on Devil's Face, a 2,800-foot vertical run that required technical expertise and nerves of steel. There was a low margin for error.

As in *no* margin for error. One little mistake was a guaranteed trip to the ER. As skilled as he was, even Hud made sure his brothers knew where he was and that his radio was in good working order.

"Hey," he called out to the girl. "You okay?"

Nothing.

He glided on his skis the last few feet between them and touched her shoulder.

She jerked and craned her neck, staring at him for a beat. Then she pulled off her helmet and dark lenses, and yanked earbuds from her ears. Tinny music burst out from them so loud that he wondered if she could still hear anything at all.

"Sorry," she said. "Did you say something?"

"I asked if you're okay."

She flashed a smile like the question was silly. "Of course."

Of course. She wore a tight ski cap beneath her helmet, also cherry red, with no hair visible and enough layers that she was utterly shapeless, but he could see now that she wasn't a girl at all. A *woman*, maybe mid-twenties. Dark eyes. Sweet, contagious smile.

Pretty.

But he'd been a cop for long enough that he could read people, often before they said a word about themselves. It was all in the posture, in the little tells, he'd learned.

Such as the layers she wore.

Yes it was winter and yes it was the Rocky Mountains, but thirty degrees was downright balmy compared to last week's mid-teens. Most likely she wasn't from around here or the mountains at all.

Then there was the slightly unsure look in her eyes, a vulnerability that said she was at least a little bit out of her element and knew it. Her utter lack of wariness told him something else, too, that probably wherever she'd come from, it hadn't been a big city.

None of which explained why she was sitting alone on top of one of the toughest mountains in the country. Dumped by a boyfriend after a fight on the lift? Separated from a pack of girlfriends and taking a break? Hell, despite appearances, maybe she was a daredevil out here on a whim.

Or it could be that she was simply a nut job. Nut jobs came in all shapes and sizes, even mysterious cuties with vulnerability in their eyes that suddenly made him feel extra protective. "You sure you're okay?"

She narrowed her eyes a little. "Why, don't I look okay?"

He knew a trick question when he heard one. Knowing better than to touch that one with a ten-foot pole, he swept his gaze over her. No visible injuries. But then again, he couldn't see much given her layers. "So you're not hurt."

"Nope." She paused. "You're probably wondering what I'm doing here."

"Little bit."

She sighed. "Did you know that people who don't understand ski maps, or maps at all really, shouldn't ski alone?"

"No one should ski alone," he said.

"You are."

Only because he had a radio at his hip with a direct connection to command central, and an entire team of ski patrol who could look up at the board in the main office and see exactly where he was. But then her words sank in and he stilled. "Are you telling me that you're on Devil's Face, the most challenging run on this mountain, by accident because you misread the ski map?" he asked, doing what he thought was a damned fine job of holding back his incredulous disbelief.

She bit her lip, ineffectually trying to hold back another smile, which didn't matter because her expressive eyes gave her away. "I realize my answer's going to make me look bad," she said, "but yes." She nodded. "Yes, I'm here because I misread the map. I had it upside down."

"This run is a double diamond expert," he said. "You're risking your life up here," he added, trying really hard not to sound like a judgmental asshole, but seriously? How many clueless people had he rescued this week alone?

"Well, I've taken lessons. Three of them. Breckenridge," she said.

Three. Jesus. "How long ago?"

She bit her lower lip. "Um, a few years. Or ten. I

thought it was like getting on a bike," she said to his groan of frustration. "I visualized it and—"

He wondered if she'd visualized the hospital bills.

"If it helps," she said, "I realized my mistake right away and was just taking in the view. Because just look at it…" She gestured to the gorgeous scenery in front of her, the stuff of postcards and wishes and dreams. "It's mind-boggling."

The wonder in her gaze mesmerized him and he found himself softening toward her more than a little. A little surprised at himself, he turned to take in the view with her, trying to see it through her eyes: the towering peaks that had a way of putting things into perspective and re-minding you that you weren't the biggest and baddest, the blanket of fresh snow for as far the eye could see, glistening wherever the sun hit it like it was dusted with diamonds.

He tried never to take it for granted but he did. It was interesting that it'd taken a little waif of a woman who shouldn't even be here to shake him out of his routine and make him notice his surroundings.

"Anyway," she went on. "I was figuring after I got my fill, I'd just head back to the ski lift and ask if I could ride it down. No harm, no foul."

He couldn't help being curious about her. Or maybe mystified was a better word. He wanted to know her story. "I'll get you back to the lift," he said.

"No, I've got it." She pulled one of her skis out of the snow and laid it down. She struggled to snap her ski in, her arms trembling a little bit. He started forward, but she stopped him with a hand.

"I've got this," she said.

A determined thing then. Fine. But he had to force himself to stay back when ski number two took her longer because she had a balance problem. When she started to tip over, he once again instinctively moved toward her, but she managed to catch herself on a pole.

When she finally clicked her second ski in, she looked up, flashing him this brilliant smile, like she'd just climbed a mountaintop. "See?" she said, beaming, swiping at her brow like maybe she was sweating now. "I'm good." And with that, she pushed off on her poles.

He caught her by the back of her jacket. Even with all those layers, she was surprisingly light. Light enough that he could easily spin her around and face her in the right direction, which was 180 degrees from where she'd started.

She laughed and damn, she had a really great laugh, one that invited a man right in to laugh along with her. "Right," she said. "Thanks. Now I'm good."

Uh-huh. At his hip, his radio buzzed, but he wasn't budging until he knew she was safely on the lift heading down.

She flashed another smile, this one a bit mischievous. "You do know that even an intelligent person can screw up reading a map, right? Despite appearances, I can assure you, I don't need a keeper."

He kept his grimace to himself, or at least he thought he had, until she spoke again.

"You don't believe me." She didn't seem insulted in the least, and in fact, still smiling, she patted Hud on the arm, like he was a poor, stupid man... "You're cute," she said, "but I bet you're single."

He blinked. He *was* single, but what the hell did that have to do with anything?

And cute?

He was cute?

He was pretty sure his testosterone level dropped at that. "Let's just get you off this mountain," he said in his usual work voice. Calm. Efficient.

But she laughed at him again and shook her head. "I've got it from here, Mountain Man. I promise."

If Hud had a penny for every time someone promised him something and actually kept that promise, he'd have... zip. Zero.

Nada.

And his doubt must have shown all over his face because she patted his arm again. "No, really," she said. "If I need help, I'll call ski patrol. But thank you."

"I *am* ski patrol," he said.

She ran her gaze up and down the length of him. It wasn't ego to say that usually when a woman did such a thing, it was with a light of lust in her eyes. Okay, maybe it was a little bit of ego. But he was athletic—big and built—and women usually gravitated to that.

Not all women, he corrected. This one in particular didn't appear impressed at all.

In fact, she looked distinctly unimpressed, so much so that he looked down at himself. "I'm not in my gear," he said, having no idea why he was defending himself. "I'm not technically on duty this morning."

She didn't respond to this, either, instead once again pushing off on her poles. Not heading down the face of the mountain thankfully, but toward the ski lift, about a hundred yards back.

He watched her go and swore to himself. She moved a little unsteadily, keeping her knees straight instead of bending them, incorrectly putting her weight on the backs of her skis. Whoever had given her those three lessons at Breckenridge should be fired. But she hadn't asked him for advice, and if he taught anyone to ski these days, it was little kids because they were actually fun.

She'd be fun to teach too, came the unbidden thought, which he shrugged off. She was on the right path now, out of his hair, leaving him free to take Devil's Face hard and fast the way he'd planned before heading into work.

Except...she'd left her helmet in the snow at his feet.

He had no idea how anyone could forget the eye-popping cherry red thing against the white snow, but she had. "Hey," he called after her. "Your helmet."

But she must have had her earbuds back in because she didn't stop or turn back.

"Well, hell," he said and scooped up the helmet.

Giving Devil's Face one last longing look, he headed toward the lift as well and caught up with her halfway there.

She'd stopped and had her weight braced on her poles. Bent over a little bit, she was huffing and puffing, out of breath. It could have been the altitude. They were at well over 8,000 feet and it affected everyone differently.

But he got the worrisome sense it wasn't the altitude at all. When he'd lifted her, she'd been light, almost...frail. People didn't realize it took a lot of strength and stamina to ski, and he was nearly positive she didn't have either of those things. He once again tapped her on the shoulder and once again she jumped.

Yep, the earbuds again. She pulled one out and looked at him questioningly, like he'd been so forgettable she hadn't even remembered he was behind her.

"You forgot this," he said.

She grimaced. "Sorry. I think the altitude's getting to me. I should really have gotten myself some caffeine first." She put the helmet on and waved him off. "Thanks again, my fair prince."

It wasn't often he found himself baffled but he was baffled now, in a big way.

"Cinderella?" she asked. "You know, her prince had her slipper and you had my helmet— Never mind," she said on a laugh when he just stared at her. "Probably I should've put far more practical things on my list than skiing."

Before he could ask her what the hell she was talking about, she'd tightened the strap beneath her chin, put her hands back into the handholds at the top of her ski poles, and pushed off.

He watched her head straight for the lift, thinking two things. One, he really hoped she knew how to stop. And two, she was definitely a nut, but possibly the prettiest, most bewildering nut he'd ever met in his entire life.

Bailey got situated on the lift and told herself not to look back, there was no reason to look back.

So of course she looked back.

Yep, he was still there. Tall, dark, and sexy ski patrol guy, and he stood on his skis like they were an extension of his own body. He was watching her as well, or so she assumed since his dark lenses were aimed her way.

She sucked in a breath. Goodness, the rugged badass mountains had nothing on the rugged badass man standing in the sunlight like a ski god. She waved at him.

He didn't wave back.

Huh. Was he always a Cranky Pants, or did she just

have a special talent in bringing it out? While she was wondering that, he planted his poles and executed a lithe jump that had his skis facing the other way now, and then he pushed off, skiing away with an effortless, easy motion that she knew she could never in a million years of lessons hope to replicate. Damn. Mr. Cranky Pants was pretty hot.

Volcanic hot.

But as Bailey had discovered the hard way, the hot ones weren't the keepers. For the most part, they'd never been disappointed or hurt by love or life, and as a woman who'd faced it all at one time or another, she had no patience for the weak, shallow, or clueless.

And actually, no patience for this line of thinking. She had other problems. She'd told herself it wasn't defeat that she hadn't skied down under her own steam. The lift would take her to the midpoint on the mountain and she could still ski down from there.

Assuming she'd read the map correctly this time.

Laughing a little at herself, she turned her head to take in the top of the mountain. And it had been the top, the very tippy top, and the stunning view had made her glad for her map incident.

She'd never seen anything like it.

For the first time she'd been the highest point, everything below her, the world at her feet. As a woman who until very recently hadn't been in control of her own destiny, it had staggered her.

In a really great way.

The lift hit a snag and jerked and she was not ashamed to admit that she gasped out loud and held on to the steel frame for all she was worth. There was nothing below her but thick pines and an endless blanket of snow. Not a building in sight, not even the comforting view of the lodge where she intended to grab a hot chocolate.

The lift jerked again and her hand ached from the tight grip. After all she'd been through, she was about to fall to her death, alone on a mountain.

And if by some miracle she didn't die from the fall, her mother would kill her.

But the lift held and she didn't fall, and ten minutes later she glided off without stumbling, and she really wished Sexy Cranky Pants could have been there to witness it. Or that *anyone* she knew could have seen.

Bailey had grown up in Denver, about two hours from Cedar Ridge. Though just about everyone she knew was a big skier, she was not. She'd gone a few times but mostly she'd been concentrating on other things. Today, with the wind hitting her face, the sun warming her cheeks, the feeling of being in control for once...it'd all given her a small taste and she wanted a bigger one—which she was hoping her business here yielded.

Beaming with pride, she straightened on her skis and glanced over at the lodge. From here she could see the entire north wall. Unlike the rest of the building, which was sided with wood and glass, gorgeous and rustic-looking, the north wall was smooth stucco. Easier to maintain than wood, especially since it took the brunt of the weather.

She'd been hired to paint a mural there.

Painting was important to her, very important. It wasn't what she did for a living, but it reminded her of her grandma, whom she missed so very much. Which was what made today such a great day—two things off her list in one fell swoop!

Smiling, she very carefully skied—okay, plowed—her way to the mid-lodge. Luckily it was only a hundred yards or so and relatively flat, but that meant she had to use her poles. Halfway there she was huffing and puffing and gasping for air.

Holy crap, this was hard work. By the time she made it to the stairs of the lodge, she was sweating. Hand to her pounding heart, she lifted her head and came face-to-face with thanks, Karma—Sexy Cranky Pants

How the hell he'd beaten her down the mountain, on his own power no less, she hadn't the foggiest. "Hey," she said, trying to act like she wasn't breathing like a locomotive on its last legs.

Not breathing like a locomotive, not sweating, in fact not exerted at all, the bastard raised a single brow. "Are you going to yell at me again if I ask you if you're okay?" he wondered.

She laughed. "I didn't yell at you."

His mouth quirked a little as he stood there, all wind-tousled perfection. He was yanking her chain in his own oddly stoic way.

And in her own *not* stoic way, she liked it. "And anyway," she said. "I'm perfectly fine so you can stop asking me that question."

"It's my job."

Oh. Right. She sighed. "I guess I didn't realize it, but that question really annoys the crap out of me."

"I'm getting that," he said dryly. "Next time I'll ask you about the weather."

Look at that, Man of Few Words had a sense of humor. And she liked that. A lot. She liked him for some odd reason, and felt the need to explain herself. She wanted to tell him that the innocuous "Are you okay" question was a trigger for her, that given how many times over the past ten years she'd been asked those three simple words, they'd long ago lost their meaning.

That instead what she heard was all the pity the words were usually accompanied by.

And she hated pity with the same level of loathing she saved for all creepy crawlies, kale, and men in open-toed shoes of any kind.

His radio went off. Without taking his eyes off her, he listened to the call, then turned down the volume. "I've got to go."

Good. Maybe when he was gone she could stop making a fool of herself.

He started to turn away, but stopped and gave her one more long look. "Stay off the top, okay?"

"Okay."

He narrowed his eyes, clearly trying to judge her for honesty.

"Sir, yes sir," she said and saluted him.

A smile threatened the corners of his mouth. "If only I thought you meant that."

And then he was gone.

She let out a slow, shaky breath. It'd been so long since she'd had any sort of interaction like this that she wasn't even sure what had just happened.

You just flirted with a man, a perfect stranger.

And she'd liked it. But Lord, she was rusty. *Sir, yes sir?* Seriously, she needed some practice being normal. Hopefully the next time a tall, dark, and sexy guy struck up a conversation with her, she'd not make a fool of herself.

Baby steps.

Now you've fallen for the gorgeous
town of Cedar Ridge,
discover Jill Shalvis's other worlds,
that we promise will capture your heart.
Turn the page to find out more...

Welcome to Lucky Harbor...

The sleepy little town that's the perfect place to escape to.

Full of characters that'll charm you.

Heartwarming stories to delight you.

And a world to make you laugh and fall in love.

Jill's

Lucky Harbor

series is available from

headline
ETERNAL

Be enchanted by Sunshine, Idaho...

The small town full of big hearts, vibrant characters,
and heartfelt emotion.

Visit Sunshine, and we promise you'll leave smiling.

Jill's
Animal Magnetism
series is available from

headline
ETERNAL

We hope you've fallen in love with Jill Shalvis.

Discover more of our books and authors by visiting our website

www.headlineeternal.com

For exciting news, competitions, and to chat to us and other fans

Follow us on Twitter

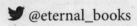 @eternal_books

And like us on Facebook

/eternalromance

headline
ETERNAL